Futures Entwined

Ardor Creek, Book 6

By

AYLA ASHER

Contents

For all the other childfree by choice romance readers out there. You deserve your happy ending too!

A Note from the Author

To the amazing readers who've stuck with me through this series and made it this far...

I write you this note with a mixture of elation and sadness because Futures Entwined is the final book in the Ardor Creek series. As someone who grew up in a small town, I never intended to write small-town romance when I became an author. A part of me left that small town behind when I moved to the NYC area, and it's impossible to write a good story without being *passionate*.

But then, the pandemic hit, and I found myself craving sweet, steamy, low-angst stories. The world was suddenly insane and I just wanted to make people feel good for a while. Ashlyn and Scott appeared in my head and the rest was history.

To my great surprise, I loved every minute of writing this series. I'm also extremely thankful for every one of you who reads, leaves a review and sends me a message telling me you love these characters too. It is so rewarding as an author and I hope this series continues to find new readers as it matures. Although the series is complete, I'm not ruling out a spin-off series down the road that focuses on the children of Ardor Creek once they grow up. I think it would be really cool to see Sebastian, Charlie, Avery, Rose and the other Ardor Creek kids get their own love stories as adults. However, that's still a faraway goal since I have multiple projects planned under both of my author names for the foreseeable future.

One thing I love about Ardor Creek is that the female characters all have traits I identify with. Ashlyn is a former medical sales rep (so was I!), Carrie, Teresa and Abby are in their forties (me too!),

Justine and Gary both had disastrous previous relationships (we've all been there, right, ladies?).

Futures Entwined is no different and perhaps closest to the mark for me. Heather is a forty-four year old childfree by choice heroine. I tuned forty-four as I was writing this book, and you guessed it, I'm childfree by choice. It's always been my path and I'm thrilled to write Heather's character because I don't think childfree heroines get enough representation in romance novels.

Unlike Heather, I actually adore children—although I do enjoy giving them back to their parents once our time is over! I wrote Heather to be warier of kids than me because it leads to some really funny moments, but deep within she doesn't dislike children. She just doesn't quite understand them sometimes. I also had a mentally ill father who exhibited some of the same traits as Heather's dad, and not having a solid foundation can make you doubt your ability to experience true emotion as Heather often does.

Seeing Heather's growing affection for Gabby and Angeline in this story was so rewarding, and having everyone in Ardor Creek support her choices was gratifying. Observing her change as a person and embrace her strength is a testament that everyone deserves a second chance at happiness.

It was important to me that Heather fall in love with Gabby and Angeline as much as Jeremy, and it was nice to write a stereotype reversal of the man pursuing a serious relationship. Since Jeremy wants something more than casual, it allows Heather to spend time with his girls, and her moments spent with them are some of my favorite in the book.

With that, I'll leave you to enjoy Heather and Jeremy's story. Thank you for spending some time with me in Ardor Creek. You'll never know how much it means. Happy reading!

Prologue

Heather Combs, formerly Connors, strolled down the bustling Philadelphia sidewalk. The early-summer heat was sweltering and she thanked all the gods she didn't believe in that she'd remembered her hat. Like most of her clothing and accessories, it was fashionable and shielded her from the glaring sun. Her two-inch heels clicked on the sidewalk as she strode toward her apartment after another day in paradise...

If one considered working as an office assistant to a misogynistic ass "paradise."

Smirking at the sardonic thought, she glanced down to step over a crack and plowed into another passerby with a solid *thunk*.

"Whoa, there," he said, steadying her as he gently clutched her upper arms. "I'm so sorry. Didn't see you."

Pushing her hat off her face, Heather opened her mouth, ready to lay into him or utter an epic curse, unsure which option would fly from her lips. Scowling, she lifted her gaze and froze. "Brian?"

"Holy shit! Heather? Heather Conners? How are you?"

Grinning, she relaxed and shrugged. "I don't think you broke any bones," she teased, drawing back and running her hands over her forearms. "I'm okay. How are you? How's Terry? What are you doing in Philly?"

Chuckling, he rested his hand on his hip. "Terry's great. Still working at the pub where I imagine she'll work until retirement. I'm good too. Here for a work meeting and can't wait to get back to Ardor Creek. I'm just not a big city guy." Sympathy entered his brown eyes. "I heard about your divorce from Butch before you left town. Sorry to hear it."

"I think we were always doomed," she said, shrugging. "He was kind of a dick and I stayed with him too long, but that's what happens when you get married when you're eighteen, right?"

"Terry and I married young but, thankfully, we've made it so far."

"True. You two were always meant for each other."

"So, I'm assuming it's Heather Combs again?"

"Yep. Took back my maiden name when we divorced. Not that it ever did me any favors but it's better than being associated with my ex for the rest of my life."

Brian's deep eyes assessed her, reminding Heather how kind he'd been in high school. His wife, Terry, had been on the cheerleading squad too and she was one of the few people Heather had liked at Ardor Creek High.

"I'm assuming you've heard Butch is engaged to Cynthia Andrews," he said softly.

Heather could barely contain her eye roll. "Yep. I figured she was going to try and seduce Chad but he shot her down to date Abby. Although I wasn't a fan of Abby's, I'm glad Chad chose someone who wasn't a Grade A hoe bag. Of course, now my ex-husband is with said hoe bag, which honestly seems quite fitting." She rubbed her chin as she considered. "They deserve each other."

His breathy laugh surrounded her. "You've still got that sharp tongue, Heather."

She shot him a droll glare. "If you're saying I'm still a bitch, it's true and I'm proud of it. I never had time to develop a filter. Too late now."

"I think a filter would be boring on you. The blatant honesty and forthright opinions are endearing in a weird way."

"Well, that reminds me of how nice you are." She flashed a grin. "So, what are they saying about me in ol' Ardor Creek? I know the rumor mill is rampant, especially since Butch and Cynthia live there."

"You know..." he said, shrugging. "Same old shit."

"Just tell me. Did Butch share that he cheated on me?"

Brian cleared his throat. "Um, not exactly."

"Well, he did. Guess he'd want to keep it secret so people didn't know what an ass he was."

Brian rubbed the back of his neck as she tilted her head.

"What is it?"

"Actually, Heather, he told everyone you cheated on him."

Bristling, she felt the anger rush in. "Excuse me? I did no such thing."

"And he also told everyone you...um..."

"Go on," she said, circling her hand. "Might as well spit it all out now."

His eyes darted to the neckline of her shirt before quickly rising. "He said you got...uh...breast surgery...and it was lopsided."

Sucking in a breath, Heather felt the rage surge as she imagined strangling her ex-husband. Closing her eyes, she steadied herself before setting the record straight. "Number one," she said, holding up a finger, "that bastard cheated on me, not the other way around. And number two, I did get a boob job. It was a breast *reduction* because I'm not twenty-five anymore and those things were heavy as shit and hell on my back. And I can assure you, they are *not* lopsided."

"Hey, I believe you," he said, showing her his palms. "You told me to be honest."

Huffing a breath, she crossed her arms over her *perfectly proportioned* breasts and tapped her foot. "I wish I could say I was surprised. This is what I get for leaving Butch in Ardor Creek and moving to Philly. I was just so ready to leave it all behind. In my absence, I left Butch to tell the story of what happened. The *false* story." Tugging off her hat, she ran a hand through her blond curls. "Bastard."

"Well, I'll be happy to tell Carrie I saw you and what we discussed. You know she'll set the record straight in five minutes."

Huffing a laugh, Heather nodded. "Biggest gossip in Ardor Creek. I heard she and Peter are finally happy. Took them long enough."

Brian's eyebrows lifted, indicating she was one to talk considering her divorce.

"Okay, you don't have to stare me down. I get it. I'm the biggest train wreck of all. How happy it must make everyone in Ardor Creek to hear these awful stories Butch is spreading about me. The bitch finally gets her due."

"I think you're being hard on yourself, Heather," he said, cupping her arm. "No one wishes you ill will."

"Even Abby?" She lifted a sardonic brow.

He squinted as he pondered. "Okay, not *too* many people."

Laughing, she replaced her hat and patted it to settle her hair underneath. "Hell, I deserve it. I was terrible to her. But I learned a long time ago it's futile to waste time on things you can't change." Glancing at the ground, she acknowledged the yearning that simmered in her gut. The desire to go back to Ardor Creek—the place with so many failures and bad memories—and rewrite the narrative. She'd promised herself she wouldn't return but could she really let Butch spread his lies without a fight?

"What are you thinking?"

"That it might be time to come home," she said, eyes narrowed as she reclaimed his gaze. "It's been several years. Do you think Ardor Creek could handle me?"

His lips formed a reverent smile. "We'd love to have you, Heather. You could always stay with me and Terry. We have a guest bedroom and it would certainly bring some excitement to Ardor Creek."

"Oh, I bet it would."

Brian's eyes sparkled with mirth before he glanced at his watch. "Well, it's been great running into you but I have to get to happy hour with my co-workers. Want to exchange numbers?"

Lifting her phone from her purse, she nodded. "I'd ask if Terry would get jealous but you've never had eyes for anyone but her and she damn well knows it."

He chuckled before they texted each other to exchange numbers. "It's true. I think I could bring Heidi Klum home and Terry would just pat my cheek and offer to cook dinner for all three of us. The woman knows I'm mad for her."

Heather smiled at him, wishing she understood the first damn thing about love. Unfortunately, some people just weren't wired for love—whether it be platonically or romantically—and she'd accepted long ago she was one of those people. "You two always had it figured out. I'm so glad I ran into you."

"Me too. Hope to see you in town one day soon. Take care, Heather." He gave her one last supportive squeeze on her arm before continuing down the sidewalk and out of sight. Heather stood firm for a moment before repositioning her bag over her forearm to resume the walk home.

As she stomped toward her apartment, she grew angrier with every click of her heels. She was practically chanting along with the firm clicks, shoring up the decision she was already sure she was going to make.

He. Doesn't. Get. To. Write. Your. Story. *Click, click, click.*

Go. Home. And. Show. That. Town. Who. You. Are.

Who you've become...

After entering her apartment, she slung her bag on the chair and fell onto her living room couch. Leaning back on the soft cushions, she stared at the ceiling.

"You ran away because you hated Ardor Creek but you also hate it here, Heather," she murmured. "You're going to hate living anywhere until you figure out how to fix what's broken inside."

The words rang true, inspired by the multitude of self-help books and meditations she'd digested after her divorce. Unfortunately, even after all the psychobabble, she'd never really figured out how to be happy. How could someone who'd never experienced love or happiness begin to understand how to welcome it or even recognize it? Based on her childhood and terrible marriage, she only understood pain and heartache.

She'd moved to Philly years ago after her divorce, thinking it would usher in a new phase of her life. One where she would meet handsome men who would wine and dine her or whisk her away to Italy or Greece. Instead, she'd met a ton of man-children who were either divorced and drowning in emotional baggage, or young and dumb as a sack of rocks. The young ones had no idea how to sexually please her and the older ones just didn't care to. She'd had lots of mediocre sex until recently when she'd discovered what she so reverently called "Netflix and vibing." The "vibe" was battery-operated and always found the spot no one else could.

Sighing, she admitted how pathetic that sounded. Now, she was a washed-up single divorcée in her mid-forties who still looked pretty damn good but was rotten inside. As much as she'd tried to become a better person in recent years, Heather always wondered if she was destined to be a mean girl.

"You were in so much pain when you lived in Ardor Creek, you inflicted it on everyone else. You became the person everyone thought you would be. Way to go, Heather."

Rolling her eyes, she expelled a huge breath, causing her lips to flap together as she pondered. Her job as an executive assistant to the most arrogant real estate agent in Philadelphia paid well but it didn't fulfill her. However, she was a quick learner and had digested a ton about real estate during her tenure. Hell, she'd probably learned enough that she could secure a real estate license and become an agent herself.

The wheels in her mind churned as she recalled the newest agent that had joined her douchelord boss' firm. He was in his early twenties and could barely spell without autocorrect. If he could become an agent, surely Heather could. Snickering, she reminded herself she was so freaking old she'd learned to type on a physical typewriter in high school. Back then, the words had to be spelled correctly or they were doused with White Out, which was a pain in the ass. Therefore, she was a damn spelling champion, in her mind, at least.

Sitting up, she rested her hand on her chin as she let the idea take hold. Yes, she could go to real estate school, get her license and move back to Ardor Creek. Chances were, the established broker in town, Chandler Grossman, was still practicing but close to retirement. He'd always glanced at her legs at church when she was a teenager—the creepy old geezer—and she bet she could charm her way into working at his firm. Hell, if she were going for gold, she probably could charm him into selling her the firm once he retired, allowing her to inherit his clients and his business' solid reputation. Heather knew he only had one child, Nathan, who was a chef, so he wasn't in the family real estate business.

It was a high aspiration but Heather had always barreled toward things once she made a decision. It would allow her to return to Ardor Creek, set the story straight, and perhaps begin the journey to healing the broken pieces inside that never quite fit together.

"It won't be easy," she murmured, rubbing her chin. "Half the people there probably hate you and you don't have much love for the place either."

Silence stretched before her lips slowly curled into a grin. "But how fun would it be to go back, reclaim your story and build a life that isn't fucking miserable in Ardor Creek?" Rising, she formed a fist and squeezed. "You might fall flat on your face but it won't be the first time. Butch doesn't get to decide who you are, Heather. Not this time."

Whirling around, she assessed her apartment, wondering how long it would take to wrap things up in Philly. A few weeks at most, and then she could return to the place that had always represented anguish and pain. Would it be different this time around? She had no idea. But one thing was for sure: it would always represent heartache if she didn't go back and try one more time.

Straightening her spine, a muscle ticked in her jaw as she gave a firm nod. Hopefully, Ardor Creek was ready because Heather Combs was coming home.

Chapter 1

One year later

Heather Combs sipped her skim caramel latte as she sat across from Justine Lancaster, hoping the decadent flavor would give her a bright spot in the otherwise unpleasant conversation she was about to have. Scrunching her features, she admitted it tasted great but wouldn't soften the blow.

"So, I'm hoping you invited me to coffee to tell me you have several competing offers on my house," Justine said, grinning over her cup.

"I wish that were the case," Heather said, sitting down her latte and shaking her head. "As we discussed, it's a buyer's market right now and there's quite a bit of inventory since Abby approved the plans the new environmentally friendly developer filed."

"Well, if I'm going to lose my buyers to new condos, I'm glad it's to a good developer instead of Rydell Industries."

"The good news is that it will lift housing prices across the board," Heather said, lifting a finger. "A year from now, I anticipate your house appreciating at least twenty percent."

Justine pursed her lips. "That's great but I really wanted to sell it before Gary and I got married. I don't know…" She wrinkled her nose. "There's something about owning the house I lived in with my ex-husband when I'm about to marry the love of my freaking life. I want to expel all the old toxic energy from my past. Does that make sense?"

"It does," Heather said with a nod, understanding this was the perfect time to bring up the plan that had been circulating in her head for the past several weeks. "I do have another option if you'd be open to it. It's a bit out of the ordinary but I figured it's worth a shot."

"At this point, I'm open to anything. Go for it."

Inhaling a deep breath, Heather straightened in her chair. "I'm forty-four and tired of living in an apartment. I've decided it's time to finally buy a house. Unfortunately, I can't afford one at the moment and I refuse to take alimony from Butch, so I'm stuck."

"I hear you on that," Justine said with a sympathetic smile. "I wouldn't take money from Dean if it was wrapped in gold and delivered by Jason Momoa himself."

Heather squinted at the ceiling. "Well, if Jason Momoa delivered Butch's money I *might* reconsider..."

Justine chuckled.

"But since I live in reality, here goes: I'd like to make an offer on your house. It's a rent-to-own offer. I can rent from you and pay down the cost of the home until I'm able to secure a mortgage. I think Chandler is going to retire next year and leave me the firm. That will increase my income substantially. Okay, there it is." She blew out a relieved breath. "Now, you can look at me like I'm nuts or scream at me because I'm a terrible agent who hasn't been able to find you a *real* buyer yet. I'm ready."

Breathing a laugh, Justine rested her forearms on the table and pondered. "I'm so glad I hired you, Heather. You've shown the place relentlessly and you don't control the market. Plus, I like supporting female business owners in Ardor Creek."

"Well, you can bet I'm going to buy a shit-ton of your fancy art after you reopen the gallery. I want to support you too."

Smiling, she covered Heather's hand and squeezed. "You're awesome. How did everyone in my brother's class hate you in high school?"

Giving a good-natured scoff, Heather rolled her eyes. "I was a huge bitch. Age has softened me."

"Um, not sure about that, but okay."

"Touché." Heather arched a brow.

"Anyway," Justine said, leaning back in her chair. "I think this could work. We don't technically need to sell my house since Gary's income can support both mortgages. One of the many benefits of marrying an adult who has his shit together. Who knew those existed?" she teased.

"You got the last one," Heather muttered.

Excitement flashed in Justine's eyes. "And I definitely like the idea of you moving next door to Ardor Creek's sexiest bestselling author. That has potential written all over it."

"Okay, let's chill with the matchmaking," Heather said, both amusement and warning in her tone. "As I've stated, I thought he was pretty sexy when I first met him but I didn't realize he was a divorcé with two daughters."

"Come on, Gabby and Angeline are the cutest little girls. Avery loves playing with them."

"Um, no thanks. This uterus is for demonstration purposes only and won't feel any tugs at cute little children, no matter how hard you try." She pointed at her abdomen. "Not to mention, I'm in my mid-forties. Give it up, Jus. You're wasting your time."

"First of all, I love that you're childfree by choice and firm in that decision," Justine said. "Society puts too much pressure on women to 'fit the mold' and I love how honest you are about what you want and don't want."

"Uh, yeah, I'm pretty sure I've never fit the mold."

Laughing, Justine nodded. "Agreed. But dating a guy with kids is different than having them yourself. Maybe Jeremy just wants some sexy times too. Who knows? It could be fun."

Heather spared her a droll look. "Jeremy has 'relationship goals' written all over him. Unfortunately, I'm a disaster in that department and have decided I'm just going to have toe-curling, sweaty, meaningless sex for the rest of my life." With a dramatic sigh, she flipped her hair. "God, it sounds so exciting...except there are zero eligible men in Ardor Creek under the age of eighty." Fluttering her lips, her shoulders deflated. "Damn, I'm screwed."

Justine's laughter surrounded them. "Now I want to see you get with Jeremy just to see what happens. He might be great in bed and make you believe in love. You never know." She waggled her brows.

Heather contemplated having sexy times with the handsome author. She certainly found him attractive—in a cerebral-hot-guy kind of way—and wondered what type of lover he would be. Inquisitive? Determined? Would he stop at nothing until he found the spots that made her scream? Scrunching her features, she debated, unable to fully envision it. Was she interested?

Possibly...as long as he was only interested in sex since that's all she currently had space for in her busy life.

"Okay, this is awesome," Justine said, sitting up in her chair. "I already see you trying to figure out what it will be like. I'll talk to Gary tonight and unless he has any reservations, we'll move forward with the rent-to-buy plan. I'll get Mark to help us with the paperwork. After all, what are genius attorney siblings for if not to do free legal paperwork for you?"

Heather grinned. "Okay, but I'll pay him. That would rock. And I appreciate you being open to this, Justine. I also appreciate your support of my real estate business. You were the first person to welcome me back to Ardor Creek with open arms and I won't forget it."

"Hey, we've all needed help leaving our disastrous pasts behind," Justine said, waving her hand. "And you seem to be on great terms with everyone, which I love. By the way, are you going to come to our cookout on Saturday? You didn't answer the Facebook invite."

Heather bristled at the anxiety she always felt at hanging with the people who knew the worst version of herself she'd been in high school all those years ago. Shivering at the memories, she pushed them away and nodded. "I'll be there. Sorry I forgot to RSVP. I appreciate you inviting me. How much booze should I bring since I can't cook worth a damn?"

"As much as you want, sister," Justine said, beaming. "I'm not pregnant yet so I'm definitely going to toss a few back. It's almost June, the weather is warm and I'm ready to enjoy the first summer in my new house with my amazing fiancé." Leaning back, she threaded her hands behind her head and grinned.

"Sweet. I'm looking forward to it." She glanced at her phone. "In the meantime, I have a showing to get to. Want anything else?"

"Nope," Justine said, rising, "I'm good. I'll let you get back to conquering the exciting real estate market of Ardor Creek."

Snickering, Heather fell into step beside her as they exited the coffee shop. It was one of a few new businesses that had opened on Main Street over the past few years and one of Heather's favorite spots. After waving goodbye to Justine, Heather sat in her car and pulled up directions to her showing. Narrowing her eyes, she realized she hadn't asked Justine if Jeremy was coming to the cookout. He'd moved into town last year and she knew he and Justine were close.

Pondering, Heather recalled his tousled brown hair and light green eyes. They had been so handsome under the staid gallery lighting when she'd first met him—before Heather realized he was a nice family man with kids. She didn't do nice family men with kids normally, but he was pretty damn handsome. Hell, maybe Justine was right. Maybe it would be fun to bang him senseless while the girls were with his ex-wife. Then, she could send him home and go on her merry way.

The idea became more firmly implanted as she drove to the home on the northern side of Ardor Creek. By the time she parked in the driveway, Heather was visualizing Jeremy staring at her from between her thighs with those sexy green eyes as he devoured her deepest place.

Hmmm...

Yes, perhaps there was potential there. Stepping out of the car, she headed inside to prepare the house for the showing, hoping the entire time that Justine had invited the handsome author to Saturday's cookout.

Chapter 2

J eremy Kramer ushered his nine-year-old twins, Angeline and Gabby, into his SUV before sliding behind the wheel and checking the mirror to make sure they clicked their seatbelts. Once they were set, he asked, "Ready?"

"Ready," they chimed in unison.

Grinning, he placed the car in gear and began the short drive to Justine's new home. She'd been his neighbor up until two months ago when she and her fiancé had closed on their new house on Cyprus Street. Justine's brother Mark and his family also lived in the development as well as Carrie and Peter Stratford. Jeremy couldn't fault Justine for wanting to move closer to family but he was bummed to lose her as a neighbor.

First off, she'd become a good friend and their daughters loved playing together. Jeremy had thought it so fortuitous he'd moved next to a single mom as cool and friendly as Justine. She'd accepted him right away and introduced him to a ton of people in Ardor Creek.

Secondly, he'd developed a bit of a crush on his new neighbor. Unfortunately, Justine was madly in love with Gary Lincoln so he didn't really stand a chance. After Justine had gently rebuffed his request for a date last year, Jeremy had resigned himself to the fact he'd always be firmly in the friend zone. It was a bummer since no one else in Ardor Creek had caught his eye, but he was happy for Justine and wished her well.

Liar.

The thought wafted through his mind before he could control it, and he allowed the image of Heather Combs' face to form. In a town as small as Ardor Creek, you were bound to run into the same people and Jeremy sure did run into Heather a lot. She was always striding around Main Street in her fancy clothes, running from one showing to another. She was a hustler, and Jeremy admired her grit. Even more interesting, he'd come to admire her other...assets too. Like her gorgeous blue eyes, the golden hair that always seemed perfectly styled, and the way her long legs fit into the tight pants and skirts she always seemed to wear. Man, the woman *loved* tight clothes...

"Can we paint our nails again when we get home, Dad?" Gabby asked.

Shaking his head to rid it of the sexy images, Jeremy smiled into the rear view mirror. "One nail painting session a day is all your old man can take," he teased. "And besides, both of you chose such pretty colors when we painted them this morning."

The girls held up their fingers, admiring their handiwork, and Jeremy chuckled. Never in a million years had he imagined he'd end up a single father with two girls intent on ensuring he knew everything about nails, hair clips, and the countless other things little girls loved. A different man might question his masculinity—after all, he'd let his girls paint his fingernails pink a hundred times at this point. But he loved his children to distraction and figured a man who adored his children was about a masculine as it could get. Giving himself an internal pat on the back, he gazed at the girls in the reflection.

"We can try the cramper tomorrow. Mom said you all enjoyed cramping your hair last time."

"It's *crimping*, Dad," Angeline said, snickering alongside her sister.

"No way," he teased, indicating he'd intentionally mispronounced the word because he knew they got a kick out of it. "Cramping all the way ladies."

"You're dorky, Dad."

"Can't argue with that." He waggled his eyebrows. "Your dad likes being dorky. Leave me alone."

The girls chatted away in the back seat as he neared Justine's home. She'd invited him to their cookout today and Jeremy was excited to see her new house. He also really liked the crew of Ardor Creek lifers she hung out with and felt he was slowly becoming friends with everyone. His ex-wife, Jennifer, lived in Battle Falls and having her close was nice. They'd been determined to stay friendly after their divorce and had done an excellent job so far. Still, Jen had her own life and her fiancé, Lou...and having your ex-wife as your only friend was super-lame. Hence, Jeremy was thrilled to be welcomed into the Ardor Creek crew.

After parking in front of Justine's house, he exited the car and grabbed the cupcakes he and the girls had made last night from the trunk.

"I'll carry them, Dad," Angeline said, holding out her hands.

"Thanks, sweetheart." Handing them to her, he reached inside for the bag of chips and beer.

"I can carry that bag."

"Whoa," Jeremy said, holding it out of Gabby's reach. "I appreciate the offer but I don't want to get arrested for letting you carry beer to the cookout. Why don't you help Angie and make sure the cupcakes are balanced."

"*Angeline*, Dad," she corrected.

"Right," he said, closing the trunk and saluting. "Sorry. Let's walk to the back of the house. Justine said to head back there when we arrived."

They began walking, Jeremy internally reminding himself that his daughter had decided sometime last year she did not want to be called Angie. He and Jen did their best to remember but it slipped sometimes. Thankfully, Gabby was perfectly fine with her nickname so he'd take the win.

When they crested the corner of the house, his girls squealed Avery's name and jogged toward her. "We made cupcakes!" Angeline announced, thrusting them at Avery.

"I'll take those," Justine said, swooping in and grabbing them before her daughter could. "Avery has already had two brownies and we're on a two-hour hiatus from sweets."

Avery crossed her arms and scowled. "I wasn't going to eat one, Mom."

"I'll pretend I believe you," she said, chucking her nose. "Want to show the girls our awesome surprise?"

The cupcakes were completely forgotten as Avery beamed and furiously nodded. "Come on," she called to Angeline and Gabby, "you can meet our new puppy!"

The girls gasped with excitement. "Puppy?"

Avery trailed to the back door and slid it open and a tiny cocker spaniel burst through. Jeremy's daughters rushed over, petting the dog with glee as it licked their faces.

"Her name is Petunia," Avery said, patting the pup's head. "Let's go play with her by the fence. Come on!"

The three of them bounded across the yard, Petunia close on their heels, and Jeremy trailed over to Justine, arching a brow. "A puppy? You're killing me, Lancaster. The girls are going to revoke my dad card if I don't let them adopt one too. What gives?"

"Blame it on Abby," she said, showing her palms. "One playdate with Kitana and Avery was toast. She finally wore me down."

Abby chose that moment to appear, strutting around the side of the house holding Kitana's leash as her husband Chad strode beside her with their daughter in his arms. "Did I hear my name? Am I getting blamed for the dog situation again?"

Chuckling, Justine hugged her before bending down to pet Kitana. "I would never disparage our esteemed mayor. If you feel comfortable letting her off the leash, she can go play with the kids." Justine gestured with her head toward the back fence and swing set beside it.

"I should probably ease her into it before I let her off the leash," Abby said. Lifting to her toes, she kissed Chad's cheek. "You keep an eye on the human kid and I've got the dog."

"Deal," Chad said, pecking her lips before she trailed off with Kitana at her side to join the revelry by the swings.

"Here you go," Chad said, handing Justine a plastic bag. "Prosecco for mimosas and vodka for later. We were going to grab some beer but Abbs thought you'd probably have enough already."

"I brought some IPAs from the local brewery in Pittston if you want some," Jeremy said, setting his bag on the nearby table and lifting one of the six-packs. "Or I have stout too. Whatever you prefer."

"Thanks, man," Chad said, eyeing the selection. "I love Susquehanna Brewing Company. Let me set up the pack and play and I'll have a stout."

"Just set it up in the yard over there," Justine said, pointing to an open spot on the grass. "And let me hold this sweet little girl while you do." Extending her arms, she took Zoey and balanced her on her hip as Chad got to work.

"Yeer-yeer," Zoey chimed, the word indistinguishable as she pointed at Justine's earring.

"That's right," Justine said, eyes wide as she grinned. "*Earring.* You're getting so big and are already so smart."

"Ah, the baby talk phase," Jeremy said, shaking his head as he began unloading the beers from the box. "Don't miss that."

"Really? I miss it all the time. I can't wait until Gary knocks me up again."

Chuckling, Jeremy opened a can and took a large gulp. "Good for you. Two and done for this dude." He pointed at his chest.

"That's nice to hear since I know of another single person in town who isn't interested in having any kids." She waggled her brows.

"Man, you're a dog with a bone, Jus. I told you, Heather's the opposite of every woman I've ever dated. I'm just not sure we'd mesh...although she's very pretty. I'd have to be blind not to notice."

"Pretty..." Justine mused, narrowing her eyes. "I can work with pretty."

Breathing a laugh, Jeremy grabbed a can of beer and extended it toward Chad when he walked over.

"What's so funny?" Chad asked.

"I think our favorite author needs to ask Heather Combs on a date," Justine said. "He's giving me grief."

Chad's brows lifted as he took a sip. "I thought you *liked* Jeremy," he teased.

"Oh, stop." She swatted his chest. "Heather is awesome and high school was forever ago. She's been nothing but gracious since she moved back."

"I'm kidding...*mostly,*" he said, grinning. "Heather's not so bad and she's always been really hot. I say go for it, man."

"Well, thanks for your approval, guys," he said sardonically, "but dating with two kids is tough. She might not be willing to put up with the weird schedule and is probably used to dating dudes way more exciting than me."

"Um, you're a freaking bestselling author, Jeremy. That's hella exciting. And you'll have to bring *someone* to my wedding in

October," Justine said, eyes widening with delight, "and so will Heather, so I think you should be each other's plus-ones."

"I'm perfectly fine attending your wedding solo, but if I meet the love of my life between then and now, I'll certainly bring her."

"Oh, you're no fun," she said, scrunching her features. "Fine. Come on, Zoey, let's go play with the doggies until everyone gets here."

They padded away and Jeremy chatted with Chad until the others arrived. Scott and Ashlyn Grillo appeared with their two kids shortly before Carrie and Peter Stratford arrived with their crew. Once Justine's brother Mark and his wife Teresa and daughter Rose arrived, the adults gathered on the back porch while the kids played in the back yard.

"Thanks to all of you for coming to our first barbeque in the new house," Gary said, lifting his beer as he saluted the group. "To many more although the next one is at Peter's house because our grill is only half the size of his."

"Hey, we can't all be grill masters," Peter said, shrugging as he lifted his iced tea. "But I appreciate your efforts, Lincoln. I'm used to having the biggest equipment if you know what I mean." He slid his arm around Carrie's waist and grinned. "Right, honey? Go on and tell them how big my equipment is—"

"Gross," Carrie interjected, palming his face and playfully pushing him away. "I apologize for my husband, his terrible sense of humor *and* his out-of-control ego," she said, rolling her eyes. "We're so happy to be here to celebrate your new home, guys."

Placing his hand by his mouth to mimic telling a secret, Peter loudly whispered to Chad, "She doesn't want to make you guys jealous. I get it."

"Well, we're happy you're here," Justine said, squeezing Gary's waist as he smiled down at her. "Along with *all* your equipment that we don't need to discuss. Make yourself at home. The coolers are stocked and I'm already pretty tipsy on this rosé." She snickered.

"Cheers to me," Gary teased before the group chimed in with a collective, "Cheers!" and clinked their glasses.

"I thought you invited Heather," Abby said after sipping from her red cup.

"I did," Justine murmured. "She's supposed to be here by now..."

As if on cue, Heather strode around the side of the house, phone in one hand as her thumb moved over the screen and a bottle of wine in the other. Focused on the phone, she didn't look up until she was steps from the group. Lifting her head, she flashed a smile.

"What?" she asked, shrugging. "I brought wine so I could be fashionably late and you wouldn't be mad." Her eyes widened. "Were you guys talking about me? How fun. Anything good?"

Justine laughed and rushed toward her. "We were just wondering where you were. Come on. You're right on time." They exchanged a hug before Justine dragged her toward the table, urging her to set the wine down before pouring her a glass. Jeremy watched their interplay, observing the woman who'd been on his mind on the drive over.

"Hot right?" Chad murmured, inching closer. "No matter how mean she was, Heather was always hot."

Jeremy studied her, clad in tight white jeans that hugged her long legs and brown sandals that had a bunch of glittery straps. She wore a necklace with large colored charms above a pretty silky blouse.

"Dude," Chad said, realization lighting his eyes. "You're into her."

"I was actually thinking that my daughters would get a kick out of all the sparkly things on her sandals." Taking a sip of beer, he lifted a shoulder. "And she's definitely hot. It's not even debatable."

"Truth. Abby is the most gorgeous woman I've ever seen, but Heather's always been a looker."

Jeremy absently assessed Heather as she laughed at something Justine said. Her white teeth flashed under the bright sun and he swallowed thickly. Yep, she was gorgeous, but there seemed to be a lot underneath the surface too. Things kept carefully hidden from the world, swirling deep beneath the pretty barrier.

"Okay, now you're staring," Chad muttered.

Clearing his throat, he faced Chad. "I was just wondering if anyone's ever bothered to look beyond her appearance. I sense she's come to rely on people either judging her or accepting her for what's on the surface. Must be tough. Everyone has a ton of layers inside but sometimes people never bother to look."

"I'm digging the way your creative author brain works," Chad said, patting his shoulder. "It generates awesome backstories and I'm here for it. How's the new novel coming, by the way?"

"Awesome. It's a thriller based on a suburban housewife who's secretly a serial killer..." He spent several minutes detailing Chad on the plot before Heather sauntered over in her sparkly sandals.

"Hi, guys," she said, clinking her plastic cup with Jeremy's and then Chad's. "How's it hanging?"

"Great," Chad said, giving a lopsided grin. "Jeremy was just giving me the scoop on his new novel."

"Do tell," she said, arching a brow.

"Eh, same ol', same ol'. Mystery, intrigue and all that jazz," Jeremy said, shrugging. "How about you? How's the real estate business?"

"Pretty good. Not as exciting as real estate in the big city but nothing in Ardor Creek ever is."

"Hey, we've got a famous author as a resident now," Chad said, gesturing to Jeremy. "We're kind of a big deal."

"Keep it in your pants, Hanson," she teased, rolling her eyes. "I know you and Abby are ga-ga over this place—" She broke off, uttering an "*oomph*" when a soccer ball pelted her stomach, causing red wine to fly out of her solo cup.

"Shit!" she muttered, swiping off the wine. "I just bought this blouse."

"Sorry!" Gabby cried as she ran over, followed closely by Angeline. "I didn't mean to kick it so hard. Angeline pushed me!"

"You ruined her shirt," Angeline whispered, covering her mouth. "You're in trouble..."

"I'm so sorry, Heather," Jeremy said as she swatted the red stains. "Let me grab a cloth." He jogged over to the table and wet some napkins before returning to her side. "Here, maybe this will help."

She grabbed the wet napkins and began to dab but it was futile. Glancing down at his girls, Jeremy lifted a brow. "What do you say, girls?"

"We're sorry," they chimed in unison.

Heather studied them as she dabbed, and Jeremy realized Gabby was seconds away from bursting into tears. Crouching down, he gazed into her glassy eyes. "It's okay, honey. Accidents happen. You both just need to be careful."

"Okay," she murmured, sniffling.

"It's what I get for drinking red wine at a cookout," Heather muttered. "I've always been a little extra." Bending down, she rested her hands on her knees so she was eye-level with Gabby.

"It's okay, kid. Go back and play. Believe me, there are bigger problems in this world than a stained shirt."

Gabby bit her lip before nodding. "Dad can buy you a new one if you want."

Chuckling, Heather glanced at Jeremy. "She's already spending your money on clothes. I'm not a fan of kids but that's pretty awesome."

Breathing a laugh, Jeremy gestured toward the yard. "Go on, girls. It's okay."

"I'll go get some club soda from the kitchen," Chad offered. "Be right back."

Jeremy stepped forward and took the wadded napkins from Heather's hand as she rose. Lifting them toward a stain on the side of her chest, he began to pat. "You missed this spot."

Blue eyes gazed into his, filled with mirth a slight bit of mischief. Jeremy was several inches taller, even though she wore the sparkly wedged sandals, and he felt a protective pull as he leaned over her.

Arching a brow, she said, "Well, this wasn't how I imagined you touching my boobs the first time, but I'll go with it."

"Sorry," he said, yanking his hand away. "I didn't even think—"

"It's fine," she said, placing her hand over his, which now clutched the wet napkins, and squeezing. "It's just a shirt, Jeremy."

His eyes dipped over the silky fabric, skating over the swells of her breasts before darting lower. Clearing his throat, he lifted his gaze, noting the arousal in her deep blue eyes. Overcome by the scent of her flowery shampoo, his throat bobbed as he swallowed. "Heather—"

"Here you go," Chad interrupted, handing her a cloth doused with club soda. "This might help."

"Honestly," she said, glancing at the shirt. "I think it's ruined. I'm just going to grab a t-shirt from Justine at this point. I like to wear blouses that show off my perfect breasts so I can squash the little rumor my ex-husband—and *others*—spread around town." She glared at Chad before batting her eyelashes. "But I think the damage is done."

"Yeah, I'm going to pay for that one for a while, huh?" Chad asked, rubbing the back of his neck. "I didn't mean to spread false rumors about your...um...chest area, Heather." He circled his hand in front of his chest as Abby approached.

"Is it salvageable?" she asked before looking at Chad. "Why are you pointing to your man boobs?"

"Man boobs, my ass," Chad muttered, appearing offended. "You've never had it so good, Miller. And I was just telling Heather how nice her chest looked—"

"What?" Abby asked, confused as she glanced between them.

"Don't worry, babe," he said, grabbing her hand. "Your boobs are the only boobs I want."

"I can't take you anywhere," she muttered.

"We're in Jus's back yard, Abbs. Chill. Would it help if we made out?" Leaning forward, he tapped his cheek. "Kiss your husband and tell him how hot you are for him."

"Uggh, you're annoying." Palming his face, she pushed him away. "I'm sure Jus will let you borrow a shirt, Heather. I'm going back to play with the kids." Chin thrust high, she pivoted and began walking away before Chad caught her and bent down, lifting her over his shoulder as she squealed.

"Put me down right now, Chad Hanson!"

"Oh, she's so cute when she's pissed like this," Chad said, waggling his brows at Heather and Jeremy. "Excuse me while I make out with my wife." Striding toward the house, he disappeared around the corner as Abby's laughter rang over the yard.

"They're cute," Heather said, wrinkling her nose. "I might barf but I'm still happy for them."

"They are," Jeremy said, turning to face her. "Thank you for being so nice to the girls. I'm really sorry, Heather. I'll definitely buy you a new shirt."

"That's not necessary." She waved her hand. "I'm going to ask Jus to borrow a t-shirt and I'll chalk this one up to collateral damage from hanging around tiny humans."

His lips curved. "I know you're not a fan of kids. They can definitely be messy."

She pursed her lips before answering. "Messy is okay. I just don't know what to do around them. I've never had the 'mommy gene.'" She made quotation marks with her fingers. "But accidents happen. Let me go grab a shirt from Jus and we can continue whatever conversation we were droning on about while you were staring at my boobs." She flashed a gorgeous grin.

"Was I?" He bit his lip, knowing he was busted.

"Yeah. I'm glad someone is enjoying the handiwork of my very talented surgeon." Leaning forward, she whispered. "You might get to look at them more often than you think."

"Really?" he asked, intrigued.

"Yep. Guess Justine didn't tell you. I'm moving into her house. You're about to be neighbors with the infamous Heather Combs." Inching closer, Jeremy could feel her warm breath against his cheek as she spoke. "Think you can handle it?"

Jeremy swallowed as his body hardened. Blood rushed to every cell in his body as his eyes fell to her luscious lips. "Honestly, I'm not sure. You're...different, Heather," he said, struggling to find the right word. "In a good way."

"Different in a good way," she repeated softly, her tongue darting out to bathe those glorious lips. "You bet your ass I am, buddy. Better get ready." Winking, she turned and strode toward the house.

Straightening, Jeremy inhaled a huge breath before running his fingers through his thick brown hair. Holy hell, she was a force to be reckoned with. Jeremy had always considered himself a mild-mannered guy and had only dated chill women in the past. His ex-wife was pretty laid back too, which was probably why they'd remained such good friends after their divorce.

Dating someone like Heather would be consuming—like being drawn into a vortex where you didn't know up from down and might spontaneously combust at any moment. It was the exact opposite of his even-keeled nature but maybe that meant it would be fun. As he stood there, fighting to control his ragged heartbeat, Jeremy realized he desperately wanted to find out.

"Whoa, dude," Chad said, sidling up behind him as Abby jogged back to join the kids. "I know that look. I pretty much had it the second Abbs returned to town."

"Yeah, I'm into her. Did you know she was moving into Justine's old house? Didn't expect that."

"Mark mentioned it to me. Certainly makes things easier. The walks of shame will be really short."

Laughing, Jeremy nodded. "I guess so. It's going to be interesting, that's for damn sure."

Heather emerged from the back door, clad in a gray t-shirt that should've looked dowdy or plain but, instead, clung to every nook and curve of her body. Swirling his tongue around his suddenly dry mouth, Jeremy realized the decision to ask her out had already been cemented in his usually logical brain.

As the father of two girls and a successful, self-employed author, he was used to being logical, but honestly, logical was boring as hell sometimes. Excited to shake things up in his regimented life, Jeremy spent the rest of the cookout anticipating the moment when he would finally get up the nerve to ask her out.

Chapter 3

Heather woke up on moving day ready to begin yet another new phase of her life. The tiny apartment she'd been living in since moving to Ardor Creek had never felt like home, and she hoped Justine's old house would one day grow to be *hers*. Somewhere she could build her future as she continued creating her new life in Ardor Creek.

Since she didn't own a ton of furniture, she'd hired two local teenagers to haul her living room furniture, dresser and other large items in their pickup truck. Once they'd moved them into the two-bedroom home, Heather returned to her apartment, loaded up her sedan with boxes, and began the transport of her other items. Although she was making good money as a real estate agent, it wasn't *great* money yet, so she decided to move the small things herself. After all, she had two working legs and wasn't helpless. Was it glamorous? Hell no. But it was practical, and Heather prided herself on not being a prima donna...*most* of the time.

Three trips across town later, she loaded the last of her clothes in her car and locked her apartment for the last time. She'd convinced the landlord to hire her as the rental agent and would keep the key for showings. Pulling into her new driveway, she exited the car, happy to finish the move. Her muscles were sore and she decided she'd treat herself with a nice long bath and glass of wine once the last load was inside. Hell, maybe a *bottle* of wine if she could keep her eyes open long enough.

As the sun set in the distance, Heather grabbed the hooks of the hangers that were tied together and gently removed some of her nice dresses from the backseat. She hadn't wanted to pack them in boxes and had decided to move them on the hangers. Carefully draping them over her arm, her ears perked when she heard a giggle from behind the nearby wooden fence.

"Shhh!" a high-pitch voice whispered. "She'll hear you."

"I didn't do anything!"

"Ouch!"

Feeling her lips curve, Heather craned her neck to peek between the wooden slats of the fence. "Hi, girls. I can see you. Are you spying on me?"

Silence stretched for a moment before the bushes bristled. Moments later, Angeline and Gabby slowly eased around the fence, stopping a few feet from Heather. One of the girls chewed her thumbnail as the other eyed the red dress that sat atop the pile in Heather's arms.

"Chewing your nail like that will stop it from growing," Heather said, her tone slightly scolding.

The girl dropped her hand and assessed her thumb. "Really?"

Pursing her lips, Heather said, "Honestly, I don't think so. My mom used to tell me that because she didn't want me to ruin my nails. Having nicely manicured nails is important to your appearance and she was kind of obsessed with that sort of stuff."

"Gabby always bites her nails," the other girl said.

"Do not!"

"Okay, so you're Gabby," Heather said with a nod. "I couldn't remember which was which."

"We're fraternal so we look different," Gabby said.

"Well, you have brown hair and green eyes like your dad, and I assume your mom has black hair and blue eyes like Angeline."

They both nodded.

"Score. Well, this has been a fun chat about genetics but I need to get these clothes inside."

Angeline stepped forward and lifted her hand toward the dresses before gazing up at Heather. "They're so pretty," she whispered.

"Go on," Heather droned. "You two have already ruined one blouse. Might as well feel up the dress before I dry clean it."

The girl ran her fingers over the red silk. "You must look like a princess when you wear this one."

"That's the idea, kid. Cost me a fortune but I bought it to impress a hedge fund manager I was sure would be ex-husband number two. Unfortunately, he burned out before we made it there."

"We have hedges," Gabby said, inching closer and pointing to the nearby row of bushes.

Chuckling, Heather grinned. "Not the same kind of hedge but you're hella smart to get the reference." Frowning, she said, "Uh, wait. I don't know if 'hella' is a bad word or not. Crap. I'm terrible around kids."

The girls glanced at each other before they faced her and beamed. "We like you. You're doing fine."

"Yeah? Thanks. Where's your dad, anyway?"

"He's in his writing cave. He thinks we're playing in our playroom but we got bored. We have a deal that we'll leave him alone if he tells us he needs an hour to focus on his writing, and we promised we won't go farther than the yard." They both made an X over their heart.

"Well, that's great but you're officially on my property now so you've broken your word."

The girls gasped before giggling and scuttling back to the grass that lined the driveway. "Don't tell our dad."

"I won't, *this* time," she warned before softening it with a wink. "But it's important to stay safe. You're both lucky you have a safe home and I know your dad would worry if something happened to you."

"Can we come over and see your dresses once you hang them up?" Gabby asked.

Heather contemplated, wondering if these tiny humans truly understood how awkward she was around kids. She'd just never felt the maternal pull and didn't have the first idea what to do around them. "I'm not sure. Let me think about it, okay?"

The girls nodded before waving. "Good night, Ms. Combs."

"Oh, good lord, please call me Heather," she said, wrinkling her nose. "I'll tell your dad I asked you to call me that too if he has a problem with it. Ms. Combs was my grandma and she had a thousand wrinkles. Uggh."

Snickering, they gave a final wave before jetting back toward the house.

"Damn, Heather, you moved *and* had to deal with kids. You definitely deserve a bottle of wine tonight." Gathering her clothes, she headed inside, already anticipating the full-bodied Malbec on her tongue.

Chapter 4

♥

A few days later, Heather finished showing an apartment above Nick's Diner on Main Street and decided she'd earned herself a beer. The renter had verbally committed and she'd already emailed him the application from her phone. After locking the apartment, she headed to Main Street, inhaling the warm air as she strode in her two-inch wedges. They were more comfortable than heels so she usually wore them when she had to show spaces with stairs.

As she sauntered along, she observed a couple approaching in the distance and her heart fell to her knees. *Butch.* Her ex-husband strolled hand-in-hand with his wife, Cynthia Andrews, and Heather debated which one she despised more as they approached. She'd caught glimpses of Butch and Cynthia around town since she'd moved back, but had always been masterful at avoiding them. Unfortunately, this time she would have no such luck.

"Well, if it isn't my lovely ex-wife," Butch said, his tone acerbic as Cynthia glared. "Figured we'd have to run into each other one day."

"Butch," she muttered, trying to sound bored even though blood was pounding through her veins. "I heard you two tied the knot. Congrats. Hopefully, this marriage will work out better for you."

"Oh, it will," Cynthia said, arching a brow. "Butch finally has a partner who isn't a raging bitch and who can please him in all the ways he needs."

Tossing back her head, Heather released a gleeful laugh.

"And what is so funny?" Cynthia snapped.

"Oh, honey, I just pity you. That's all. You can pretend there's 'pleasure' in your relationship all you want." She made quotation marks with her fingers. "Your husband could never find the speed bump in my roadway if you catch my drift. I doubt he can find yours."

"That's enough, Heather," Butch warned. "We told each other we'd be cordial after we divorced."

"Was that before or after you spread the rumor that I cheated on you, even though we both know it was the other way around?" she asked, rubbing her chin. "By the way, Cyn, Butch and I were never together after that but he did have some weird creams in the bathroom. I'd get tested if I were you—"

"You'll never change, will you?" Cynthia interrupted, thrusting her finger in Heather's face. "You'll always be the skanky bitch we knew in high school. Derek Combs' degenerate daughter who made people feel like shit and who we all knew would never amount to anything!"

Heather flinched, the words cutting to the bone. After all, they rang true deep in her core where she'd always felt rotten and unlovable. So many years she'd lived that way, and so many years she'd tried to shed the feeling...but how did you discard something that was a part of you? Something you'd inherited from your shitty parents and would always believe about yourself no matter how many self-help books you read and self-love meditations you tried?

Working her jaw, she tried to form a witty yet scathing comeback. Quips and zingers were usually her specialty, but she found it hard to speak with the huge lump burning the back of her throat. Feeling her breath quicken, her chest heaved as she struggled to move her lips.

"Hi, sweetheart," a deep voice said above her ear before a strong arm slid around her waist. "I didn't realize you were going to meet me on Main Street before our date."

Heather glanced up at Jeremy Kramer, a goofy smile on his face as he gazed into her eyes. Breaking their stare, he thrust his hand toward Butch. "Jeremy Kramer. You must be the ex-husband. Nice to meet you."

Butch's eyes narrowed but he shook Jeremy's hand before Jeremy extended it to Cynthia. Her eyes widened with delight as she shook. "J.R. Kramer," she breathed. "It's so nice to meet you. I absolutely loved *Alternate Destinies*. I left you a five-star review."

"Well, thank you..."

"Cynthia."

"Thanks, Cynthia. Those even out the bad reviews, for sure."

"Oh, you," she said, playfully swatting his chest as Heather gaped, wondering when in the hell *she'd* entered an *alternate destiny*. "I can't believe anyone would give you a bad review. You're such a good author and so handsome—"

"Okay, dear," Butch interjected, sliding a possessive arm around her waist. "We need to head to the diner before it gets busy."

"And I have to get this one to the pub for our date," Jeremy said, squeezing Heather's waist. "I feel like the luckiest guy in town to be with the real estate agent who's setting Ardor Creek on fire. Ready, sweetheart?" He smiled down at her before tucking a strand of hair behind her ear that was wafting in the light breeze.

Tilting her head, she murmured, "Are you daft?"

"Come on, Butch," Cynthia said, taking her husband's hand and leading them away. "Let's leave these two to their dinner. Jeremy, don't be a stranger, okay? Bye for now." She waggled her fingers before they scuffled down the street. Turning to face Jeremy, Heather placed her palms on his chest and shoved.

"What the hell do you think you're doing?" she asked through clenched teeth.

His features contorted before he stepped back and held up his hands, palms facing her. "Whoa. I was just trying to help. I could hear Cynthia from a block away."

"So you made up some fake story about us dating?" Stepping forward, she jabbed a finger in his chest. "Cynthia is an ass and I can handle her just fine." Adding another finger, she pressed again. "And I don't know what gave you the idea I was some damsel who needed saving but you swooped in on the wrong woman, buddy. Got it? *Wrong. Woman.*" She jutted her fingers into his pec to emphasize each word.

"Wow," he said, encircling her fingers as he gazed at her with those light green eyes. They had deep honey-colored flecks that simmered with confusion and a slight bit of frustration. "I did *not* expect this reaction."

Drawing her hand away, she lifted her chin before crossing her arms over her chest. Jeremy's eyes darted toward the globes before lifting back to hers. "That's right. Eyes up here, buddy." Forming a "V" she pointed into both eyes. "You've got a lot of fucking nerve."

Expelling a breath, he shook his head before harshly rubbing his forehead. "Am I in the wrong here? I was just trying to help a friend—"

"You don't know me," she said through clenched teeth. "I know we've been friendly but the last thing I need is for people to think I need a man to save me. Not in a million years. Got it?"

"Got it," he said, a muscle ticking in his jaw under the stubble that she was too irritated to admit was extremely sexy.

"Good." She tapped her foot on the ground as he gazed at her with those kind, hooded eyes, and she began to feel the remorse set in. Realizing she'd overreacted, she tamped down the emotion, determined to stay strong now that she'd already made an ass of herself.

His eyes darted between hers, contemplating before he leaned closer and spoke in a low tone that sent shivers through her frame. "I'm sorry for trying to save you. Somehow, I got the notion you've gotten used to fighting alone and I thought it might be cool to have an ally."

Backing away, his lips curved into an empathetic smile, transforming his features into an expression so handsome, Heather's breath caught in the back of her throat. "I'm on your side, Heather. See ya." Saluting, he pivoted and trailed away.

Deflated, Heather emitted a frustrated groan and watched his broad shoulders disappear down the street. Damn, she'd really messed that up. First, she'd let Cynthia get under her skin, and then she'd lost it with Jeremy. Feeling like a Grade A chump, she scuffled into the pub and slid onto one of the barstools.

"Hey, Heather," Terry said, grinning as she approached behind the bar. "You're just in time for happy hour. What can I get you?"

"How about a do-over on life?" Heather muttered.

"That bad, huh?"

"Yeah." Glancing at the bottles of liquor, she decided she needed something strong to clear her head. "Jack neat."

"Sure thing." Terry poured the drink and Heather took a sip, grimacing as Terry arched a brow. "I'm a good listener, you know?"

Sighing, Heather twirled the glass above the bar as she contemplated. "Why am I such a dick, Terry?"

Her friend's features drew together before she reached over and squeezed her wrist. "I'm going to need a *bit* more clarification." She held her thumb and forefinger an inch apart.

Heather stared at her, pondering. "I guess I just wonder if a person is rotten in their core, are they destined to be that way forever? Can a person like that change?"

"Good lord, Heather," Terry said, picking up a glass and shining it as she spoke. "You're nowhere near rotten. Were you Little Miss Sunshine all those years ago? Nope. But I saw your dad around town and he was nastier than a hornet without a nest. Your mom was no picnic either."

Glancing down, Heather felt the old pain and anger well inside. "I didn't realize you noticed."

"Well, you were too busy being a mean girl to let anyone get too close, but I understood why you put up all those walls and pushed people away. Maybe other people didn't, but I did."

Shaking her head, Heather stared at the brown liquid, wishing she could swirl away all the old pain as easily as she could churn the whiskey. "I keep telling myself I'll wake up one day and finally be an awesome person, but I'm pretty sure I'm destined to be fucked up until I croak."

"If that's what you believe, then that's what will happen," Terry said, lifting a shoulder.

Breathing a laugh, Heather sipped the whiskey. "When did you become a psychologist?"

"Um, have you *met* a bartender before? Therapy is all I do around here, hon. And I assure you, you're not fucked up. Maybe a little scared. Becoming the person you truly want to be is painful, and most people are afraid of pain."

"Not me," she said, tossing back the rest of the drink. "Not this time. I can't afford to be scared anymore, Terry. I've got to figure out a way to be happy. Forty-four years of misery is enough."

"Hear, hear." Sauntering toward the liquor rack, Terry grabbed the Jack and poured Heather another round. "On the house. I'll call a rideshare for you if you need one, or Gary's on patrol tonight and he'd always be happy to take you home."

"Thanks, Terry." Lifting the glass in a salute, she smiled at the kind woman before she sauntered toward the kitchen and disappeared behind the flapping doors. Running her hand over the smooth wood of the bar, Heather replayed the conversation with Butch, vowing to remain unemotional the next time she encountered him and his *wife*.

The word caused a burning in the back of her throat which she doused with a sip of Jack. And then, she allowed her thoughts to drift to her handsome neighbor. The man who'd been so kind to try and help her—before she jumped down his throat in the middle of Main Street.

Huffing a laugh, Heather realized it was kind of funny in the big scheme of things. Would Jeremy have a sense of humor about it? She had no idea. But one thing was certain: she'd find out soon. Because Heather needed to apologize to her new neighbor and she needed to do it in person.

Chapter 5

♥

Jeremy flinched when the firm knocks sounded on his back door. It was Friday and the girls were with Jen so the house was blissfully quiet. Clicking "save" on the document, he closed his laptop and trailed from his home office to the back door. Heather stood on the other side, grinning through the paned windows as she held up a bottle of red wine.

"Truce?" she called through the door.

Unable to control his smile, he pulled open the door and crossed his arms before leaning on the frame. "Hello, neighbor. I'd invite you in but I still have bruises on my pec where you jabbed me the other day."

She scoffed and rolled her eyes. "Are all authors this dramatic?"

Closing one eye, he glanced at the dusky sky. "Not sure. But I prefer *creative* to dramatic."

"I bet you do." Breezing past him, she pushed inside, her body grazing his as he inhaled the flowery scent of her shampoo.

"Come on in," he muttered, closing the door behind him.

"Nice," she said, gazing over the kitchen, which Jeremy had recently remodeled. Setting the wine on the island counter, she pointed to the drawer beneath. "Is the corkscrew in here?"

"You know, I could be busy. It *is* Friday night."

She shot him a deprecating grin. "Are you?"

"Actually, I just finished a chapter," he said, striding over to the counter and opening the drawer. Pulling out the corkscrew, he extended it toward her before drawing it back. "But I could have a hot date."

"*Ohhhh*," she said, those gorgeous eyes lighting with excitement. "Do tell. Let me guess: you were going to invite her over and read *Pride and Prejudice* until her panties got so wet she'd show you her ankles before swooning?"

Shooting her a sardonic glare, he clenched the wine bottle and dragged it close. Inserting the corkscrew, he began to twist. "I'm not sure if I should be offended at your assumption of my sexual prowess or impressed that you've read Jane Austen."

"Darling, every woman has read Jane Austen. I think it's embedded in our DNA." Reaching for the glasses that hung from the ceiling rack, she grasped two before lowering her voice to a sultry tone. "This is a great opportunity to stare at my boobs. Perfect angle and all that."

Tossing back his head, he laughed before lifting the bottle and shaking it. "I'm not sure one of these is going to be enough to make it through an evening with you, Heather."

Setting the glasses on the counter, she arched a brow. "I think you'll survive. And I have more at home."

He poured them each a glass before lifting his in a salute. "To your epic apology?"

"Don't push it," she muttered, clinking her glass with his. "You'll get one when I'm ready."

"Can't wait." Swirling the liquid, he noted the fullness before sniffing and taking a sip. "It's good. Thanks."

"Sure. Can we sit?"

"The couch is comfortable but I wasn't expecting company and there are about a thousand dolls of various shapes and sizes strewn around. If you're cool with that, we can go into the living room."

"Sounds creepy. I'm in."

Armed with the wine, he led her to the living room, noting the toys and dolls that lined the carpet. "Told you," he said, lowering to one corner of the couch.

"It's not so bad." She sat on the other corner and kicked off her sandals before drawing one leg to curl under the other. "This is a pretty big house for a single guy and two little girls."

"I wanted something big when I moved from Philly," he said, shrugging. "The girls and I were cramped into a two-bedroom condo there and this house allows them to have their own rooms."

"Good looking out, Dad," she said with a smile. "I wasn't sure thoughtful dads existed until I returned to Ardor Creek. There are some good ones in our crew."

"Are we part of the crew?" he asked, excitement lacing his tone. "I wasn't sure but I definitely want to be. The Ardor Creek lifers are fun."

"I *think* we're part of the crew. Justine made me apologize to Abby so I should've earned my 'crew card.'"

"What did you do to Abby? She seemed fine with you at the cookout."

Sighing, Heather shook her head. "I was a dick to her in high school. Kind of like I was to you on Main Street the other day."

"Eh, you weren't that bad. I man-fouled by trying to swoop in and save you. My ex-wife says I always try to fix everything. It drives her crazy."

"Oh, god, you have a savior complex. Yikes. Your chances of getting laid just diminished tenfold."

His brows lifted. "I wasn't sure I even had a chance, so score one for me." He raised his finger as she chuckled.

Bringing the glass to her lips, she studied him over the rim as she drank. Jeremy stared back, determined not to squirm under her heated gaze. After swallowing, she lowered the glass and said softly, "I'm sorry. I didn't mean to freak out on you the other day. I know you were trying to help."

The corner of his lips curved. "It's okay, Heather. I'm sorry too. I promise I won't try to save you again."

Sighing, she glanced at the dollhouse in the corner of the room before running a hand through her golden curls. "It was kind of nice, actually. You were right about always fighting alone. I've never really had anyone in the bunker with me."

Pursing his lips, Jeremy debated how far to push. He definitely wanted to get to know her better but didn't want to pry. Scooting closer, he reached over and glided his hand over her thigh, just above her knee. Gently squeezing, he felt the denim of her white jeans as he stared into her eyes. "Is this okay?"

She nodded before covering his hand with hers. "I'm terrible at this crap."

Breathing a laugh, he asked, "What crap?"

"Relationships...intimacy...friendship...you know," she circled her hand, "basic human emotions. I really suck at them."

"Well, if it's any consolation, my girls seem to really like you. They already think you're best friends because you offered to keep their secret when they came onto your property."

"Those little shits," she teased, wrinkling her nose. "They were supposed to keep that between us."

"Parenting rule number one: kids are the worst at keeping secrets."

"Noted."

"So," he said, relaxing into the couch as his palm tingled atop her thigh. "Tell me. Why are you so bad at emotions?"

Her chest lifted as she inhaled a deep breath before slowly exhaling. "That's a heavy topic for neighbors who barely know each other."

"But it's a perfect topic for neighbors who are on the path to becoming great friends. Maybe with benefits?" he teased.

"Stay in your lane, buddy," she said, grinning. "I'm not down with kids. You've figured that out, right?"

"Um, I'm not sure what your perception of dating with kids is, but they're definitely *not* present when the 'benefits' portion is being enjoyed."

Laughing, she bit her lip as her eyes sparkled. "Touché."

"Come on." He squeezed her leg. "No judgement. And then I'll tell you how things fell apart with my ex. It's only fair."

Her lips twerked as she settled father into the couch. "Fine. I'll give you the basics, but just to be clear, this isn't a sob story." She held up her finger. "I stopped feeling sorry for myself a long time ago. It's not conducive to creating a productive life."

"Agreed," he said with a nod.

Drawing a breath, she gave a slight shrug. "I am the product of two people who should've never been parents. They were from a different time when many people married if they got pregnant. I was an unwanted surprise that tied them together, and I'm not sure they ever forgave me for that. They also both struggled with mental illness, although only Dad's was diagnosed."

His eyebrows drew together. "What did he have?"

"Manic depression according to the doctors but this was decades ago." Taking a sip, her lips tightened as she swallowed.

"Mental health just wasn't something that was addressed as it is now. Dad certainly had mood swings but he also had a serious mean streak."

"Did he hurt you?" Jeremy asked, appalled.

"No, thank god." Shaking her head, she straightened a bit, pulling her leg closer. The action was protective, as if she was fortifying her defensive shell, and he ached to comfort her. "He never hurt me but he became more unhinged as I got older. His main form of entertainment was torturing animals, which was awful. He had a BB gun and would shoot squirrels and even cats who were unlucky enough to wander into our back yard."

Jeremy frowned. "That's psychopathic behavior, Heather. I've researched it thoroughly since I write thrillers with some pretty fucked up characters."

"Well, it certainly meant we didn't have any pets, that's for damn sure. I knew he'd probably hurt them if we adopted one so I never asked."

"Sounds lonely," he said, aching for her as he imagined his girls having to grow up with a father who wasn't mentally sound. Jeremy wasn't perfect but he did everything in his power to make sure Angeline and Gabby felt loved and weren't exposed to the darker side of the world. He couldn't shield them forever but they would only be little once and he wanted them to experience childhood with openness and innocence. Frustrated that Heather hadn't been protected in the same way, sympathy welled deep within.

"And your mom?"

"Mom was self-absorbed and extremely focused on her appearance. I'm no psychologist but I'm pretty sure she had narcissistic personality disorder. According to the scientific musings of Google, that means she exhibited exaggerated feelings of self-importance, an excessive craving for admiration, and struggled with empathy."

"So you were a child stuck in a home with two people who had no idea how to support you."

"Yeah," she murmured, toying with her lower lip with her teeth. "It's why I never really learned how to have empathy or had any desire to be a parent myself. I have zero foundation for that."

"Were you at the same cookout as me last weekend?" he asked, leaning closer. "You showed so much empathy to my girls. Honestly, it was that reaction that made me look at you differently."

Her eyes narrowed and curiosity swirled in the blue orbs. "How did you look at me before?"

Glancing at the ceiling, he pondered. "Gorgeous but kind of...cold. Hope you don't mind the blatant honesty."

"No, it's pretty spot on. Believe me, I've been called worse," she muttered.

Breathing a laugh, he nodded. "Go on."

Sighing, leaned her temple against the couch. "I think Mom had dreams of leaving Dad and finding a new husband. Since she was a housewife and had no discernable skills, she felt the best way to do this was to somehow attract a *new* husband. The amount of anti-wrinkle creams we had in the house could've fortified an entire senior citizen community," she joked before playfully grimacing. "Being beautiful was her life's goal."

Jeremy gnawed his lip. "I'm trying not to spout some cheesy line about how beautiful she must've been since you're so pretty too."

Wrinkling her nose, she scoffed. "Please don't."

"Heard." He gave a small salute. "I'm rusty at this. Go on."

She studied him before continuing. "Since she was so obsessed with her looks, she taught me all her beauty tricks too. She would reinforce that I needed to be pretty so I could attract the right husband."

"So there was no focus on your skills as a person? That's pretty shitty."

"Yeah. It took me a long time to grow into myself and believe I had value apart from my appearance. I still work on it, to be honest, but it's gotten better over my *many* decades on the planet." She dramatically rested the back of her hand on her forehead.

"Wait, how old are you? I know Justine is close to my age and I assumed you were too. I recently turned forty."

"I'm forty-four and fondly remember when I was *only* forty. Sometime shortly thereafter, my back began to hurt like a tractor truck hauler in the World's Strongest Man competition."

Jeremy snickered, admiring her sense of humor. "I think you've got a few good years left," he teased, winking over the rim of his glass.

"Maybe." Slowly tracing the pad of her finger over the glass, she seemed to ponder. "Anyway, as I got older and these began to grow in," she pointed to her chest, "Dad began to look at me weird. He never crossed the line but it was creepy. Mom would catch him sometimes and they would get in terrible fights. She would accuse him of not wanting her anymore and he began to destroy things around the house. You know...throwing chairs into mirrors and shattering them and shooting things with his BB gun."

"Inside the house?" Jeremy asked, his features contorted into a horrified expression.

"Yep." Sighing, she ran a hand through her hair. "I just wanted out and didn't care how. Somewhere along the way, I decided that marrying Butch was my ticket out."

Releasing a breath, Jeremy's lips flapped as he digested her words. Unable to imagine living through something like that as a child, sympathy welled as he gazed into her eyes.

"I'm so sorry. That's awful."

"Thanks, but it wasn't your fault. Honestly, it wasn't mine either but it took me a long time to realize that."

Grasping her hand, he held it as he tenderly stroked her soft skin with his thumb. "Well, it seems you eventually got out."

"I did. Butch fell head over heels for me the first time I let him see my boobs in tenth grade and I seized the opportunity."

"In the interest of adding a little levity, I will confirm that—as a former teenage male—I completely get that sentiment."

Laughter bounded from her throat. "The levity is appreciated. Butch was pretty hot—in a football jock sort of way—and he was really popular, so I went with it. He proposed two weeks before graduation and we married a week after I turned eighteen."

"Did your parents attend the wedding?"

"They did. It was one of the happiest days of my life since it meant I'd be free from my parents' toxicity."

"Then, I'm glad it happened, even if it didn't work out."

"Me too." Swirling the last bit of wine in her glass, she hesitated before continuing. "I knew Butch wasn't the love of my life. But he was a mechanic and was going to inherit his dad's auto repair shop when he retired, so he could support us while I figured out what I wanted to do. He was kind of a jerk but nicer than my dad, and he certainly appreciated my looks. So, I guess my mom's beauty tips paid off after all."

"Are your parents still alive?"

"Nope." Lifting the glass, she tossed back the remaining sip. "They both croaked a few years after I married Butch. Dad from a heart attack and Mom from a stroke. I buried them and stayed married to Butch for a decade until I finally divorced him and moved to Philly."

Jeremy pursed his lips as he debated asking her for more details.

"It's your typical 'married too young' story," she said, a despondent shadow crossing her features. "We fell into the typical roles of what we thought marriage should be. Even though I worked part-time as a secretary to a lawyer in Battle Falls, I made pennies. Butch supported us and thought I should be the little wifey." She grimaced. "When he was home it was always, '*Babe, bring me a beer*' or '*I expected my wife to be a better cook*.'" She spoke in a low tone to mimic his voice. "Gross. That's when I realized I hated marriage."

Leaning forward, Jeremy tilted his head. "Marriage should be a partnership, Heather. Seems like you didn't really have one with Butch."

"More like a prison," she murmured. "Eventually, I became disillusioned and couldn't imagine letting him touch me anymore. So, he went looking somewhere else. Honestly, it was the best thing that happened because his infidelity spurred me to file for divorce."

"And you headed to Philly to start over," he said, impressed by her fortitude. "That took a lot of courage."

She squinted one eye. "Maybe. Regardless, I don't think anyone in Ardor Creek mourned my departure," she said, her tone acerbic. "And now I'm back because somewhere along the way I decided to reset the story about my dreadful past in this podunk little town."

"We both left the big city behind for Ardor Creek. Maybe it's fate."

Scoffing, she wrinkled her nose. "You are way too romantic for me. Do you write romance too?"

"No, but I could give it a shot if I had some inspiration," he joked before inching closer. Studying her, he realized how honored he was that she trusted him enough to tell him about her past. It was the first step in building a friendship and was quite meaningful. "I didn't expect you to open up this much."

"Don't get too excited, Mr. Famous Author. I'm telling you this because I'm highly considering sleeping with you, but..." she leaned forward and lifted a finger. "I want you to know my backstory so you fully understand why I'm only capable of a casual fling. I'm not wired for romance and want nothing to do with your cute little spawns if we cross that bridge."

Jeremy's eyes narrowed. "If you really wanted nothing to do with them, I don't think you'd mention how cute they are. And they *are* really cute, by the way. Oh, and they're kind of already obsessed with you."

Tossing back her head, she gave a jubilant laugh. "Not interested."

"We'll see."

Shooting him a playful glare, she thrust her glass against his chest. "Well, this has been fun but I need a refill. And then you're going to tell me about *your* backstory. Capisce?"

Chuckling, he took her glass and rose. "Got it. Be right back."

As he strode to the kitchen, he digested her words, thankful she'd shown up on his doorstep on what would've been an otherwise quiet Friday night. Excited to spend more time with her, he refilled their glasses and grabbed the take-out menu from the drawer, ready to buy her dinner for their first unofficial date. Pizza and wine on the couch weren't what he'd expected when he finally asked her out, but Jeremy was perfectly fine with it as long as he could convince her to stay for a while...because whether he was ready or not, Jeremy was honest enough to admit he really liked being around Heather Combs.

Chapter 6

"Wait a minute, you did *not* help your ex-wife pick dry shampoo flecks out of her hair," Heather said, devolving into laughter as she sank into the couch. "I can't see that being remotely sexy."

"I know," he said, shrugging as he bit into the half-warm pizza crust. They'd both just polished off the last two pieces of the large pepperoni, as well as two bottles of wine. Now, happily full and sated, Heather struggled not to snort at her handsome companion's admission. "Once we fell into the pattern of being extremely unsexy with each other, we both realized it was the beginning of the end. One day, we looked at each other and admitted we had zero sexual attraction left."

Chewing the last bite of her crust, Heather swallowed before wiping her hands on the paper napkin. "Another marriage bites the dust."

"Truth."

"And you can't even blame it on your parents because they sound like the Cleavers," she said with a cheeky grin.

Admiration along with a bit of sadness laced his features. "They were pretty great."

Compassion seeped into her veins, tugging at the emotion she mostly kept locked away as she gazed at him. "I'm so sorry you recently lost them both. I guess the one silver lining is that it caused you to move closer to Ardor Creek and the girls get to be closer to their mom."

"Thank you. It's a nice consolation, for sure. The girls love it here and I do too." Sitting up, he wiped his hands before tossing the napkin on the table. Reaching for the bottle, he poured the remaining portion evenly into his and Heather's glasses. "Well, I'm officially drunk."

A high-pitched hiccup leapt from Heather's throat. "I'm sotally tober," she joked.

Grinning, he relaxed back on the couch, drawing her foot to rest in his lap. Goosebumps formed under his touch as he slowly caressed her ankle while he sipped the wine. "To wrap up my little saga, I'll say that Jen and I realized it was futile to try and make our marriage work but we really wanted to remain friends. We were great friends all those years ago when we became roommates and had one drunken night together that resulted in our babies. We were always meant to be friends instead of lovers. Just took us a while to realize it."

"God, that's so fucking healthy," Heather groaned, leaning her head on the couch. "I'm not ready to deal with an emotionally healthy person. They're like kryptonite to me."

Emitting a deep laugh that sent shivers down her spine, Jeremy stared at her with slightly glassy irises. "That sucks because I'm having a really good time, Heather. I don't want this to be the last time we hang like this. Do I need to morph into someone who's not emotionally healthy? Because I'll do it."

Amusement, along with a hefty side of desire, twinkled in his light-green eyes, causing Heather to swallow thickly as something welled in her chest. The unnamed emotion was paralyzing and her heart began to race. Wanting to bang her sexy neighbor was one thing, but she wasn't interested in getting romantically involved with a single dad. Anxious to make that distinction extremely clear, she straightened on the couch and chugged the last of the wine. Setting the glass on the table, she stood, wobbling on her feet before Jeremy rose to help her.

"Whoa," he said, placing his glass on the table so he could steady her. "You okay there?"

"I only want sex," she blurted, incapable of having any sort of filter since she was tipsy. "I thought you understood that." Hiccupping, she wiped her lips with the back of her arm. "I can't offer more, especially because you're...you..." she finished lamely, gesturing over his body.

His eyebrows lifted as he assessed her. "Should I be offended? I can't tell if that was an insult."

"Not at all." She rapidly shook her head. "You're a good guy with two kids, which is why you should have some fun with me and send me on my way."

Emitting an awkward laugh, he crouched down so he was eye-level with her. "Maybe I'm not interested in just having sex, Heather."

"That's ridiculous. You're being offered hot, sweaty sex with Heather Combs. Twenty guys in Ardor Creek would've given their right nut for that offer before I left town."

His lips twitched as his eyes darted over her. Straightening, he brushed past her and took her hand. Tugging, he said, "Come on, sweetheart. I'll walk you home."

Frustrated, she yanked back, drawing him to a stop. "You don't want to sleep with me?" Glancing down, she assessed her body. "Wow, I guess I've finally lost it. After forty-four years, I'm washed up."

Chuckling, he tugged again. "Come on."

Disbelief coursed through her that he was actually kicking her out, especially after the fantastic time they'd had together. Heather hadn't experienced a night like this in a long time—hell, maybe not ever. One where she relaxed enough with a man to laugh and open herself up, only to be ushered out the door when she offered to sleep with him.

Annoyed, she slipped on her sandals before silently following him through the house. When they reached the back door, he stepped into the athletic slippers before leading her outside and across the damp yard, wet with mist. They crossed the concrete back porch before Heather fumbled in her pocket for her keys. Grabbing them, she unlocked the door and pushed it open, disconcerted as he stood behind her.

"Hey," he said, encircling her arm and turning her before she could enter the house. "Give me a sec here, sweetheart—"

"It's fine," she said, her tone curt even though she tried like hell to hide the emotion swirling inside. "I'm a lot to take and we're very different people."

"We are," he said, moving closer so she was forced to back against the frame of the open door. "And that's why I don't want to sleep with you tonight, Heather."

Confusion and tipsiness warred in her brain, making her feel fuzzy. "Yeah, I got that message loud and clear." Emitting a hiccup, she flattened her lips to stop another one from escaping.

"Spending time with you tonight was awesome. I'm not really into casual sex, Heather. I want to get to know you before we take that step. I think that will make it ten times better."

"Damn it," she whispered, shaking her head against the frame. "I knew you were a relationship person. I should've stayed home and eaten pizza with my vibrator tonight."

His lips curled into a sexy grin. "The visual I have in my head right now is *not* making this decision any easier."

"Then come inside," she almost whined, grasping his shirt and tugging. "We can have a playdate—you, me and my vibrator. I promise he doesn't bite." She waggled her brows.

"Heather," he whispered, sliding his palm over her jaw. "I'm a dad with two kids and busy life. I'm at the point where I want *some* sort of connection. My last few attempts at casual burned out and I don't want that to happen with us. Let's give this thing a real shot."

Her eyes narrowed. "Meaning...?"

"I want to date you."

"No," she said, her tone firm and unwavering.

"Come on, sweetheart. A few dates won't kill you."

Arching a brow, she asked, "Do any of these dates involve your spawns? Because that's a hard no."

Mirth sparkled in his eyes as he considered. "We go hiking up by the reservoir on nice sunny days. I think they'd probably do backflips if you agreed to come with us one day."

"No."

Playfully rolling his eyes, he leaned closer, barely grazing the tip of her nose with his. Arousal sparked in every cell of her body at the brief touch. "Come on, Heather. Four dates and some hikes with the girls."

"I can't imagine your ex would like me hanging around the girls. Shouldn't I meet her first?"

"She knows you already met them at the cookout and that you moved in next door," he murmured. "Like I said, she's really easy-going. I think it's fine, but if you agree, I'll certainly tell her we're dating."

Lifting to her toes, she gently touched her lips to his. A groan rumbled from his throat and she tightened her fist on his shirt. "I can't believe I'm negotiating with you," she rasped, lips brushing his as she spoke, "but I'll give you two dates and a one-hour hike with the spawns. That's it, buddy. Take it or leave it."

Staring into her with half-lidded eyes, he extended his tongue and drew it across her bottom lip. Heather's knees buckled before he swooped in, supporting her as he slipped his free arm around her waist. Gliding his hand from her jaw to her nape, he threaded his fingers through her hair and gently tugged. "Three dates and a hike, and you've got a deal."

Heather stared back at him, her body vibrating with lust as she contemplated. Jeremy's hand tightened in her hair and she gasped. Arching her body against his, she capitulated. "Fine. Three dates and a hike, and then you're going to screw my brains out—"

The words were swallowed by his mouth as it swooped over hers, claiming her lips as he groaned. Feeling her muscles turn to mush, Heather arched into him, thrusting her tongue inside his mouth as he moaned in approval. Their tongues mated and warred, sliding and tasting until she emitted another hiccup. Drawing back, Jeremy chuckled, the deep rumble surrounding every inch of her burning skin.

"You're so cute when you hiccup," he said, placing a soft kiss on her lips. "Damn, I never expected you to be cute."

"I'm not cute." Her lips formed a pout. "I'm a bitch with no filter. Don't romanticize me. You'll set yourself up for disappointment."

Softly stroking the hair at her temple, he shook his head. "I don't think so, sweetheart. I'll reach out this weekend to plan our first date. Is there anything you don't like?"

"Dating," she muttered.

Tossing back his head, he gave a joyful laugh. "Besides dating."

"I don't like Indian food and I hate anything involving water sports."

"So, my favorite Indian restaurant and jet skiing are out. Got it."

Groaning, she rolled her eyes. "I'm definitely going to regret this. You'd better be amazing in bed, buddy," she said, jabbing his chest with her finger. "Like, superhero sex god status."

Snickering, he leaned in for one last kiss. "You're funny as hell, Heather. I didn't realize how much I needed that. Thanks for coming over tonight. Sleep well, hon." Drawing back, he waved and grinned, adorable in the moonlight, before shuffling back home.

Leaning back on the frame, Heather glared at the sky and huffed. "Dating," she muttered, stepping inside and closing the door behind her. "What red-blooded man turns down sex so he can date? Good grief."

Slogging up the stairs since she was tipsy, Heather finally managed to drag off her clothes and halfheartedly brush her teeth. Then, she fell into bed naked and drew up the covers before snuggling into the soft sheets. In the last moments as she drifted to sleep, she realized something quite strange: her lips were curved into a sated grin as she basked in the evening she'd spent with her sweet, sexy neighbor.

T he next morning, Heather woke up and grumbled into the pillow, cursing the extra bottle of wine that was now wreaking havoc on her liver. Gone were the days when she could toss back alcohol and recover like a champ. Mumbling incoherent musings about her old age, she managed to stumble to the shower.

After her morning routine, she felt better and threw on her yoga pants and sports bra to take a walk. Jogging would require too much energy after last night, but she could manage walking to the deli in the nearby strip mall to grab an egg-white spinach wrap. Glancing down, she decided she'd leave off the tank top and just wear the sports bra that exposed her stomach.

Heather ate pretty healthily—*most* of the time. Last night's pizza dinner was a splurge but she enjoyed exercising and tried to get her heart rate up at least once a day. She also took the stairs whenever possible and walked quite a bit for her job. Hence, her body was in shape and she vowed to give Jeremy a glance at what he'd passed on last night as she strode by his house.

Sure enough, he was outside watering the pretty flowers that lined his front yard as she walked by. Waving, she called, "Hi, neighbor. You missed a good time with me and the vibe."

His lips formed a huge grin as his eyes widened, assessing her body in the workout attire. "I'm pretty sure you passed out after you headed inside but it's hard to formulate words when you're walking around in those tight pants."

"Oh, these old things?" she called, pointing at her yoga pants. Tugging off her sunglasses, she batted her eyelashes.

Chuckling, he shook the hose and moved to the next bush that was covered with flowers. "You still going to help Justine today?"

"Yep. It never hurts to help a friend and cement possession of my 'crew card.' Make sure you watch my ass as I stride away. It looks really great in these pants." Placing her glasses back on her nose, she swayed as she resumed walking. Unable to resist, she looked over her shoulder and noticed him standing slack-jawed as he held the hose.

Oh yeah, he wanted her.

And she sure as shit wanted him. So, she'd go on his stupid dates and get to know him better so she could satisfy whatever hang-up he had about dating before they banged. Then, Heather would bang him for the foreseeable future until one of them got tired of the arrangement and moved on.

"Easy-peasy, Heather," she murmured as her sneakers padded on the concrete. "Just don't fall in love with him. He's a dad and a semi-public figure who needs to settle down with a woman who wants the same things. Sexy-times is all you can have."

Firm with the boundaries she'd set, she exited the cul-de-sac and picked up the pace, determined to burn some calories along the way.

Chapter 7

♥

Several hours later, Heather poured blue paint from the large can into a tray. Straightening, she swiped the curl that had fallen from her sloppy ponytail behind her ear before grasping the roller. Gliding it around the tray, she coated it with the paint and lifted it to the gallery wall.

"I like this color," she said, contemplating as she painted. "Gives the place some brashness and makes the walls pop."

"Thanks," Justine said beside her, maneuvering her roller against the wall. "I was sure Kristoff was going to hate the idea of painting the walls anything but white, but he said he trusted my judgement. It's nice to have a partner who lets you flex your creative muscle."

"Well, you've got creativity in spades, Jus," Abby said, sitting on the floor as she studied the instructions of the display table she was assembling with Ashlyn. "I, on the other hand, thought I'd be better at assembling stuff than painting, but I might be wrong."

"I think it goes in here..." Ashlyn said, fitting the base of a leg into the table as she held her tongue between her teeth. It popped into place and she grinned. "Got it. Who says my husband is the only one who can build things?"

"You two are putting a table together, not constructing Rome, but good job anyway," Carrie teased from across the room where she was jimmying open another can of paint.

"I'm still taking credit," Ashlyn said, patting herself on the back before reaching over to do the same to Abby. "Nice job, Mayor Hanson. Don't listen to grumpy-pants over there."

Carrie playfully scrunched her features at Ashlyn before carrying over the paint. "I think one more can should do it."

"Yep," Justine said, planting her fists on her hips as she observed the walls. "I promised Kristoff I'd only paint two walls blue. Any more was pushing it, I think. He's still financing this venture and I don't want the money to dry up."

"That's never going to happen," Carrie said, supportively rubbing Justine's arm. "I'm so happy for you, Jus. This place is going to be amazing when you have the reopening."

Justine beamed and looked each of them in the eye as she spoke. "I'm so thankful to you guys for helping me. When I told Kristoff I wanted to open my own gallery, I figured he'd tell me to go to hell and be pissed since there isn't enough demand for two art galleries in Ardor Creek."

"But it's so glamorous," Heather chimed, her tone sardonic.

"We know you've secretly fallen in love with this place all over again," Justine said, swatting her arm. "You're not fooling anyone, Heather."

Shrugging, she conceded. "It's not terrible...and I'm really happy to see you seize your dreams, Jus."

"Thank you," she said with a nod. "When Kristoff informed me he wanted to spend more time in the city, and that he would offer me sweat equity if I became his partner, I was floored. It's the perfect solution and I get to run my own gallery. Holy shit. Never in a million years did I imagine this when I was married to Dean and drowning in unhappiness. Things really can change."

"You worked hard to make those changes," Carrie said, squeezing Justine's wrist. "Teresa would say the same thing if she were here. I wish she didn't have the health fair today because Ashlyn and I brought a little surprise to celebrate."

Justine's eyes lit with excitement. "Do tell."

Ashlyn snapped in the last leg of the table before she and Abby stood and turned it upright. "This puppy will hold one of your fancy sculptures soon," Ashlyn said, patting the table, "but for now, it's going to hold our mimosas!"

Carrie disappeared into the back and returned with two cloth bags. Striding toward the table, she pulled out several bottles of prosecco and orange juice, along with a bag of plastic champagne flutes. Lifting one of the prosecco bottles, she said, "We can drink while we paint, right ladies?"

They uttered a resounding, "Hell yes!" before Carrie removed the cups and Ashlyn popped open a prosecco. They began to mix the mimosas and Heather held up her hand. "Just half for me...to start, at least. I'm kind of hungover."

The women stilled, their gazes filled with rampant curiosity. "And with whom did you get drunk?" Justine asked, excitement in her voice.

"Maybe I got drunk by myself," she said, striding over and taking the half-full glass Carrie handed her. "I'm allowed to do that, you know."

"*Ohmygod*," Ashlyn breathed, her green eyes sparkling with excitement. "You got drunk with Jeremy. Tell us *everything*."

Heather spared them each an annoyed glance before lifting the glass to her lips and tossing back the entire contents. Lowering it, she wiped her mouth with the back of her arm. "Hell, fill me up. I need some hair of the dog for this story."

The ladies giggled with glee as they concocted the extremely strong mimosas. Then, they faced Heather, their expressions inquisitive. Laughing, she assessed them and shook her head. "You all are *way* too excited about this."

"No way," Justine said. "We all want you to fall in love, Heather. It's your turn and we're ready for all the juicy details."

"Okay, hold your knickers," she said, showing them her palm. "I am absolutely, one hundred percent *not* falling in love with Jeremy. Which is exactly what I told him last night." Her eyebrows drew together. "Well, it's sort of what I told him. Huh. Things got fuzzy after we opened the second bottle of wine."

The ladies shrieked with joy before Heather snickered. "You guys are too much. Okay, here's the lowdown because I'm not really into 'love stories,'" she mocked, making quotation marks with her fingers. "I told him I only wanted sex, he said he would only bang me if we dated, so we're going to go on a few dates and then we're going to knock boots."

Justine gaped as she held her glass halfway to her lips. "Wait...so you guys negotiated dating terms?"

"Precisely." Heather lifted her glass in a salute. "He's a dad, guys, and a famous author...I think?" She glanced at the ceiling. "He needs a respectable woman on his arm who loves tiny humans.

That, my friends, is not me. So, we'll have some fun and I'll send him on his way to find someone more...*palatable.*"

"Palatable," Abby droned. "Good luck with that. Take it from someone who swore she wouldn't fall for her own husband: it's not as easy as it sounds."

"And Scott and I swore we were only in it for the sexy times," Ashlyn said, waggling her brows, "until we weren't. The more you swear it's not going to work out, the more the universe pushes you together. Mark my words."

"Not happening, ladies," she said, shaking her head. "I appreciate all your sappy sentiments but this will only be a sordid sexual affair."

Carrie gnawed her lip. "Is it weird that I'm dying to know how Jeremy is in bed? I'd ask you not to tell Peter but he'd probably be turned on by it. He's kind of kinky and I'm here for it."

"Um, you both are kinky, judging by the adult costumes I accidentally opened in the package that was mistakenly left on my front porch by the delivery guy," Justine teased. "But who am I to judge? At this point, Gary has 'borrowed' three pairs of handcuffs from the station that I've made him promise never to return." Blushing, she bit her lip.

"Impressive," Heather said, sipping her mimosa. "You ladies are my people. I was telling Jeremy last night how much I wanted to be in this crew when I came back to town."

"Well, you're in it now," Justine said, throwing her arm over Heather's shoulders, "and we might be nosy but we care about you, Heather, and want you to be happy." Leaning in, she spoke in a stern but reverent tone. "And you're a perfectly lovely person for Jeremy to date *and* to settle down with. I don't want to hear you say you two won't fit. Even the most jagged puzzle pieces can find a match. Just be open, Heather. That's all I'm saying."

"Well, I agreed to go on a hike with him and the girls, so I'll try. He drives a hard bargain. I swear, if I go through all this trouble and he can't find my clit, I'm going to bill him for time wasted."

Abby covered her mouth with her fist, attempting to prevent the drink from rushing from her lips as she laughed. "Damn, Heather. You're vicious."

"Just honest," she said, lifting a shoulder. "I promise, I'll keep you guys updated. Carrie, do me a favor and try not to tell *everyone* in town. But if you want to pass along the news that I'm dating Jeremy to anyone who frequents Butch's auto body shop, I won't be mad." She flashed a grin.

"Duly noted," Carrie said with a salute.

"And on that note, refill my glass and let's get painting. I've got a showing at four I'll need to be halfway sober for."

Snickering, the ladies refilled their glasses and got to work.

Chapter 8

♥

Jeremy threw himself into planning the dates with Heather, understanding they were an opportunity to prove that getting close to someone didn't mean imminent disaster. After she opened up during their wine and pizza night, he recognized she associated any sort of true connection with pain. It made sense, considering her experiences with her parents and ex-husband, but Jeremy was determined to show her that opening up didn't always lead to disaster.

Somewhere during their spontaneous night together, he'd acquired the longing to develop a deeper bond with his stunning neighbor. Perhaps the yearning for something more profound sprang from his desire to fix things. As he'd explained to Heather, that constant inner drive to help and nurture had always bugged his ex-wife.

But Jeremy possessed a huge empathetic streak—most likely inherited from his parents who were extremely caring and kind—and since the world was a dumpster fire half the time, he aimed to make it a better place. Especially for his girls, whom he wanted to grow up surrounded by love and affection. It might be slightly naïve, but they had time to learn the world was harsh. For now, he would protect and support them.

He hadn't expected the innate desire to protect Heather too, but when he'd seen her on the street with Cynthia, he'd felt compelled to step in. Of course, she could defend herself, but he'd genuinely wanted to help. Grimacing, he swiped his hand over his face, realizing Jen would've had a field day at his reaction. She always teased him for his savior complex and it drove him nuts since she was right most of the time.

Jeremy's thoughts drifted back to Heather, and he grinned as he recalled her stubbornness. She projected a tough exterior but deep down, she possessed compassion and genuineness. He'd seen it in those deep blue eyes as he'd told her about his parents passing, and in the recounting of her yearning to be part of the local crew. No matter how thick her walls, Heather Combs had a layered, vulnerable core under her carefully manicured appearance, and he wanted to connect with that deeper part of her.

Of course, he longed to connect with her when they were sweaty and sated on his bed...or her bed...or any surface, really. Despite her chiding, Jeremy definitely wanted to sleep with Heather. But he'd dated sporadically after his divorce and no one ever stuck. Eventually, he'd realized he wanted the connection too. That was hard to find on dating apps—especially when you had two young children—so he didn't spend a ton of time cultivating his love life.

When he'd developed the crush on Justine, he hadn't asked her out because he'd wanted their friendship to progress first. Of course, that left her to fall deeper in love with Gary. Grinning, Jeremy acknowledged it was for the best. Gary and Jus were meant for each other and he was extremely happy for them. However, it lit a fire under his ass and he vowed not to waste time if he happened to meet someone he was attracted to and could possibly build something with.

Heather moving in next door was fortuitous and he wouldn't squander the opportunity. The fact they were attracted to each other was a bonus, but Jeremy wanted more than attraction. He wanted someone who felt comfortable with him, and eventually the girls, because he no longer possessed the desire or will to foster a purely sexual relationship. His life was consumed by his children and work, and he would rather spend time with someone he enjoyed being with.

He had no desire to change Heather—hell, he loved her brashness and her ability to vocalize exactly what she wanted. It was something he wanted to foster in his girls, and regardless of her objections about being a good influence on them, he knew they would benefit from being around a strong woman. Heather had left an unhappy home, and then an unhappy marriage, before reshaping her life and seizing control. It was incredibly inspiring and one of the things he found most attractive about her.

But he did want to see her open up and connect with someone. To see her realize that letting down her walls didn't always spell tragedy. It was something she deserved and something he could easily give her. Go figure. He was ready to go full force into wooing a woman for the first time in years. Sighing, he ran his hand through his shaggy hair, realizing the first thing he needed was a haircut.

"Time to get back into dating mode, dude," he murmured, absently clicking through Yelp as he tried to find the perfect place to take her for their first date. "You're rusty but you can do it."

Suddenly, his finger stopped scrolling as his mouse hovered above one of the Yelp listings. "Perfect," he muttered, clicking to open up the listing. Excitement bloomed in his chest, causing him to take a moment and acknowledge the feeling. Rubbing his pec, he realized how complacent he'd become. Being a dad and an author had filled the well, but not completely. His statement to Heather the other night had been true: he needed some fun and laughter in his life. Some *adult* fun with a sexy, adorable neighbor who possessed a wicked sense of humor.

Unable to contain his grin, he picked up his cell to call her and schedule their first date.

Two weeks later, Heather was pretty sure she was going to croak before ever having sex again. Jeremy had taken her on two dates—which she begrudgingly admitted were extremely enjoyable—but her vagina was at full-on cobweb phase.

Date #1 had been at the local mini-golf course, located north of town between Ardor Creek and Battle Falls. Heather hadn't been mini-golfing since childhood and chided Jeremy as he drove them to the course.

"I expected we'd do something more...*mature*," she said from the passenger seat, gazing at the facility as they approached.

"I thought dinner and a movie would be boring," Jeremy said, shrugging as he parked and clicked off the car. "I want this to be fun, Heather. I want you to enjoy hanging with me. Come on."

He jogged around to open her door, and she inwardly kicked herself as her heartbeat quickened. Butch had rarely performed such acts, and she'd always told herself she didn't need them. After her divorce, she'd had some flings with some chivalrous men, but none of them caused the organ in her chest to flutter as it was now. Stupid hormones. Chalking it up to being strung out from wanting to bang a man who insisted on dating her first, she took his offered hand and stood.

Once they had their clubs, balls and adult beverages from the surprisingly adequate facility bar, they began putting through the course.

"You looked pensive by the car," Jeremy said, focused on the orange ball as he took some practice swings with his club. "If you hate it after nine holes, we can stop." He clinked the club against the ball, shooting it to the far wall a few feet from the hole.

"I was just thinking about my ex," she said, handing him her plastic cup before she spread her feet to line up her shot. "We never really got in the habit of treating each other with respect. We were so young when we married. It took me a while to figure out I hated being in a relationship." She struck the ball, shooting it forward before it dropped in the hole.

"Woo hoo!" she cried, lifting her hands in the air, club held tight as she beamed.

"Wow, you're going to cream me," he said, chuckling as he handed back her wine. "Good thing I like women who are inherently better than me at everything."

Heather playfully scrunched her features, acknowledging his teasing. As they maneuvered over the course, they continued to chat.

"So, you never want to get married again? Or be in a relation-ship?" Jeremy asked as he leaned over the ball, ready for his next shot. Heather sensed his interest in her answer, even if he was pretending to be focused on the game.

Pursing her lips, she pondered. "After my divorce, I always said I'd only get married again if I was a trophy wife to a rich man who didn't need me for anything except as a fixture on his arm when the occasion called for it. That seemed to fit into my wheelhouse and exemplify how I could offer value. I've never wanted kids so marriage seemed kind of pointless." She brushed the green turf with her club, wondering if she sounded pathetic. Most people wanted companionship and relationships, right? Keeping her eyes averted, she stepped into place after Jeremy took his shot. Setting the wine on the ground, she planted her feet and lined up her stroke.

"A person can get married for a lot of reasons," he said, his voice thoughtful as he stood behind her. "Children are one factor, yes, but I know plenty of couples who marry and don't have kids. To me, companionship seems like a pretty good reason to take the plunge if you love someone."

Heather completed her shot before lifting her cup and taking a sip. "But you're already a dad, so you need to marry someone who's interested in kids." She arched a brow, a challenge in her gaze.

The corner of his lips curved. "I'm done having kids, Heather. I don't need anyone who still wants to have them. If I ever settle down again, I'd just need someone who loves them too. They can detest every other kid on the planet for all I care."

Huffing a laugh, rolled her eyes. "I don't hate kids, okay? I just don't understand them. I think it's because I never really got to be a kid myself or something. Who knows?"

"That's understandable." Stepping closer, he leaned in, his green eyes glistening in the waning sunlight. "Why do you think we're mini-golfing? I'm showing you that being a kid can be fun."

Her mouth dropped open in mock exasperation. "Are you buttering me up to bring the girls here together? Because it's not happening." She playfully jabbed her finger in his chest. "One hike with them was all I agreed to."

"I know, woman," he said, grabbing her finger and bringing her hand to his lips. Coyly biting the fleshy skin below her thumb, a naughty gleam entered his eyes. "But I think I can get you to agree to more."

Arousal flared at the wicked sentiment in his gaze. Biting her lip, Heather acknowledged the rush of fire along her skin and the heaviness of her breaths. "Don't make this something it's not," she whispered, noting the slight plea in her voice. "I'll only end up letting you down..."

"Impossible," he murmured, kissing her knuckles. "Come on. The senior citizens behind us are pissed we're moving so slow."

They continued, effectively ending the serious conversation, and Heather ended up having a fantastic time. On the way home, they stopped for hot dogs at the local stand that resided on the corner of Main Street during the summer. And then, her handsome companion dropped her off at her front door, gave her a thorough but rather short kiss (in her opinion!), and headed home after confirming their next date.

Date #2 had basically followed the same pattern. Jeremy took her to a sushi-making class at a fancy restaurant in Scranton. She had a fabulous time getting to know him better and eating the delicious food before he'd driven her home, kissed her, and hopped back in his car to pick up the girls from the babysitter.

In the scheme of things, spending a few weeks getting to know someone wasn't *that* long. But Heather was quite confident in her appearance and sex appeal, and held the inner belief Jeremy wouldn't be able to complete their "date deal" without caving and deciding to have sex with her. Scowling at her inability to inspire her handsome neighbor to rip her clothes off, she harshly answered the phone when it rang.

"Whoa," Jeremy's deep voice echoed through the phone. "Did I catch you at a bad time? You sound pissed."

"I was just remarking on the fact I'm dating *without* having sex," she droned. "Seems like a lot of work for zero orgasms."

His chuckle reverberated through the phone, causing her skin to tingle, which only further incited her annoyance. "Come on, Heather. You put on a good show but you're not *that* great of an actress. I know you've had fun on our dates."

"Mini-golf was nice," she said, tracing the counter with her finger as she stood inside the kitchen. "Although now that I think back on it, you should've taken the opportunity to put your arms around me and show me how to swing. That could've been some good ol' fashioned clichéd fun."

"True...except you were a thousand times better than me. *You* should've put your arms around *my* waist and shown me the ropes."

"Another opportunity missed," she said, unable to stop her grin. "Story of my life."

"You enjoyed the sushi-making class, right?"

"The premium sake made that one mildly enjoyable," she teased.

Silence stretched and she could almost see his smile—the vexatiously adorable smile he always seemed to have around her. Hating how handsome he was, especially with the new haircut he'd recently gotten, she leaned on the counter and pondered.

"Can we kill two birds with one stone on Date #3 and take the girls hiking?" she asked. "It's supposed to be nice tomorrow and all my showings are in the morning. I could be ready by two p.m."

"I knew I'd get you to volunteer to hang with the girls," he said, excitement lacing his tone. "Just had to employ the Kramer charm."

"Okay, Casanova, relax." She bit her lip to contain her grin. "I'm only offering to streamline things. For the thousandth time, I'm only doing this to get laid."

"So you've indicated, and I appreciate the honesty." The low timbre of his voice surrounded her, causing tiny bumps to rise on her arms. "I think it's pretty obvious I want you too. But I've really enjoyed getting to know you. I'd even go out on a limb and say we're becoming friends. Now, I can live up to the 'friends' moniker when we enter the 'friends with benefits' stage."

Heather chuckled, overcome with how adorable he was. Fuck. She'd just used the word *adorable*. About her sweet, sexy neighbor she had no business thinking any such thoughts about.

Gnawing her lip, Heather reflected on all the times in her life when she'd felt alone. When no one had ever given a damn about her or gone out of their way to get to know her. She'd accepted it, chalking it up to the fact some people just weren't worth being cared for. That she didn't *deserve* to be cared for. As much as she chided Jeremy, deep down, she appreciated his efforts more than he would ever know.

"I haven't had many friends in my life," she said softly, "so I'm glad you feel that way."

"That's a shame, because you're very likeable, sweetheart," he said, the endearment causing her heart to skip. "You just need people who aren't scared of those walls. They're pretty thick."

"Yeah," she said, suddenly feeling the insane urge to cry. One thing Heather hated was crying. It never solved anything and just made you feel like utter shit. "Well, I'm glad you're as stubborn as

I am. It makes me hate you a tiny bit less when I'm falling asleep with lady blue balls."

Laughter sprang through the phone. "We'll get there soon, hon. I promise. So, why don't you come over at two o'clock tomorrow? I'll have the girls ready and we'll go to the reservoir."

"Sounds good. Jeremy?"

"Hmm?"

"Don't let me sabotage this, okay? I kind of like you too. But I still mostly want you for sex."

He breathed a laugh. "I've got you, sweetheart. See you tomorrow."

"See ya."

Clicking off the phone, she emitted a frustrated groan and tossed it on the counter. Narrowing her eyes, she contemplated how deftly Jeremy Kramer had woven himself into her life over the past few weeks. Understanding that her vow to remain emotionally unattached was in serious jeopardy, Heather straightened and inhaled a ragged breath.

"Sex, Heather. Don't get it twisted. You do not have space in your life for heartbreak right now."

Unfortunately, her heart seemed to disagree, judging by the way she all but skipped up the stairs so she could decide which hiking outfit to wear that would be child-appropriate but would also give her sexy neighbor a fantastic view of her cleavage.

Chapter 9

Unfortunately, Saturday's hiking session never materialized. After her morning showings, Heather headed home to change and stretch before the excursion. Once she'd slipped on her yoga pants and tank top, she was about to put on her sneakers when she heard the pounding on the back door. Rushing downstairs, she yanked open the door.

"What the hell? Where's the fire?"

Jeremy stared back at her, raw emotion lacing his features, and she immediately knew something was wrong.

"Jeremy?" she asked, clutching his wrist. "Come inside. What is it?"

"It's Jen," he said, cradling his forehead as he paced around the kitchen. "She and her fiancé were in a car accident. I have no idea what to do but I have to get to the hospital. Her parents are visiting her sister in Colorado."

"It's going to be okay," Heather said, gently encircling his forearm. "We'll figure this out. I'm sure we can call Jus or Carrie to watch the girls and I can drive you to the hospital."

"The crew is at the lake fishing," he said, shaking his head. "I called Jus but I don't want to wait for them to get back. Hours could pass by the time they pack up and head home."

Heather nodded, remembering Justine had mentioned going to the lake with the rest of the crew. "What about Kara?" she asked, referencing the local college student who was the most beloved babysitter in town.

Facing her, Jeremy inhaled a tattered breath before swiping a hand through his hair. "She's waitressing at Nick's Diner today. I already called her." Gorgeous green eyes lifted to hers, inquisitive and hopeful.

"No," she said, balking as she took a step back. "I can't watch them, Jeremy. I have no idea how to supervise children."

"They're very well-behaved, Heather. I wouldn't ask you if I had any other options but this makes the most sense. Please."

She shot him an exasperated look. "You want them to remain alive, right? Because leaving them with me is *not* a guarantee that will happen."

Stepping forward, he gently gripped her upper arms. "Please. I trust you and know you can do this."

Her nostrils flared as terror shot down her spine. How much clearer could she have been that she had zero skills or intuition when it came to kids? "Let me call Jus. Maybe I can go pick her up at the lake—"

"Please, Heather," he said softly. "I need to get to the hospital. She's their mother. I need your help."

Heather exhaled a breath...and then another...pretty sure she was on the way to hyperventilating as he slowly began to rub her arms. "Breathe, sweetheart. You'll do fine. I swear, they're harmless."

Lifting a finger, she stared him dead in the eye. "I'll do it, but if something terrible happens, I won't be held accountable. You're seriously taking your children's lives into your hands by leaving them with me. This is a horrible idea."

"Thank you," he whispered, leaning in to give her a sweet kiss. "You'll never know how much this means." Gently running his hand over her hair, he cupped her jaw. "Just call my cell if you need anything. And you can call Jus too. She's already offered to be moral phone support."

Heather's eyes narrowed. "Fine. Let me go put on my sandals." Disengaging, she marched toward the stairs and up to her room. Once her sandals were fastened, she headed downstairs, heart pounding at the knowledge she was going to be stuck with two tiny humans for the foreseeable future. Clicking off all the kitchen lights, she led Jeremy out the back door, locking it behind her. They trailed to his house and he led her inside.

"They don't know about the accident yet," he said softly as they walked to the living room. "I don't want to say anything until I know more."

Nodding, Heather followed him, observing the girls as they lay on the couch and recliner playing with their tablets. They both looked up when Heather and Jeremy entered. Gasping, they sat up and flashed wide grins.

"Did you come to show us your dresses?" Angeline asked.

"Ummm, not this time," Heather said, glaring at Jeremy to indicate he was the one who should explain her presence.

"I have some work stuff that's come up so Heather is going to watch you until I get home. It might take the rest of the day into the night, so if I'm not back by bedtime, I expect you both to brush your teeth and go to sleep on time." He arched an eyebrow. "Got it?"

"So, you're having a sleepover with us?" Gabby asked excitedly.

Blowing a breath through puffed cheeks, Heather nodded. "I'm going to be here until your dad gets home, so maybe a half-sleep-over."

"Yay!" The girls cheered and rose, the tablets tossed on the coffee table as they approached. "Mom just let us start practicing with makeup last month but we can't wear it outside the house," Angeline said. "Maybe you can help us practice since your makeup is so pretty."

Heather grinned. "Thank you. I can do that if your dad doesn't mind." She glanced at Jeremy.

"That's fine, as long as it's in the house."

"Okay," the girls said in unison.

"And we got these really cool press-on nails we were going to put on after our hike," Gabby said. "We can put them on you too!"

"Oh, joy," Heather droned.

Jeremy flashed a grin, acknowledging her tone, and Heather decided the torture was worth it if it helped her friend. Yes, some-where along the way, they'd become friends and she genuinely wanted to help him.

"Girls, I'm going to talk to Heather in the kitchen before I leave. Give me a hug."

They ran toward him and he crouched, tightly embracing them as Heather looked on. If she were sentimental or sappy, her throat *might* have tightened at the poignant gesture of affection and her eyes *might* have welled just a bit. Reminding herself she was neither of those things, she chalked up the sensations to allergies.

Rising, Jeremy extended his hand. "Let's talk in the kitchen."

Grasping his hand, Heather followed him until they stood in front of the island. Exhaling a relieved breath, he gazed at her as he tucked a curl behind her ear. "Thank you, Heather. I have no idea when I'll be home. It could be really late."

"Take all the time you need," she said, wondering why her voice was so gravelly. "I'll try to keep them alive."

Breathing a laugh, he tilted his head. "I see you in there." He lightly tapped his finger over her heart before resting his palm over the now rapidly-beating organ. Tracing his thumb over the sensitive skin of her collarbone, he leaned forward and whispered, "You don't have to hide from me, Heather. I wouldn't leave my girls with someone I didn't trust." He tenderly brushed his lips over hers. "Nor with someone I didn't care about."

"I never asked you to care about me," she rasped.

Grinning, he slowly shook his head. "You didn't have to. It seems to come pretty damn naturally with you, hon." Giving her one last sweet peck, he straightened. "I'll call and update you when I know more."

"Okay," she breathed.

Releasing her, he grabbed his keys and phone and trailed to the back door, giving a salute before he exited. Heather's lips fanned together in slight exasperation. Grasping her upper arms, she rubbed them, unconsciously consoling herself for signing up for hours of alone time with two children. Then, she lifted her chin and strode to the living room.

"Well, girls," she said, standing firm at the entrance of the room. "What should we do first?"

Several hours later, Heather sat on Jeremy's living room couch marveling at how humanity had survived for thousands of centuries. It seemed impossible, considering they had to spend excessive amounts of energy raising children, who by their very nature, were designed to suck every last drop of energy from one's veins. Sighing, she stared at the ceiling as Gabby trailed the makeup brush through one of the several palettes Heather had jogged over and grabbed from her stash. If she was going to get the worst makeover in history, might as well be with the good stuff.

"Over the cheekbone, like we did with Angeline," Heather said, turning her face so Gabby could apply the blush.

"It's too pink," Gabby said, wrinkling her nose. "Let's use this one instead." Reaching down, she grabbed a darker palette.

"Sure, cake it on," Heather muttered. "Why not go for the gold?"

The girls snickered, one standing on each side of her as she sat on the couch. Angeline took her hand and began filing one of Heather's nails. "We have to make your nails shorter so we can put on the new ones."

Realizing her nails would take a few weeks to grow back, Heather flattened her lips and let the girl file away. Who needed nice nails anyway? It's not like she could dig them into Jeremy's back during sexy times since he refused to sleep with her. Bastard. She'd rail at him if she weren't so worried about him and the situation with his ex-wife. Glancing down at her phone, she noticed the unread texts and reached for it with her free hand.

Jeremy: Jen is really banged up with a broken leg but she's going to be okay. Her fiancé has a broken nose and arm. They'll both be fine but will need some recovery time. How are the girls? Are you surviving?

Relief swished through her as she typed.

Heather: I'm so glad they're going to be okay but sorry they're hurt. The girls are fine. Me...not so much. You could've warned me they have limitless energy.

"There," Gabby said, patting Heather's face with the makeup brush. "Now I need to do the other one."

Heather sighed and turned her other cheek to the girl.

Jeremy: You'll never know how much I appreciate this. I owe you.

Heather glanced at the girls, both adorable as they focused on her makeup and nails. Begrudgingly, she texted back.

Heather: They're cute, okay? Don't tell anyone I said that. It will ruin my ice queen reputation. Come back soon or I'm going to go full Tammy Faye Bakker.

Jeremy: Who is that again?

Heather: Way to remind me you're four years younger. I despise you even more now.

An emoji with laughter and tears appeared.

Jeremy: I know who she is. Just kidding. The girls are heavy into makeup right now. We let them play around with it at home.

Heather: Obviously. We'll also need to have a memorial service for my perfectly manicured fingernails.

Jeremy: Damn, they're giving you a full-on makeover. You're sweet to let them. Thank you, Heather.

Arching a brow, she typed a sardonic reply.

Heather: Sweet as a cat under a cold faucet. What time is bedtime by the way?

Jeremy: Around 8:30. I probably won't be home by then but they know the routine. Don't let them talk you into staying up later. They're monsters if they don't get enough sleep.

Heather eyed the girls.

Heather: Aaaaand you left me stranded with them. Forget it. I've decided I don't want to sleep with you. You don't deserve my sweet lovin' after this torture.

Jeremy: Weirdly, that makes me want you more.

Heather: Whatever. Be safe. See you later.

Jeremy: See you later, sweetheart.

Glowering that the sweet words made her heart pound, Heather tossed the phone on the couch and let the girls do their worst. By the end of the makeover, Heather guessed she had several pounds of makeup covering her face, her hair was sectioned into multiple ponytails—some braided, some not—and she had three different colors of press-on nails covering her once-perfect manicure.

She ordered pizza for dinner and they ate on the carpeted living room floor before Heather instructed them as they put makeup on each other. It was the perfect task for her since she was an expert at honing her appearance if nothing else, and the girls seemed to glow under her instruction.

When it was time for bed, the girls went through the nightly routine and Heather said good night to each of them before switching off the lights and leaving each door cracked. Heading downstairs, she lay on the couch, wondering if she'd ever been so exhausted. Pressing her palms together, she slid them under her cheek, cushioning her head as she relaxed.

"You can lay here just a few minutes, Heather…" she mumbled, wondering when her eyelids had begun to weigh a thousand pounds. "You can clean up the kitchen in a minute."

She'd left the extra-large pizza box open on the counter with two slices inside and would wrap them up and place them in the fridge when she had some energy. First, she just needed a *tiny* recharge. Yes…just a slight respite and she'd pack everything up…

Chapter 10

Jeremy sat by his ex-wife's hospital bed as they discussed what to tell their children. He'd been granted immediate access due to the fact he was still listed as her emergency contact. They'd decided ages ago to remain listed that way, agreeing to discuss changing the arrangement if either of them remarried. It ensured they would be able to support each other, and therefore their children, if either was injured or worse. Once Jen was married to Lou, they would discuss changing the designation, but for now, it worked perfectly.

Jennifer's words were sluggish but she was conscious and had insisted on deciding what to tell the girls before he left the hospital. After talking it over, they decided Jeremy would tell them she'd been in an accident and was hurt, but that she would be okay. Jen desperately wanted to see them, and they agreed he would bring the girls to the hospital in the morning. Jeremy also offered to watch them as often as needed during her and her fiancé's recovery, which seemed to soothe her.

"You know, for an ex-husband, you're pretty fantastic," she rasped, taking his hand as she lay in the hospital bed. "Lou doesn't even think it's strange that we're best friends anymore."

Smiling, Jeremy clutched her hand and leaned forward, swiping the dark hair from her brow. "We are. It's so important for our kids, Jen. Thank you for being the best worst wife I've ever had."

A laugh escaped her throat as her eyes roved over his features. "I want you to fall in love again," she said softly. "Lou makes me so happy. You deserve that too."

Jeremy nodded, recalling the conversation he'd had with Heather. She'd been pretty clear she wasn't interested in the serious relationship or marriage route, but he attributed that to her past experiences. After all, how could one crave relationships or affection when they'd only resulted in pain?

The people who were supposed to care for her had failed her. She was righteous to take responsibility for the failures too, but she deserved to have a connection with someone that was easy. Healthy. Nurturing.

"Oh, boy," Jen said, shaking her head on the pillow. "You're really tangled up in this Heather."

"Please don't call her *this* Heather," he said, wrinkling his nose. "And yeah, I think I am."

"The girls tell me she *soooo* pretty," Jen teased. "You never really messed with the pretty ones. You always went for dorky girls like me who played video games and can name all the hobbits from Lord of the Rings."

Jeremy laughed. "Very true. Honestly, I wasn't sure about her in the beginning. I had a crush on Jus and totally blew that, so I figured I'd just write and hang with the girls. I assumed if I was meant to meet someone, it would happen along the way. But Jus kept insisting Heather and I would be great together, and then she showed up to that cookout wearing those sexy white jeans..."

Jen squinted one eye. "Weird ex-wife conversation territory."

"Um, I'm pretty sure you told me two months ago that you and Lou christened the renovated shower, like, four times, but whatever."

"We did," she sighed, gazing toward the ceiling. "He likes to use the massager on the removable showerhead—"

"Moving on," Jeremy interjected, grimacing. "Anyway, Heather's pretty great. There's so much more to her than her looks, although she hides behind them. Her exterior projects this hardened, brash woman, but she's mush inside. I just have to dig deep to find it."

"Don't try and save her," she said, lifting a finger. "It's so annoying."

"I know, Jen, all right?" Straightening, he ran a hand through his hair. "I'm not taking dating tips from you."

"Fine." With an exasperated look, she smoothed the covers. "I just want you to be happy and want our girls to be happy. Once I've recovered a bit, I want to meet her."

"Okay. I have to take it slow because meeting you will probably scare the shit out of her."

"A commitment-phobe who hates kids. You really know how to pick 'em."

"She doesn't hate kids, Jen." Rising, he kissed her forehead. "And on that note, I'd better go save her. She did me a sold watching the girls tonight."

"It's really nice of her," Jen said, eyes glossy from the pain medication as she glanced up at him. "I'm being hard on you. I can't wait to meet her."

Patting his pockets to make sure he had his phone and wallet, he tilted his head. "Feel better. I'll bring the girls to see you tomorrow."

"Thanks," she murmured, eyelids drooping as she relaxed into the mattress. "You're my favorite ex-husband."

Grinning, he trailed from the room and headed home.

J eremy drove home under the silver moonlight, nerves frazzled from the harrowing day. Thanking the universe Jen was okay, he cupped his chin as he neared the driveway. Once parked, he rubbed his eyes, wishing he could scrub away the exhaustion that laced his bones. Exiting the car, he trailed to the back door, locking it behind him out of habit. The house was dim and he strode down the hallway toward the soft light of the living room lamp.

When he crested the open doorframe, he saw Heather on the couch, palms pressed together beneath her cheek as she snored. Quietly approaching, he lowered to the carpet and placed his hand on her shoulder, bare beneath her black tank top.

She mumbled something incoherent before smacking her lips and relaxing into the couch. Jeremy's lips twitched as he assessed her face—caked with makeup—and her hair, which was pulled into a bunch of ponytails. Lifting his hand, he traced his finger over one of the haphazard braids.

She swatted him away and he snickered. The sound must've registered because her eyes snapped open and focused on his, angry and disoriented.

"Jeremy?"

"Hey," he murmured.

She blinked several times as her eyes darted around the room. Emitting a soft curse, she groaned. "I fell asleep in the makeup. Meant to wash that off."

"Tammy Faye's got nothin' on you, kid," he teased, running his finger over her extremely pink cheek. "It's hot."

"I hate you," she said, scowling. "And my hair's a mess too. The little liars have no idea how to braid. They're heathens. You should send them to a boarding school in Switzerland."

Unable to control his grin, he cupped her jaw and ran his thumb over her bottom lip. "I like seeing you all stretched out and sleepy on my couch. Is that too weird...or too serious? I have no idea. I'm exhausted."

"*Way* too serious," she said, narrowing her eyes. "And now I resemble *Hit-By-A-Truck Barbie* so you probably don't even want to bang me anymore."

Tenderly caressing her lip, his body hardened as he gently slipped the pad of his thumb deeper, touching the wetness within. She inhaled sharply and he shifted on the carpet since he was now sporting a rapidly growing erection inside his khakis. "I want you so much, Heather. How do you not know that?"

Her throat bobbed as she studied him. "Usually, if a guy wants to fuck you, he tries to fuck you. I assure you, I *do* have experience with this."

Something tightened in his chest at the thought of her having *experience* with anyone else. It was possessive and misplaced, but he felt it nonetheless. "There won't be any *trying* when I fuck you, sweetheart. Trust me."

Her eyes widened, causing his lips to curve.

"What?"

"Ummmm, where has *this* guy been the whole time?" She circled her hand over his face. "Are you a dirty talker?" Sitting up, she pushed her hair off her face before lifting her hands in prayer and glancing at the ceiling. "God, it's me, your favorite atheist. Please tell me he's a dirty talker."

Laughing, he extended his hand and pulled her to her feet. She held on tight and swayed into him.

"I know I'm so gross right now, but the possibility of dirty talk has *really* turned me on."

"If the girls weren't upstairs, I'd make better use of the couch," he said, arching a brow. Sliding his hand around her waist, he glided it over her yoga pants, palming her ass as he pushed his throbbing shaft into the juncture of her thighs. "But it's definitely time we consummate this relationship, sweetheart."

"After I watched your spawns and you tortured me with *dates?*" she chided, lifting to her toes and brushing a kiss on his lips. "It's past time, buddy."

Leaning down, he kissed her, slow and tender as she arched against him. Drawing back, he murmured against her lips, "Let me walk you home."

Nodding, she disengaged and slipped her hand in his. The sweet gesture caused his heart to clank in his chest, and he laced their fingers, squeezing as he stared into her drowsy eyes. Tugging, he led her down the hallway and to the back door where she slipped on her sandals. Clutching her hand again, he walked her to her back door, making sure she entered safely.

"Thank you, Heather." Sincerity laced his tone as he stood under the small awning. "I'll call you tomorrow."

"Okay." Her gorgeous eyes seemed to glow in the moonlight, probably enhanced by the plethora of makeup she wore. "And they're great kids, Jeremy. I...don't mind hanging out with them...as long as we make time to bang." She lifted a finger. "Banging time is essential."

"Understood." He gave a salute. "We're going to carve out a *lot* of time for that, hon. Good night."

Her whispered *"good night"* followed him home, across the wet grass, enveloping him like a warm blanket as he stepped inside. Realizing tonight had been an important step in his burgeoning relationship with Heather, he released a breath, thankful the exhausting day was over. After wrapping up the leftover pizza on the counter, he clicked off the lights and padded upstairs to kiss his children.

Chapter 11

T he following two weeks were a whirlwind as Jeremy took care of the girls so Jen and Lou could recover at their home in Battle Falls. It left little time for him to pursue Heather, which royally sucked due to the fact she'd taken up residence in his brain. Ever since he'd come home to find her sleeping on his couch, his imagination had been working overtime. Seeing glimpses of her vulnerable and open had shifted something inside him.

Jeremy had seen the inner-goodness in his gorgeous neighbor—the quiet empathy and emotion she kept locked away—and he wanted *more*. He wanted to see that emotion burning in her stunning blue eyes as he buried himself deep inside her...slow and measured so he could observe every quiver of her lips and the reddening of her flushed skin...

Clearing his throat, he straightened at his desk and glowered at the blank screen in front of him. Obsessing about making love to Heather had all but destroyed his creative flow, and he desperately needed it back. Assured it would return once he'd scratched the itch, so to speak, he lifted his phone and texted the object of his musings.

Jeremy: Hey! My babysitter canceled on Saturday. You available?

The text bubble appeared, and he bit his lip to contain his grin as he imagined her scowling as she typed.

Heather: To think, I was once convinced we were going to sleep together.

She sent a thinking emoji.

Heather: Now, you've been relegated to hot guy I used to know who will never touch my lady parts. Too bad. It could've been fun.

Chuckling, he typed back.

Jeremy: I take it back. I'll give them up for adoption if I can still touch your lady parts. I've kind of been obsessing about them.

Heather: Tell me more. There are great families out there who'll take your heathens, I'm sure.

Huffing at her feigned disregard for the girls, he settled into the chair as his fingers roved over the screen.

Jeremy: Jen is taking them this weekend. She and Lou are recovered enough to have them over and her parents are back from Colorado. I'm childfree (temporarily).

Heather: Woo hoo!

Narrowing his eyes, he continued.

Jeremy: You're joking though, right? I can't sleep with someone who doesn't like my little angels. It's against dad code.

An eye roll emoji appeared.

Heather: You're trying to get me to admit I like your girls, and I will say no such thing (although IF I were GOING to like kids, I'd certainly like them because they're sweet and kind and sort of amazing...but this is all hypothetical, of course).

Releasing a breath, he grinned.

Jeremy: Message received. And I'm glad you like them, Heather. They can't stop talking about you.

Heather: Stop trying to make me FEEL things. Ew. Sex only, remember?

Jeremy glanced at the ceiling, reminiscing about the thousands of times over the past two weeks he'd imagined looking into her eyes as they made love. Swallowing thickly, he realized a "sex only" relationship with Heather might already be doomed...on his end at least. Jeremy was already pretty wrapped up in her, but he didn't want to scare her away so he forged ahead.

Jeremy: Sex only. Does this mean I should bring the dirty talk?

Heather: Sweet lord, yes! I never expected it from you. I was sure you were going to recite Wadsworth while we banged. Bring all the dirty talk and sweaty adult activities. I'm ready.

Feeling his muscles tense with arousal, he clenched his jaw, ready to show her he wasn't the boring intellectual type she accused him of being—in bed, anyway. Little did she know he liked hot, mindless sex just as much as the next guy. Sure, he liked slow, meaningful sex too, but if she wanted hot, he'd give her hot. Fuck yes. After adjusting his rapidly-swelling cock in his pants, he replied.

Jeremy: I'll be over at 8 pm tomorrow. Leave the back door unlocked.

Heather: Ohhhhh, I'm intrigued. I'll order in. Any requests?

Jeremy: Anything, as long as it can sit for a while. We're taking care of business first.

She sent a prayer emoji and then a wide-eyed emoji, causing him to laugh.

Heather: Finally. My penance is done. See you tomorrow, lover.

Tossing his phone on the desk, Jeremy rubbed his chin as he contemplated the laptop. Unable to concentrate, he rose and headed upstairs before yanking open the bathroom cabinet. Reaching for the box, he tore off a few extra condom packets and stuffed them in his wallet, determined to show Heather Combs he was worth her efforts over the past few weeks.

Heather took her time getting ready on Friday, vowing to have the best sex of her damn life since she'd certainly earned it. After her afternoon showing, she headed home and took a long, hot shower, scrubbing her skin with the loofa that would make it extra smooth. After shaving her legs, she used the sweet-smelling moisturizer over her whole body, imagining the lust in Jeremy's eyes as he inhaled her skin.

Would he gaze at her from between her now-silky thighs as he swiped his tongue over her deepest place? Arching a brow, she placed an extra dab of moisturizer between her legs for good measure. Just in case. After all, a lady could never be too prepared to have mind-blowing sex.

Gazing at her reflection in the mirror, Heather noticed the frown lines that had appeared between her eyes somewhere after her fortieth birthday. She hated them and had tried all sorts of creams to eradicate them to no avail. Tracing her finger over them, she acknowledged the self-doubt.

Sure, she talked a good game and still was a very confident woman, but Heather hadn't had sex in a while. Squinting at the ceiling, she tried to recall the last time.

"Barry from the bar at the fancy steakhouse in Philly," she murmured, reclaiming her gaze in the reflection. "Over a year ago and he ran out the door the next morning as fast as his little legs could take him." Sighing, she reached for her makeup bag and dug out the eye shadow. "Plus, his name was *Barry*. Good god, Heather. Hopefully, this time will be better."

As she began to swipe on her makeup, nerves curled in her gut. Sex had always been a physical act for her, even with Butch whose favorite thing about her had been her looks. But with Jeremy, he seemed to actually want *her*, regardless of her flaws and brash demeanor. Feeling a moment of panic, she stared at the frown lines and the tiny creases under her eyes.

"We'll cover those right up," she murmured to herself, determined to maintain her appearance for her lover. She'd made progress on her habit of basing her value on her looks, but Jeremy was four years younger and she didn't want to push it. Vowing to never let him see her without makeup, she forged ahead, completing her regimen. Once finished, she pressed her lips together, noting the cherry red lipstick enhanced her deep blue eyes under the shadow and eyeliner.

After styling her hair, full and bouncy over her shoulders, she strode to her closet to find something that would knock Jeremy's socks off. She was pretty much planning on banging him upon arrival, so she didn't need to put on *too* many clothes. Perusing her closet, her fingers swiped across several dresses until they landed on one in particular. Grinning, she pulled it from the closet.

It was a flowy black dress she wore to semi-formal functions and it clung to every curve of her body. Every time she wore it, she received a plethora of appreciative glances. Removing it from the hanger, she slid it on, reveling in the soft feel of the silky fabric. Walking to her full-length mirror, she turned side-to-side, admiring the way it fell to her knees, showing off her legs. Damn, but she had nice legs.

Smiling at the fact Jeremy's hands would be all over said legs shortly, she trailed to her dresser and pulled open the drawer. Functional cotton underwear stared back at her and she shook her head.

"We're going to need the big guns tonight."

Sliding the drawer closed, she opened the drawer underneath, revealing her sexy lingerie. Reaching inside, she grabbed a pair of barely-there thongs.

"Perfect," she murmured, stepping into them and shimmying them up her legs. After adding her earrings, she nodded to her reflection and headed downstairs in her bare feet.

After opening a bottle of red, she poured it into the decanter and left it on the counter to breathe. The doorbell rang and she padded to the front door, taking the Cuban food from the delivery driver. She took out the containers and set them on the stove, ready to heat after Jeremy had settled in...and hopefully banged her senseless.

Inhaling a deep breath, Heather placed her hand over her heart and gave it a slight warning.

"Don't fall for him, Heather. He's a temporary distraction you damn well deserve. Nothing permanent, okay? We don't have time for that shit."

Closing her eyes, she embraced the words, willing them to remain true.

A knock sounded on her back door and she swiveled her head, locking onto Jeremy Kramer's intense green gaze.

And just like that, her heart shot to her knees and damn near exited her terrified body.

Chapter 12

♥

Jeremy knocked on the door, spying Heather through the glass as she stood facing the stove. Her head whipped around and she stared at him for a moment, seeming stunned. Then, she regained her composure and sauntered through the kitchen, past the island counter to the back door. Those blue eyes lasered into his as she gripped the knob and turned before slowly opening the door.

"Why, if it isn't famous author J.R. Kramer," she said, fanning herself as she arched a seductive eyebrow. His gaze trailed down her body, wrapped in a black dress that hugged every crevice before he noticed her cute bare feet. "I hope you're hungry because dinner just arrived."

Feeling like a caveman who was barely capable of grunting, much less speaking, Jeremy leaned in, conscious of the organ in his chest that was now ceaselessly pounding. "I'm fucking ravenous," he growled.

Shallow breaths exited her ruby red lips as they stood there, frozen in desire and anticipation. And then, she snaked out a hand, clutching his shirt in her fist and dragging him inside.

The door slammed behind him, and then, all hell broke loose.

Lunging for her, he drew her against him, cupping the mound of her gorgeous ass as he thrust his other hand in her thick curls. Tugging, he reveled in her arousal-laden gasp before lowering his lips to hers. She moaned, squirming against him as he thrust his tongue in her mouth, swirling...savoring...wondering if he'd ever tasted anything so intoxicating.

Unable to control his body, he undulated into her, pressing his erection into the juncture of her thighs as she mewled. The sexy, high-pitched sound reverberated in the back of his throat as he swallowed it, determined to make her scream even louder.

She snaked a leg around his waist, clutching him as he dragged her to the island. Their tongues mated and warred until he thought he might go mad if he didn't bury himself inside her.

"I wanted to go slow," he rasped, pressing her back into the counter as he spoke between hurried kisses. "But I'm not sure I can—"

"Screw slow," she interjected, breaking the kiss and turning around. Pressing her palms to the cold surface of the island counter, she planted her feet and gazed at him over her shoulder. "Fuck me. Now."

Overcome by her glistening lips as she panted above the counter, Jeremy took a moment to appreciate his fortune. He hadn't made love in quite some time, and here was this stunning woman whom he was coming to care for, begging him to fuck her. Damn, he must've done something right along the way. Grateful for her trust, he gripped the hem of her skirt and slowly dragged it up her thighs. She whimpered, beckoning to him as she silently gazed over her shoulder.

"You little tease," he murmured, wondering how much dirty talk she actually wanted. Mainly, because he was turned on as hell and could go full-on filthy. Bunching the fabric over her waist, he bared her ass, thankful his knees didn't buckle. Covering the twin mounds with his palms, he slid them over the smooth skin. "You're dripping wet."

Hooking his finger beneath the string of her thong, he gently ran it along the fabric. "Look how soaked these naughty panties are."

"Oh god..." she breathed, dropping her head to the counter. "*Jeremy...*"

"That's right, sweetheart," he said, grasping the underwear before slowly sliding it down her legs. "Get used to moaning my name. That's going to happen a lot tonight." She stepped out of the underwear and he rose, lowering over her body and pressing his jean-clad erection into her bare ass.

Lifting the thong to his nose, he stared into her eyes as he inhaled. "Soaked through. I want to taste you before I fuck you."

Her eyes glazed over as she panted beneath him. "I swear to god, you weren't supposed to be this hot. You were supposed to fuck me like the nice dad next door—"

Tossing the scrappy underwear aside, he thrust his fingers in her hair and gently yanked before pressing his lips to hers. "Careful what you ask for, sweetheart. Now, open those sexy legs for me." Giving her a frenzied kiss, he rose and ensured the dress was securely bunched around her waist. Lowering to his knees, he palmed her ass and spread her apart.

"*Ohmygod...*" she cried, pushing into him when he buried his face in her deep, wet center. Holding her apart, he extended his tongue and began the pleasurable task of getting her off with his mouth before he fucked her.

Alternating between long, drawn-out strokes and intense flicks of his tongue against her clit, Jeremy drank her in, dying to please her. Bringing his thumbs to her puckered hole, he tenderly flirted with it as he lathered her clit with his tongue.

"More!" she begged, pressing against him. "I'm close...need more..."

Lowering his hand, he thrust a finger into her slick channel, gliding it back and forth as he flicked her clit with his tongue. Sliding his other index finger into her wetness, he coated it with her honey before dragging it to the swollen nub. Drawing back, he fucked her with his hand as he drew firm, concentric circles over her clit with the other one.

"Yes!" she cried, tossing back her head. "Oh, god...I might collapse..."

"I've got you, hon," he growled, determined to support her. "Give into it. You're so fucking sexy right now."

Her hips gyrated as she pushed herself into his fingers. "*Ohhhh...coming now...fuck!*"

Her back snapped as she fell headlong into the orgasm, sending a jolt of pleasure to every cell in Jeremy's body. Still drowning in the taste of her on his lips, he squeezed the mounds of her ass as she came, the gesture possessive and raw. Her body spasmed atop the counter before she collapsed, gripping the surface and emitting a ragged groan. Enraptured by the glistening evidence of her desire on her deepest place, he gently caressed her wet opening.

"Don't give out on me now, hon," he said, easing his fingers inside, wondering how his eyes didn't cross with lust. "We're just getting started."

"I don't have the energy to bang like teenagers anymore," she muttered into the counter. "I wasted all that good energy when I should've saved it for you. Damn."

Chuckling, he eased his fingers from her and rose. Swiping the hair from her neck, he rubbed the essence over the sweaty skin.

"What are you doing?" she mumbled, gazing up at him with half-lidded eyes as her cheek pressed into the counter.

"You smell so fucking good, Heather," he said, his low tone causing her to shiver. "I want it everywhere. Later, when we cuddle on the couch, I want to bury my nose right here and remember this." He lightly tapped her neck.

"I'm not cuddling with you," she said, the curve of her lips negating the words.

"You're a terrible liar." Lowering, he brushed his lips against hers as he reached for his wallet and threw it on the counter. "Tell me another one."

Those luminous eyes searched his. "I only want sex," she murmured, a slight hint of fear in the softly spoken words.

Jeremy's heart slammed in his chest. Tenderly cupping her jaw, he rested his forehead against hers. Giving her a poignant kiss, he gazed deeply into her eyes.

"I'm not going to hurt you, Heather," he said, needing her to know that caring about someone didn't always result in heartache. "We're writing a new story this time."

"Do flawed characters really deserve a new story?" she asked, her voice gravelly as she stared at him with such vulnerability, he struggled to breathe.

"Yes," he whispered. "Take it from this bestselling author who knows a thing or two about writing flawed characters."

Rising, he unbuttoned his jeans, tugging them off and tossing them away before shirking his underwear and shirt. Heather gazed at him from the counter, limp and sated as questions swirled in her eyes.

"No thinking right now," he commanded, reaching for his wallet and digging out a condom. Opening it, he tossed the wrapper on the counter and eased the condom on. Seeing her sprawled open, ass up as she waited for him to take her did all sorts of things to his insides. Stepping behind her, he aligned their bodies and lowered, resting his lips on the shell of her ear.

"Open wider," he demanded softly.

She complied, spreading her feet and planting them firmly on the floor. Gripping the base of his cock, Jeremy slid the head along her wet slit, hissing as he aligned himself with her core. Needing to stare into her gorgeous eyes when he finally claimed her, he buried his fingers in the hair by her temple and gently turned her head. Resting his forehead against hers, he gazed into her blue orbs as he began to ease inside.

A ragged breath escaped her lips as he jutted between her soft folds, the pleasure almost unbearable as he clenched his teeth. Needing more, he slowly increased the pace of his hips, sliding his shaft to the hilt before dragging it back through her tight channel...only to claim her once again.

"Feels good," she whispered, her hips moving in tandem with his as he fucked her, deep and slow. "But you can go faster if you want."

"In a minute," he said, nodding against her forehead. "I just need to feel you first."

"*Jeremy...*"

"I know, sweetheart." Closing his eyes, he pressed his cheek against hers, reveling in their closeness. She huffed one of those sexy little mewls, setting his body on fire and spurring him into action.

Pressing a feverish kiss to her lips, he rose and realigned their bodies. Gripping her hips, he pulled back, overcome at the sight of his cock against her wet opening, ready to surge inside.

"I'm going to go hard. You okay with that?"

"Yes!"

Breathing a joyful laugh, he tightened his fingers and thrust, surging inside as her heels lifted from the floor. Lust consumed him as she balanced on her cute painted toes, and he began to hammer her, eager to release all the pent-up arousal that had built over weeks of courtship. Although she pretended to hate it, Jeremy was thankful they'd dated because he doubted she would've been as open with him now otherwise.

And good lord, was she open.

His woman gripped the counter with open palms as his fingers dug into her hips, marking her as he maneuvered her body against his. She gave him control, for which he was imminently grateful, and he gladly took it, claiming her body with firm, rapid strokes. Her slick walls were so tight around him, choking his cock, and he felt the tingling at the base of his spine.

Lowering, he gripped her hair in his fist and rested his lips over her ear.

"Whose cock is inside you?" he demanded, his tone low and laced with lust.

"Yours. Oh, god...*Jeremy*..."

"That's right, honey." Clenching his jaw, he reached for the peak, feeling his balls tighten as his release drew close. Sliding his free hand between her legs, he delved between her folds, searching for her clit.

"You don't have to..." she groaned, shaking her head. "You can make me come again later. Just fuck me. Hard!"

Following her directive, Jeremy moved his hand to her hip, gripping and anchoring her for the final push. Clutching her hair with his other hand, he relentlessly pounded into her tight body. Grunting with desire, he claimed her, his chest swelling with pride as she balanced on the tips of her toes. Closing his eyes, he buried his face in her neck and began to come.

Jets of release spurted from his body as he screamed her name, his fingers digging into her flesh, holding her close while he drowned in the abyss. Her joyful laughter surrounded him like a warm blanket, enveloping his heated skin as he experienced true bliss. His body quaked and shuddered against her, bucking as he shot the last pulses of release. Circling his hips, he inhaled her scent, still lingering on her damp skin. God, it smelled amazing, and he wanted to be buried in it for the rest of his fucking life.

Feeling the energy leave his muscles, he collapsed over her, his body liquifying as he balanced on wobbly legs. The cool surface of the counter pressed into his cheek and he lifted his lids to stare into her hooded eyes.

"Hey," he murmured, tenderly swiping the hair from her sweaty forehead.

"Hey," she softly replied.

They stared at each other, cheeks resting on the counter, as their bodies cooled.

"Still think I'm boring in bed?" he asked, arching a brow.

She closed one eye, contemplating. "Technically, we never made it to a bed."

His lips curved into a sultry grin. "Semantics, sweetheart."

Leaning in, she placed a sweet peck on his lips, sending his decelerating heartbeat back into overdrive. "You were pretty damn good. I stand corrected."

Grinning, he ran the pad of his thumb over her lips, wishing he didn't have to move to dispose of the condom. "Let's eat and then we'll cuddle."

An amused challenge flared in her eyes. "I'm not cuddling with you."

"Man, you are so damn cute when you lie. Don't ever stop."

Kissing the tip of her nose, he avoided the lazy swat of her arm before chuckling and rising. Pulling from her gorgeous body, he removed the condom and tossed it in the nearby trash can. Returning to her, he grazed his palms over her ass one last time, unable to resist. Then, he lowered her dress, helping her to stand before he began to tug on his clothes.

"I'm a useless pile of limp muscles right now," she said with a sly grin. "Help."

"I'm not much better but I think I can load food onto a plate and work the microwave." Tugging over a nearby stool, he urged her toward it. "Want to sit and direct me?"

"Sure." Sliding on, she observed as he trailed over and opened the containers atop the stove. "I ordered Cuban food. Hope that's okay."

"Perfect," he said. "Plates?"

She lifted a weak arm, pointing to the cabinet above the microwave.

Jeremy opened it, unable to control his grin as he grabbed two plates. Her sated expression and relaxed posture sent a jolt of satisfaction down his spine. Thankful the first time had gone so well, Jeremy vowed to make each subsequent lovemaking session better and better.

Heather cleared her throat and he jumped to attention, recognizing he was daydreaming about the future, which would probably scare the hell out of her. Determined to keep things light, he prepared two plates, ready to replenish their energy so he could love her all over again.

Hours later, Heather lay sprawled over Jeremy's naked body, sweaty and sated as they melted into her couch. Dinner was followed by another steamy encounter on the kitchen island before he carried her to the couch to finish the deed. Snuggling into him, she wrinkled her nose at the tickling sensation from the spiky hairs on his chest. Sighing, she ran her fingers in a lazy pattern over his pec.

"Why are you dramatically sighing?" he teased, his deep voice surrounding her from above.

"Because I swore I wasn't going to cuddle with you."

"Mmm-hmm..." was his soft reply as he gently stroked her hair.

Feeling her eyes narrow, Heather attempted to push down the anxiety that welled in the pit of her stomach. She'd let her guard down with him earlier, indicating she might want more than sex, and it terrified her. After all, she sure as hell wasn't wife or stepmother material. Anyone with basic observational skills could see that the moment they met her.

And yet, somewhere deep in a tiny crevice of her heart, she wondered what it would feel like to love someone again. She'd only ever loved Butch, and that was a love borne more from necessity than affection. Once she was free of her parents, whatever love she'd felt for her ex-husband had dissipated. And she doubted he'd ever truly loved her. If anything, he'd been in lust with her looks and her brashness.

In the end, no one had ever truly loved her. It was something she'd accepted long ago and stopped craving along the way. But now, locked in her lover's arms, she allowed herself to channel that buried yearning for just a moment, vowing to acknowledge it before stowing it away again.

"The girls and I are going hiking up by the reservoir next Saturday," he murmured, dragging her from her thoughts. "I'd really like you to come with us."

She tensed, letting the words sink in as she contemplated. Part of her felt almost giddy at his request while the other half was stone-cold terrified.

"Hey," he said, placing a tender kiss on her head. "It's not formal, Heather. Just a low-key day with me and the girls."

Gathering the courage to look him in the eye, she shifted and rested her chin on her palm as her elbow balanced on his chest. His green eyes glowed with sated desire and sparks of hope she'd say yes.

"I'm not interested in being a mother or sliding into a family unit. I don't understand those things, Jeremy."

His eyes darted between hers as he slowly trailed a finger over her jaw. "I'm not asking you to be anyone but yourself, Heather." His lips curved, making him look so handsome as he gazed at her with affection. "I understand you're scared. Everyone who was supposed to love you let you down. And yet, here you are, opening a part of yourself to me. That takes a lot of strength. I know you're strong enough to offer something more than just the physical stuff."

"The physical stuff is easy," she whispered.

"Easy is boring and I never pegged you as boring, sweetheart."

Chuckling, she nodded. "I am definitely *not* boring."

Mirth sparkled in his eyes as he continued to caress her jaw. "Be open with me, hon. With us. It could lead somewhere fun." He waggled his brows.

"Or it could lead to me being crushed. I vowed I'd never allow that to happen again. I'm over needing people."

"Then let us need you," he murmured, cupping her face. "I really like needing you, Heather."

Her heart pounded against his at the poignant words. Feeling her nostrils flare, she relented. "Okay, let's go hiking. I guess I technically still owe you a date...or two?" She gazed at the ceiling. "I lost count."

Laughter rumbled in his chest. "Me too. How about this? I'll continue to ask you to hang—with me alone and sometimes with the girls—and you say 'yes' when you're available."

Her eyes narrowed. "Sounds a lot like a relationship to me."
"Yep."
"I'm not interested in a relationship."
"Okay."
Huffing, she rolled her eyes. "I'm not."
He flashed her a shit-eating grin. "All right."
Shaking her head, she tried to contain her smile. "Fine. I'll hang around here and there...as long as you continue to fuck me like you did tonight." She arched an eyebrow and gave him a sultry glare. "Holy shit. I did *not* see that coming."
Chuckling, he encircled her with his arms and squeezed. "I'm definitely going to develop a complex about why I give off vibes that I suck in bed. Are you trying to decimate my ego?"
Shimmying against his warm skin, she bit her lip. "Sorry. You're just kind of...goofy sometimes...and a bit dorky with the author vibes—"
Gasping, Heather latched on to his biceps as he flipped them over, pinning her to the couch as he growled. "I think you're just goading me so I'll fuck you again, you little tease."
Encircling his neck, she speared her nails into his nape. "Well folks, I think he's finally catching on."
Desire sparked in his eyes before he lowered his head, nudging her nose with his. "Can you take another round? We really went for it tonight."
Pressing her lips to his, she murmured, "I'm game if you are."
And then, all talking ceased as he plunged his tongue into the wet depths of her mouth before taking her to heaven once more.

J eremy eventually headed home after midnight, his expression adorable as he slipped on his shoes by Heather's back door.
"Guess you're kicking me out," he said, his lips forming a cute pout. "Not ready for a sleepover yet, huh?"
"Definitely not." Rising to her toes, she pecked his lips. "I had fun. Thank you."

"Me too." Stepping outside, he turned and tilted his head. "I have to write tomorrow but you could come over after seven if you want. We could have dinner."

Leaning on the door, she arched a brow. "Dinner and sex?"

Breathing a laugh, he nodded. "You drive a hard bargain but I'll concede."

"Then, I'm in. I'll text you tomorrow so we can decide what we want to order. Good luck writing your next bestseller."

He squinted one eye. "Have you read any of my books?"

"Nope. Busted."

"Do you like sci-fi and time travel? You might like *Alternate Destinies.*"

"Not really." She scrunched her nose. "But I guess I could try it. It's hard to find the time to read."

"You can listen to the audio for free from the Ardor Creek Library," he said. "Might be more conducive to your work schedule. You know, listening while you're prepping a place for a showing or whatever."

"Maybe I will." Rubbing her upper arms, she smiled at him as he stood firm, silently asking to stay. "Good night, Jeremy," she whispered.

Sadness flashed across his features before he straightened and gave a tiny salute. "Good night, sweetheart. See you tomorrow."

Heather watched his broad shoulders as he trailed across the yard. Then, she softly closed the door and rested her forehead against it, acknowledging how close she'd come to asking him to stay. Sighing, she turned off the lights and headed upstairs. Once in bed, she hugged the extra pillow close, disbelief coursing through her at how attached she already was to her new lover.

Chapter 13

After some successful showings on Saturday, Heather headed over to Jeremy's at seven on the dot. Not that she was anxious to see him again or anything. She just preferred being punctual. Of course, that was why.

They had another amazing night of sex, laughter, and Greek food delivered from Nick's Diner. Jeremy offered to take her to his bed, which scared the shit out of her for some reason, so she performed a nice little striptease in front of the couch so he would just bang her there. Something about banging on the couch was less intimate, and it was all she could allow herself since she was having all sorts of unwanted feelings about her sexy neighbor.

When eleven o'clock rolled around, Heather disengaged from Jeremy's sweaty body atop the sofa and began to dress. His green eyes observed her, sated and curious, as she slipped her shirt over her head.

"Don't get up," she said, leaning down to kiss him. "It's cute that you walk me home but I'll let you stay there and recover."

Grasping her hand, he laced their fingers as affection simmered in his eyes. "You can stay," he finally said, the plea in his voice almost buckling her knees.

"I'm not ready," she whispered, squeezing his hand. "I don't know if I'll ever be. I tried to tell you." She gave a slight shrug.

His lips formed that lazy, knowing grin she was becoming addicted to. "Okay. I won't push you. You've given me a lot this weekend. Thank you, hon."

She smiled back, wondering why her throat was suddenly tight. "What time should I come over next Saturday for the hike?"

"Eleven a.m.?" His eyes narrowed. "Does that work for your schedule?"

She nodded, not wanting to tell him she'd spent an hour earlier that day rescheduling next Saturday's afternoon showings to early morning so she'd be available. Her excitement about spending the day with him and the girls had been palpable as she'd shuffled the appointments, and she just wasn't ready to examine why. Heather had never looked forward to spending time with kids but, damn, she missed the two little heathens.

"Sweet." Bringing her hand to his lips, he kissed the back of it before letting it go. "Night, sweetheart."

Reaching for the blanket from the nearby recliner, she covered him with it before placing a parting peck on his lips. "Good night, lover. See you Saturday."

Blatant desire laced his handsome features as she straightened, stalking out of the house before her resolve crumbled. Once home, she lay down on the couch and nestled into the cushions. Placing her nose to the fabric, she inhaled, closing her eyes as she caught the slightest trace of his scent, still lingering from the previous night.

Sighing, she acknowledged that she was in serious jeopardy of falling hard for Jeremy Kramer.

Jeremy spent the week huddled in his writing cave each day while the girls were in day camp. He and Jen had decided to send them there during summer break and they loved the activities. Unfortunately, the week brought heavy thunderstorms so the girls were relegated to staying inside the rec center most of the week. Still, the camp directors had various projects for them to do and it freed up time for Jeremy to write.

Making love to Heather had restored his creative drive, and he wrote a multitude of chapters as the week wore on. By Thursday, he realized he was almost finished. Sitting at his laptop, he laced his fingers and stretched, thrilled to have another manuscript under his belt.

"Dad!" Gabby called, bounding into the room. "Check out my painting. Do you like it? The head counselor said it was the best one in class."

"Wow," he said, rising to look at the canvas. It displayed a beautiful landscape with what looked to be a farmhouse by a lake. Taking it, he tilted it as he studied, impressed. "This is fantastic, sweetie. I'm so proud of you." Leaning down, he kissed her soft hair. "We need to show this to Justine. I'm going to need her advice on how to hone your talent."

"Thanks," she said, excitement glowing in her eyes. "Do you think Justine would let me paint with her in the studio in her new house?"

"I think so," he said, chucking her nose with his finger. "I'll talk to her."

"Well, mine is awful," Angeline said, trailing into the room and showing him her painting. It certainly wasn't a Picasso, but Jeremy didn't want to rub salt in the wound.

"Hey, at least you tried. A-plus for effort right?"

"Sure," she said, wrinkling her nose.

"You have such a pretty singing voice, though," Gabby said, patting her shoulder. "I got the painting skills and you got the voice. It's only fair."

"Well, look at our sweet angels being nice to each other," Jen said from the doorway, balancing on her crutches. "You would barely know they were screaming at each other in the car."

"That's what siblings do, dear," Jen's mother, Nadine, chimed in, appearing beside her. "You and your sister used to scream so loud the walls would shake."

"That's a bit dramatic, but okay," Jen muttered.

"Thanks for driving the girls over here, Nadine," Jeremy said, striding over to kiss her cheek. "You've been so helpful now that Jen is useless."

Jen swatted his arm as he chuckled.

"Thanks for taking them a day early," she said, rubbing his arm where she'd just smacked him. "Guess I should be nice to you."

"You should. I'm Dad of the Year over here, right girls?"

The twins looked at each other and snickered.

"*Anyway*," he continued after shooting them a good-natured glare, "I hope Lou's surgery goes well tomorrow. Call me if you need anything."

"I will. Come on, Mom. Let's get on the road. You're the best free Uber driver in Ardor Creek and I need to prep my fiancé for surgery."

Leaning down, they each gave the girls one last hug before exiting through the back door.

"Can I wear mascara on our hike on Saturday, Dad?" Angeline asked. "We'll be outside and no one will see me. I want to put it on and show Heather."

"Um, no and no," he said, stroking her silky hair as she frowned. "No makeup outside the house until you're a teenager. Mom and I aren't budging."

Sighing, she nodded.

"Let me save my work and I'll make us a snack before dinner. Go wash your hands and I'll meet you in the kitchen."

They both nodded and trailed from the room. Jeremy sat at his desk, gnawing his lip as he pondered Angeline's words. She was becoming a bit obsessed with makeup and clothing—more so than Gabby—and he and Jen had discussed it at length. They'd decided that letting the girls play with makeup in the house wouldn't do any harm but maybe they'd been wrong.

His girls needed to learn their worth and beauty came from within. He and Jen always reinforced that notion, assuring them that outer beauty would follow. Lifting his phone, he located Heather's number and dialed.

"Hello," she answered, her voice rushed. "I'm caught in a monsoon. Help!"

Laughing, he asked, "Where are you?"

"Just finished a showing in north Ardor Creek. One sec, let me get you on Bluetooth."

He heard a car door slam and then she chimed, "You there?"

"I'm here."

"Whew! It's freaking pouring. So, to what do I owe the pleasure of this afternoon call, lover?"

"I want to ask you something. You might think it's kind of weird."

"Shoot."

"You've mentioned that you've done some work in the past to focus on placing value on what's inside versus your appearance."

"Uh-huh," she said, sounding confused.

"When we go hiking on Saturday, can you maybe talk to Angeline about that progress? I know it's a strange request but she's become a bit obsessed with appearance and she thinks you're gorgeous. I just...I don't know...I think it would resonate with her more than hearing it from me or Jen."

Silence stretched as the soft patter of rain sounded in the background.

"Did I lose you?"

"Jeremy, I have no discernable skills whatsoever when it comes to speaking to children."

His eyebrows drew together. "I don't know why you say that, Heather. The girls are enamored with you. Come on."

She expelled a deep breath. "I guess I can try. You're really pushing it here, buddy. I'd be pissed except I want to keep sleeping with you now that I know you're a secret sex god."

His lips curved. "Am I? That certainly helps restore my ego from your previous decimations."

Her breathy laugh sounded as he waited.

"If you don't feel comfortable, you don't have to, hon. I just had a dad-moment where I saw an opportunity. It's no big deal."

Sighing, she cleared her throat. "Okay, I'll try to talk to her if it comes up naturally. If I mess it up, you can't deny me sex for the foreseeable future. I've earned sexy times until this thing runs its course."

"You say that as if it's inevitable."

"It is."

He grinned. "Is it?"

"Yes."

"Okay."

She huffed a laugh. "I'm only capable of casual and temporary, Jeremy."

"Okay."

"Uggh, you're annoying."

"You're adorable," he chimed, thoroughly enjoying their banter. "And I'm always going to want to have sex with you, Heather.

Unfortunately, we can't on Saturday night since I'll have the girls but you can stay and watch a movie with us after we hike."

"Let's not push it," she droned, although he saw through the façade. He bet his left arm she'd end up staying for the movie.

"I don't want to have you stay over when the girls are here until you've met Jen and she gives the go-ahead. Since you won't stay over when the girls *aren't* here, I figure I have some time."

"We just started banging last weekend," she said, exasperated. "Give me a break. This is a lot for me."

"Okay, drama queen, it's not that bad."

"Emotions and kids and fabulous sex...I mean, you're really layering it on. My stoic shell of a soul can barely handle it."

"Wow, you should be an author. This is good stuff. Very descriptive."

"Whatever." He could envision her rolling her eyes. "I have to get to another showing. I'm going to try and squash my terror about advising a nine-year-old. Yikes."

Laughing, he shook his head. "This is gold. I'm co-authoring a book with you one day. Can't wait to see you. I'd tell you I miss you if I wasn't scared it would freak you out."

Rain sounded over the phone as she digested his words.

"I'd tell you I miss you too if I wasn't incapable of basic human emotion."

"You're no such thing, sweetheart. Good luck at your appointment."

"Thanks."

The screen went dark, and Jeremy bit his lip, anticipating the moment he could hold her again. Rising, he noted his growling stomach and headed to the kitchen to scrounge up some snacks.

Chapter 14

Heather finished her early showings on Saturday and headed home to change and stretch before the hike. Once ready, she tied her sneakers by the back door and stood. Shaking her hands at her sides, she delved into a last-minute pep talk.

"Just a fun day hiking, Heather," she said, jumping up and down a few times to get the jitters out. "You've spent time with the girls before and didn't croak. Stop being dramatic."

Bracing herself, she fastened her small black fanny pack and headed out the back door. When she arrived at Jeremy's, she lifted her hand to knock but was met with two beaming smiles as the girls raced to the door.

"Hey, Heather," Gabby said, drawing open the door. "Dad's upstairs putting on his sneakers."

"Sweet," she said, stepping inside. "I like your shoes."

"Thanks." Both girls lifted their feet, showing off their hiking boots. "Mom bought us new boots since we've been well-behaved since her accident. Dad says it's going to be muddy because it rained so much this week but we can clean them when we get home."

"For sure. From what I remember, the trails from the reservoir are pretty flat, right?"

"They are," Jeremy said, breezing into the kitchen. He was wearing shorts, sneakers, and a t-shirt that hugged his toned chest. Tiny hairs dotted his legs and Heather felt a jolt of lust, remembering having those legs pressed against hers as he fucked her on the kitchen counter. *Down girl.*

"Apparently, new hiking boots are the trend on TikTok so we caved, even though the girls don't have phones yet," he continued, striding over. "Ready?" he asked the girls, stroking Angeline's hair.

"Ready!" they chimed.

Jeremy smiled at Heather, causing her heart to clank in her chest. "You ready?"

"Ready," she said, grinning.

"You guys can totally kiss if you want," Angeline said, rolling her eyes. "We know you like each other."

"Is that so?" Heather asked, arching a brow as her eyes darted to Jeremy's. He gazed back before winking.

"Yep," Gabby said. "It was the same when Mom met Lou. We told him he could kiss her too. It's not a big deal."

"There will be plenty of time for kissing down the road," Jeremy said, turning to grab their small packs from the counter. Lifting them, he handed them to the girls. "These are stocked with snack packs, tissues and sunglasses. Strap them on and let's go, ladies."

The girls strapped on their packs while Jeremy stuffed his wallet in his pocket. He ushered them out the door and they climbed into the SUV. Once Heather was settled in front, she slid on her sunglasses, noting she was excited for the day ahead. It was beautiful without a cloud in the sky, and she would relish the nice weather.

When they arrived at the reservoir, they parked in the lot and Jeremy did one last check for supplies before they started on the path. They walked at a brisk pace, and Heather inhaled the fresh air.

"It's so pretty today," Jeremy said, taking her hand and lacing their fingers as the girls walked in front of them on the dirt path. "Thank you for coming with us. Is it torturous so far?"

She shot him a good-natured glare. "It's awesome, actually. I thought I'd be freaking out at the 'day of family fun,'" she made quotation marks with her free hand, "but it's pretty chill. Thanks for inviting me."

"You're welcome."

He squeezed her hand, and she squeezed back, wondering when she'd turned into a lovesick teenager. Something about holding his hand while his children strode in front of them was poignant.

Gabby and Angeline chatted about summer camp and the shows they were watching on Netflix as they padded along.

Eventually, they crested the hill at the top of the path, coming to stand on a grassy knoll that overlooked the lake below. The view was stunning and Heather took a moment to appreciate the tiny sliver of the world that was Ardor Creek. She'd had so much heartache in the tiny little town but perhaps her luck was finally changing.

"The people look like ants," Angeline said, pointing to the walking path that surrounded the lake. "I can barely see them."

"Yep," Jeremy said, placing his arms over each girl's shoulders as they blanketed his sides. "Feels like we're at the top of the world."

Angeline slipped her hand into Heather's and grinned up at her. "Are you having fun? Dad said he had to ask you a few times to come with us and we had to be on our best behavior."

"Did he?" she asked, sneaking a glance at Jeremy over Angeline's head.

He bit his lip and chuckled. "Busted."

"I'm having fun."

Angeline giggled, small white teeth flashing in the sun as she beamed. Suddenly, the ground below them trembled, crumbling beneath Angeline's feet. Time seemed to still as the girl gasped and began to tumble down the side of the cliff...dragging Heather behind her as she clutched her hand for dear life.

Heather landed with an *oomph!*, sucking in a breath as something hard jutted into her side. Patting the space below her, she realized it was a rather large rock. Placing her palms on the ground, she pushed herself up and searched for Angeline. The girl was bawling beside her, and Heather crawled across the ground, placing a hand on her shoulder.

"Angeline? Hey, it's okay. You're okay."

"My leg," the girl wailed, reaching for her shin as she lay on the ground, covered with dirt and grass.

Heather shuffled, reaching to wipe debris off Angeline's leg. Feeling her eyes widen, she forced herself not to gasp at the wound. A small piece of Angeline's bone was sticking directly out of her leg. Jumping into action, Heather unclasped her fanny pack and dug inside.

"You're going to be okay," she said, looking at the meager contents. Some gum, sunglasses, tissues and her cell phone. Realizing that wasn't going to do jack shit, she eyed the blood rushing from the girl's leg. Reaching for the hem of her tank top, she yanked it off, leaving the sports bra beneath and focused on keeping her voice calm.

"Your leg is bleeding, Angeline," she said over the girl's cries. "I'm going to wrap it in my shirt so we can stop the bleeding."

"It hurts..."

"I know, but we have to stop the bleeding. Roll over on your back and look at the pretty sky while I wrap it, okay?"

Sniffling, she followed the directive, her chin wobbling as her cries diminished to smaller sobs. Heather realized she was probably experiencing a huge shot of adrenaline and wanted to wrap her leg before it wore off. Getting to work, she gently maneuvered the girl's leg and began to wrap the wound.

"Heather!" Jeremy called from above. "I called 911 and they're sending an ambulance. Are you guys okay?"

Heather glanced at her own rapidly swelling ankle, realizing it was likely sprained. In the scheme of things, not a huge deal, although it would probably hurt like hell once her own adrenaline rush wore off. For now, it slightly throbbed as she wrapped Angeline's leg.

"Angeline's leg is broken. Are they going to be able to rescue us?" She glanced around, figuring they'd fallen at least twenty feet. They were anchored on a patch of land that seemed sturdy atop a cliff rock. Thanking the universe for that small miracle, she continued to wrap. Once finished, she placed her hands over the wound, applying pressure to halt the bleeding.

"Gary just called and he's coming too," Jeremy yelled. "He assures me the paramedics can lift you both up. The ground must be unstable due to all the rain."

"Fucking perfect," Heather muttered.

Angeline's wet eyes widened and focused on Heather. "You said the F word."

"Yep," Heather said, balancing more firmly on her butt so she could extend the leg with the swollen ankle while she applied pressure. "I told you, I'm not kid-friendly. I'd ask you not to tell your dad, but I hear you and Gabby are terrible at keeping secrets."

Her lips trembled as tears glistened in her eyes. "Gabby's worse than me."

"I bet she'd say the same about you."

Angeline nodded before grimacing and beginning to wail again. Wanting to soothe her, Heather figured she'd try to keep her distracted with conversation.

"So, your dad tells me you want to wear makeup out of the house. Instead of focusing on the pain, let's talk about it. Want to tell me why?"

Sniffling, she shrugged. "I don't know. I think it makes me prettier."

"Well, take it from me, it doesn't. You can put on all the makeup in the world but it won't cover up who you really are inside. That's where the *real* you comes from."

"Mom and Dad say the same thing."

"Well, they're right."

Sighing, Angeline wiped her nose with her arm. "There's this girl at day camp, Debbie. She's really popular and all the boys like her. She wears makeup and her parents don't care."

"Well, that's their choice but I think you're too young."

Angeline's wet blue eyes assessed her. "You wear makeup."

"I'm a tad older than you," Heather droned. "Anyway, tell me more about Debbie. Is she your friend?"

She nodded. "Gabby is friends with Laura and Cecile, and they're nice but they're *her* friends. Debbie told me I could hang with her and eat lunch at their table...but she said I need to be one of the girls who's pretty and who boys like. Otherwise, I'm not invited."

Heather sighed, remembering how brutal being young could be. In truth, she'd been one of the mean girls, and Debbie sounded right up that alley. However, this gave Heather some inside intel on how to counsel Angeline.

"Look, Debbie sounds like she has her own issues and that manifests as her trying to control the people around her. I speak from experience, and she's not worth it. You need to be yourself around her, and if she doesn't accept you, you'll find other friends."

"But I want to be popular," she said, frowning.

"I get it. I really do. But are you popular if you have to change yourself so someone will like you?"

Heather could see the wheels churning in the girl's mind as she pondered while her wet cheeks glistened in the sun. "No. But what if no one likes the real me?"

"I like the real you," Heather said, smiling and lifting a hand to squeeze her shoulder. "And I think *I'm* pretty cool."

"You're so cool," Angeline breathed. "Gabby and I really like you."

Heather's nostrils flared as tears stung her eyes. Annoyed at the spark of emotion, she replaced her hand over Angeline's wound. "Thanks. I like you both too."

Shallow breaths exited Angeline's lungs as she struggled against the pain. "Do you like our dad?"

"Yeah," Heather said, swallowing thickly as her voice turned to gravel. "I really like him."

"He likes you too. Sometimes, he gets this weird look on his face, and Gabby and I tease him that he's daydreaming about you."

Feeling her lips twitch, she tilted her head. "Yeah?"

She nodded. "Are you going to marry him like Mom's marrying Lou?"

"Who knows, kid? I always said I'd only get married again if it was to someone old who wouldn't bother me."

"That doesn't sound fun," she said, wrinkling her nose.

Laughing, Heather shook her head. "It doesn't. Being married to your dad would probably be lots of fun." Blood pulsed through her body at the serious words. "But I'm not ready to think about that yet."

"Okay. You can always hang out with me and Gabby if you don't want to hang out with Dad. Mom says he can be a pill sometimes."

Heather breathed a laugh. "I need to meet your mom. She sounds awesome."

"She is." Angeline pursed her lips, squirming as she fought the pain. "My leg really hurts, Heather."

"I know, sweetheart." Looking to the embankment above, Heather prayed the paramedics would arrive soon. Voices sounded atop the hill, followed by Jeremy who pointed down at them, directing the paramedics.

"Heather!" Gary Lincoln shouted, hands cupped around his mouth. "We're going to lower a backboard down. We're going to instruct you on how to strap Angeline to it and then we'll lift her up."

"Got it," she said, giving a thumb's up.

"After that, we're going to drop a rope and reel you up unless you need to be strapped too."

"My ankle's hurt but I'll be able to hobble to a rope. That's fine."

"Okay, get ready."

The paramedics lowered the backboard and Heather followed the shouted instructions, securing Angeline to the contraption. Once she was stable, the team lifted her to the top. Afterward, they lowered a rope toward Heather with a loop on the end.

"If you can seat yourself on the rope, we'll bring you up," Gary shouted. "It's going to be bumpy so use your hands and uninjured leg to maintain distance from the cliff."

Heather hobbled to the rope, balancing most of her weight on her good ankle and situating herself. The lift to the top was no picnic, but she avoided any major injuries. Once she crested the top, two paramedics grabbed her arms and lifted her to solid ground.

"Thank god," she breathed, balancing on one of the men. "Did you address Angeline's leg wound? It's bad."

"Jen met them in the reservoir parking lot and they're already in transit to the hospital," Gary said, leaning in and assessing her. "Are you okay?"

"Yeah," Heather said, noting her ankle was now the size of a softball. "Relatively."

"Heather," Jeremy's voice called behind her, laced with affection. He slid around her and drew her into a solid embrace, holding her so tight she could barely breathe.

"Too much," she said, tapping his shoulder.

"Sorry." Drawing back, he cupped her face and ran his thumbs over her cheeks. "Thank you for taking care of Angeline. Thank god it wasn't worse. My heart damn near collapsed when you fell."

Swaying into him since she couldn't really balance on her sprained ankle, she allowed herself to take comfort in his embrace.

Now that the adrenaline was wearing off, she realized how close she'd come to biting the bullet.

"Holy shit, we fell down a fucking ravine."

A ragged laugh escaped his throat. "You fell down a fucking ravine. Maybe hiking was a bad idea."

Uncontrollable laughter bounded from her throat. "I told you I suck at dating." Glancing at her ankle, she dug her fingers into his shoulders. "I need to get an X-ray. I'm probably fine but I'll definitely need a brace."

"Okay." He placed a sweet kiss on her forehead before leaning down and lifting her into his arms. "I'll carry Heather to the car and drive her to the hospital," he said to Gary. "Since Jen's already in the ambulance, I'll meet up with her and Angeline there."

"I'll drive Gabby to my house and she can hang with Avery and Justine," Gary said, leaning down and resting his hands on his knees to look Gabby in the eye. "Sound good, sweetheart?"

Gabby nodded and took Gary's hand once he straightened.

"Thanks so much, Gary, and thanks to all of you," Jeremy said, addressing the remaining paramedics. "I'm grateful for your help."

"You don't have to carry me," Heather murmured, sliding her arms around Jeremy's neck as he began to traverse the trail. "If the paramedics have some crutches, I can manage."

"It's okay, hon. Let me take care of you."

Wracking her brain, Heather realized it might have been the first moment in her life someone offered to take care of her. Too exhausted to argue, she buried her face in his neck and let him carry her through the woods.

Chapter 15

♥

After an X-ray and thorough examination by the orthopedist at Ardor Creek Medical Center, it was confirmed that Heather's ankle was sprained. The doctor prescribed an ice press, ankle brace and lots of ibuprofen. Thankful it wasn't worse, she allowed the doctor to wrap her ankle as she sat atop the exam table. When he was finished, he directed her to wait for the nurse who would bring her some crutches.

Jeremy entered as the doctor exited and observed her wrapped ankle. "How's it feeling?"

"Eh, I've had worse," she said, shrugging atop the exam table. "Is Angeline on the way to Scranton?"

He nodded and sat beside her. "Jen is on her way too. Angeline will be in surgery at the orthopedic hospital to repair her leg and there's no reason for us both to sit in a waiting room. I'll head to Scranton once I have you home and settled in. Jus and Gary are going to keep Gabby tonight."

"You should go to Scranton now, Jeremy. I'm fine."

He nudged her with his shoulder. "You really not a fan of being taken care of, huh?"

"Honestly, I don't really know. I don't think anyone's ever offered."

Brushing a lock of hair from her forehead, he tucked it behind her ear. "You've got someone in the bunker with you now, Heather. Whether you like it or not."

She squinted one eye. "I'm not sure if I like it. It makes me uncomfortable, that's for damn sure."

Chuckling, he slid his hand over hers and squeezed. "Good. I want you on your toes."

"I'm not sure how I feel about that coming from an author who writes about serial killers," she teased. "Should I be worried?"

He gave her a goofy grin before the nurse walked in with her crutches. Heather stuffed them under her arms, ready to get home and put the harrowing day behind her.

Jeremy drove them home, holding her hand the entire time, fingers laced atop her thigh. Once they arrived, he jogged around and helped her out before crouching down and lifting her.

"This is ridiculous," she said, feigning annoyance although there was something primal and sexy about him carrying her. "I have crutches, Jeremy."

He shushed her and trailed to the door, opening it and carrying her upstairs before placing her on the bed. "I'm going to go down and get your crutches and fanny pack, and I'll be right back."

After he retreated, she stood on her good leg and tried to remove her yoga pants, although she didn't make much progress. He returned, setting her crutches and pack in the corner before rushing over. "Let me help you."

Sighing, she collapsed on the bed. "I didn't imagine this scenario would be the first time you took off my pants in my bed, but thanks."

His lips twitched as he helped her remove her pants. Glancing at her legs, he trailed his fingers over them. "Do you want to take a bath? You've got dirt everywhere. I can help you."

"I bet you can," she said, arching a brow.

"And you accuse me of being cheesy," he muttered. "Come on, let's get the rest of these clothes off and I'll run the bath."

She tugged off her sports bra and panties, feeling her body flush as he helped her. Once she was naked, he grabbed her robe and slung it over her shoulders before he prepared the bath. Once it was ready, she leaned on him as she hobbled to the adjoining bathroom. She removed the robe, feeling self-conscious since he was all business. It made sense, considering his daughter was hurt and having surgery several miles away, but she was uncomfortable nonetheless.

Jeremy helped maneuver her into the bath and she relaxed into the warm water, full of bubbles.

"Here," he said, dropping to his knees on the bathmat as he reached for the washcloth. "Let me help."

Heather's ankle rested on the rim of the tub, still wrapped and above the water. Biting her lip at the fact she was basically spread eagle in front of her lover, she watched him caress her skin with the cloth. He dragged it over one leg, then the other, careful not to wet the bandage. Eventually, he trailed it up her torso, over her breasts, causing her to shiver as he brushed her nipples.

"Jeremy," she whispered, grasping his wrist.

"Sorry," he said, tenderness in his gaze as his hand stilled. "I want you, Heather, but I'm so worried about Angeline. I just can't right now. I want to take care of you and get you situated, and then I'm going to go to her." He shrugged. "This is what being a parent is. They're the most important things in my world."

"I get it," she said, gently rubbing his arm. "I'm really worried about her too. The break was awful. I hope the surgery is a success."

His eyes drifted to her collarbone and he resumed washing her. Eventually, her skin began to shrivel and he helped her out. Grabbing the towel, he began to dry her and she laughed. "I can do it."

"Please, hon," he said, tenderly patting her skin. "You saved my little girl and got hurt in the process. Let me help you."

Clutching onto his shoulders, she balanced against him as he dried her. Once finished, he replaced the towel on the rack and lifted her, carrying her to the bed. Heather shimmied under the covers but left her ankle exposed, resting it atop the pillow Jeremy placed at the foot of the bed. Once she was situated, he sat beside her, gently stroking her hair as it fanned the pillow.

"Okay, you've got the remote and I'll grab you some water. Want me to heat up some food and bring it to you?"

"Honestly, I kind of just want to veg here and maybe take a nap. I'll manage to hobble around if I need something."

"Angeline's surgery is supposed to be done around ten o'clock tonight. Once they're finished, Jen and I will probably set up alternating shifts. I'll let her go home and catch some Z's before I do the same. I'll text you when I'm on the way home and see if you want me to grab you some food."

"You don't need to worry about me—"

"I'm already worried," he interjected, placing his thumb over her lips. Ever so gently, he began to trace it back and forth. "Worried at how close I came to losing you today. When you disappeared over that cliff, I was terrified, Heather."

"Well, your little girl was in danger."

"Yes," he whispered, the caress of his thumb so soothing against her lips. "But *you* were in danger too."

"I'm fine," she said, shaking her head on the pillow.

Light-green orbs darted over her face, his expression serious as he contemplated her. "I'm in this for more than sex, Heather. I fully accepted that today and need you to know."

She inhaled a deep breath, gaze locked with his as fear shot to every cell in her body. Unable to respond, she contemplated him while trying to digest the words.

"Thank you for saving Angeline. It was so brave."

"I didn't save her. Man, you are really dramatic right now. I'm the one with the injury, remember?"

He huffed a laugh. "I remember. Jen and I are grateful to you, sweetheart."

Grasping his hand, she placed a tender kiss on his palm as she stared into his eyes, showing him with the gesture what she wasn't ready to vocalize yet. "Go see your daughter. I'll be fine."

Leaning down, he brushed a kiss across her lips. Rising, his broad shoulders disappeared through the door before he returned with a glass of water and a box of crackers so she had something to munch on. With one last wave, he left, promising to lock the front door behind him.

Sighing, Heather snuggled into the bed, closing her eyes and imagining he was still above her...imagining he was saying even more sweet words she insisted on pretending she didn't want to hear...

Chapter 16

The next day, Heather was sprawled on her couch, ankle high on the backrest, as she balanced worrying about Angeline and the general unfairness of life. The latter was spurred by the fact she'd become invested in the former or, in other words, she was pissed that she cared.

Sighing, she threw her arm over her forehead, wondering when she'd become the woman who wanted more than sex. The woman who cared about a sweet, precocious little girl whose leg was severely broken and her dad, who pretty much now inhabited her every thought.

Loud knocks sounded at the door, jarring Heather so she damn near fell off the couch. Muttering to herself, she hobbled to the door and yanked it open.

"What the—"

"Surprise!"

Five beaming faces stared back at her, attached to hands that each held a bottle of wine, vodka or a various mixer. Grinning, Heather placed her hand over her heart.

"You guys scared the shit out of me."

"Um, hi," Justine said, waving her free hand. "As I told you, Heather, you're in the crew whether you like it or not."

"We're here to offer support and lots of alcohol," Carrie chimed.

"The men are sequestered with the kids and watching baseball," Ashlyn said, "and we took rideshares over. Looks like it's a Sunday Funday!"

Overwhelmed they would rearrange their days to check on her, Heather swallowed the lump of emotion at the back of her throat. "That's really nice, guys, but you don't have to—"

"Oh no, I'm ready for some day drinking," Abby said, shaking her head. "Come on, Heather, let us in. We all need this, believe me."

"I've learned to just go with the flow with this crowd," Teresa chimed in. "When they're dead set on day drinking, there's no arguing."

"All right," Heather said, unable to control her grin as she ushered them in. "The place isn't sparkling but it's passable."

"We don't give a damn," Justine said. "Come on ladies."

Carrie and Abby handed off their supplies to the others and wrapped their arms around Heather's waist so they could help her to the kitchen. Once there, they commenced making various rounds of drinks.

"I'd say we could sit outside but I never bought any lawn furniture," Heather said. "And now, summer's halfway over so I probably won't."

"The living room's fine with me," Justine said, mixing a vodka soda atop the island. "Although, the back yard is nice. You might want to remove the swings and treehouse so you can make it more adult appropriate."

"About that," Heather said, glancing at Ashlyn. "I was wondering if I should offer to move the swing and other kid stuff to Jeremy's yard so the girls can play with them. Do you think Scott would be willing to help? I'm not sure if the treehouse can be moved or rebuilt?"

"I'm sure he'd love to help," Ashlyn said, sipping her drink. "I'm not sure if it can be moved but, if not, he can disassemble the old one and junk it. I know he wouldn't mind building a new one for Jeremy's girls."

"Are they too old for that?" Heather asked. "Do almost ten-year-olds still like swings and treehouses and things? You all have to help me. I'm dreadful at this shit."

"I think they'll love it," Carrie said. "And Peter will help too."

"I'd offer for Chad to help but he'd probably just end up breaking something or playing on the swings more than moving them," Abby said. "But he can offer moral support, I guess."

The ladies chuckled.

"We'll figure it out," Ashlyn said. "Let's go sit in the living room."

They maneuvered into the living room, relaxing on the couches and chairs Heather had assembled over her years of residing in various parts of Pennsylvania.

"Do you want to elevate your ankle?" Teresa asked beside her on the couch. "I can sit on the floor. The carpet looks soft."

"I'm good," Heather said, gesturing for her to stay. Lifting her glass, she made eye contact with each of them as she spoke. "Wow, ladies, I don't know what to say. Never in my bitchy teenage years did I think you'd all be here supporting me during my disastrous injury." She dramatically rested the back of her hand on her forehead. "I guess we really are the poster children for moving on, growing up and becoming our best selves. Cheers!"

The group gave a resounding, "Cheers!"

"Honestly, guys, thank you," Heather said, snuggling into the couch. "My ankle is fine and the doc said it will probably be back to normal in a week or two. But I still appreciate you checking on me."

"How's Angeline?" Justine asked. "Jeremy said her break was awful."

"The surgery to repair the leg went well," Heather said, acknowledging the concern that bloomed in her chest. "He promised to give me updates as they know more but she's anticipated to have a long but full recovery."

"Sounds like you saved the day when you fell, Heather," Carrie said, placing her hand over her heart. "I heard you were extremely calm and collected. I'm not sure I would've reacted the same way. It's admirable."

"You would've. Intense situations always bring out your inner fortitude. I learned that lesson at a very young age. It probably hardened me a bit too much but it made me strong too." Smiling at Teresa, she asked, "What do you think, doc? Valid assessment?"

"I think so," she said with a nod.

"Sweet. So, what's up with all of you? How are the various spawns and balls and chains doing?"

"Hold it right there, lady," Justine said, showing her palm. "We are not here to talk about our *boring* lives. We're here to talk about you and Jeremy. Mainly, we're all dying to know how he is in bed. Spill, sister."

Heather slowly sipped her drink, drawing out the anticipation. "I mean...isn't that between me and Jeremy?" she asked with a shit-eating grin.

"No!" the ladies chimed in unison.

Tossing back her head, Heather gave a joyous laugh. "Fine. I'm dying to tell you anyway. Do you think he'll be mad?"

"We all discuss our sex lives and our husbands damn well know it," Carrie said. "It's a prerequisite to being married to us. Now that you're in the crew, you will be held to the same standard." She rapidly blinked her eyes as Abby snickered beside her.

"If Jeremy wants to date one of the crew, he needs to accept we're going to know *all* the juicy details," Justine said. "We're waiting..."

Inhaling a huge breath, Heather took one more gulp for courage and plunged ahead. "He's so much better than I thought he would be. Ladies..." she glanced at each of them as mischief crossed her expression, "...he's a dirty talker!"

Excited gasps echoed in the room.

"Jeremy?" Abby asked, wrinkling her nose. "Really? He's so...Jeremy."

"I know," Heather said, eagerly leaning forward as she brimmed with excitement. "The first night we were *soooooo* ready and he banged me on the kitchen counter." Fanning herself, she exhaled a breath. "So. Damn. Hot."

Her friends squealed with excitement as Heather detailed them on their first weekend together. "Of course, it's hard to have sexy times when we're both so busy and he has two kids, but I'm dead set on banging him as much as humanly possible."

"Til death do you part?" Ashlyn asked, arching a brow.

"Debatable," Heather said, squinting. "I'm hesitant to tell you guys this because I don't want to make a big deal out of it, but I do experience all these weird...*feelings* around him. And around the girls." Leaning her head back on the couch, she scoffed. "Gross. I hate feelings."

"Sympathetic friend here gets it," Abby said, raising her hand. "I had so many feelings for Chad and it was infuriating. Of course, *now*, I adore said feelings. It just took me a while."

"So, maybe you'll come around," Justine said, waggling her eyebrows at Heather. "Having feelings for someone isn't a death sentence, Heather. When it's the right person, it's actually pretty great. Dean wasn't the right person for me so I thought I sucked at relationships. Turns out, I'm pretty awesome at them now that I'm with Gary." She huffed on her nails and rubbed them on her shirt.

"Okay, Dr. Ruth, relax," Heather teased. "We all know you're an expert on relationships now that you've found your soul mate."

"Who's Dr. Ruth?" Justine muttered.

"God, I'm old," Heather groaned. "Forget it. Anyway, I was having a nice time with him until shit hit the fan. Now he's got a hurt daughter and I'm not a paragon of health over here myself." She pointed at her ankle. "We might bang again when we're eighty."

"You guys will find the time," Carrie said. "Peter and I always find the time even though we have three kids." She bit her lip atop a playful smile. "And the sex is way better when you're married. Don't let anyone tell you differently."

"Whoa," Heather said, holding up a hand. "Let's chill with the 'M' word. Right now, I'm into having fun and trying to handle basic human emotions here, ladies."

The women chuckled as they fell into conversation about marriage and relationships. Eventually, everyone passed the point of tipsy to full-on drunk and called a rideshare. Heather hugged them as they left, assuring them she would be okay.

Once the house was quiet, Heather limped to the kitchen, noticing an envelope on the counter with her name scrawled on it. Lifting it, she read it as tears began to blur the words.

Heather,

Life is long and we all deserve our second chances. Sometimes, even third or fourth chances. You've overcome a lot of adversity in your life to be where you are today. We're not sure you give yourself enough credit for having the strength to plow through life, even when you fail and times are tough. You are a true fighter and we admire you for it.

Since we love to meddle, we'll remind you that strength comes from within but there is also strength in allowing yourself to be supported by others. That requires trust and vulnerability. Even a five-star general would admit he can't fight a war alone. We're happy to have you in the crew and help fight too.

Love, the Crew

The note was signed by six women, including Terry, whom Heather assumed was working at the pub or she would've been present today too. Closing her eyes, she folded the note and rested it on her chest, overwhelmed by the emotion that was coming to embody this phase of her life.

After cleaning the kitchen, she headed upstairs and located the old yearbook she'd kept through numerous moves and iterations of herself. Thumbing through the pages, she observed the pictures—in her cheerleading uniform, at the lunch table sitting with the other mean girls, at the football games leading the cheers. She'd been so pretty and so popular—on the outside. Inside, she'd been wretched.

Flipping to the last page, she ran her hand over the smooth inside cover. It didn't have one signature. Not one note from a fellow student saying, "*Have a good summer,*" or "*Good luck in your future endeavors.*" No one had wanted to sign her yearbook because she'd been a pretty shitty person. She hadn't been spawned from the best people, so it made sense, but she just hadn't possessed the capacity to be a better person at that point in time.

Placing the letter from the crew in the back crease, she closed the yearbook and ran her palm over the etching on the front.

"Well, Heather, took you a while but you finally have some signatures in your yearbook. Nice job."

Resting her forehead on the soft leather, she hugged the yearbook tight as she rocked back and forth on the soft carpet.

Chapter 17

Heather spent the week recovering, pleased as her ankle decreased in size a little each day. Jeremy came over to check on her often, which was sweet considering he had a hurt child, a hurt ex-wife, and a million other things to deal with in his busy life. Since she didn't want to push it, she called her clients and rescheduled showings that weren't urgent. It freed her up to have time to rest, which made her realize something pretty quickly: she was freaking *bored.*

Since the doctor had urged her to rest—and since her body wasn't fresh off the boat anymore, so to speak—she understood it was imperative to heal so the injury wouldn't cause her lingering issues down the road. But for someone as active as Heather, sitting around watching your ankle heal was maddening.

After she'd binged two shows on Netflix, she sat on her couch one afternoon, drowning in boredom. Suddenly, a thought flickered in her brain and she pulled up the browser on her phone. After typing *J.R. Kramer* into the search tab, she awaited the results, deciding she'd finally read *Alternate Destinies.*

His face popped up immediately, and rather than clicking on his website, she clicked on the Wikipedia page. Scrolling through, she read about his accolades and accomplishments as an author. Impressed, she realized he had several bestselling books and was quite popular.

Her finger hovered over his most recent projects and her eyes widened as she read:

Alternate Destinies *has been optioned by Netflix and is currently in pre-production. Kramer will be credited as a producer and* *screenwriter alongside four-time Oscar-nominated screenwriter Layla Short.*

"Damn, Heather," she murmured to herself as she scrolled, "Jeremy is kind of a big deal. Who knew?"

Transfixed by his accomplishments, she read every one as her heart began to pound. What in the hell was he doing with someone like *her*? The way it appeared, he could be dating famous supermodels and actresses. Flummoxed, she continued reading.

*Kramer has a dedicated Facebook fan group called **Kramer Junkies** which has over fifty thousand members. The group is run by fans and Kramer insists he has no affiliation with the group.*

"Kramer Junkies?" she whispered in disbelief. "He's got a whole damn fan club."

Overwhelmed by the info, she pulled up her contacts and dialed his number.

"Hey," he said, breathless. "I'm walking Angeline around the neighborhood to get some blood flowing in her good leg. You okay?"

"Hell no, I'm not okay," she said, mock incredulity lacing her voice. "I just googled you."

"Oh, lord. Were there pictures of me naked? My publicist says people are nuts and can put my head on other people's bodies. Although, maybe if they use someone like The Rock or Jason Momoa, I won't be mad."

"Kramer Junkies?" she asked, exasperated. "Jeremy, you could've told me how famous you are."

"Oh, that's just a Facebook group. It's a bunch of fans who geek out about my books."

"Fifty thousand fans! That's massive."

"I guess it's pretty cool. Honestly, that stuff is so weird to me. Authors are pretty introverted. We like hanging with the people in our head more than most people in the real world."

"I feel like I'm dating a celebrity. You got a freaking movie deal, Jeremy!"

"My agent negotiated that but, yeah, it's been in pre-production for a while. At this rate, the movie will get made when I'm seventy. These things move slow."

Grinning from ear to ear, she shook her head. "I'm really intimidated and I'm *never* intimidated. This is major, Jeremy."

His deep chuckle drifted through the phone. "I'm still the same guy I was before you googled me, Heather."

"Okay, go walk with Angeline while I pull up your book. Now I *have* to read it."

"I'm kind of terrified you'll hate it. Hope it doesn't scare you away since you're not a sci-fi time travel fan."

"I'll let you know. I'm buying the e-book when I hang up. Hug the girls for me."

"Aw," he said, affection in his tone. "That's sweet. I will."

"Oops, I said that without thinking," she teased. "I still detest children."

"Right. Talk to you later, hon. Call me if you need me."

Still reeling from her discoveries, she pulled up his website and purchased *Alternate Destinies* before opening it on her phone. Settling back on the couch, she began to read, ready to see what all the fuss was about.

On Friday afternoon, Heather chewed her thumbnail as she anxiously read the last chapter of Jeremy's book. All of her mother's training not to bite her nails flew out the window as she glanced at her reading progress, seeing she was at 99%. How could that be when she still needed to know if the protagonist was alive in the parallel timeline? Tapping her phone, she scrolled to the last page, reading the final paragraph before exclaiming, "What?"

Swiping forward, she was taken to Jeremy's bio and list of other books. Frustrated, she swiped back and reread the last page. Exasperation welled deep within and she rose from her flat position on the couch.

Reaching for her sandals, she slipped them on, one of them looser over her bandaged ankle, and began to limp to Jeremy's house, thankful she no longer needed crutches. She banged on his back door, noting the afternoon sun was still rather high in the sky. He was probably working but she didn't give a damn.

"Hey," he said, confusion lacing his expression as he opened the door. "You were supposed to come over at six. I won't be done writing for two hours."

"You son of a bitch," she said, crossing her arms and tapping her bound foot.

"Um, excuse me?"

"A cliffhanger? You've got to be kidding me."

His lips curled into an adorable grin as he regarded her. "It's not really a cliffhanger. The reader is meant to assume Shannon is still alive in the parallel universe."

"Okay, but is she alive with Jackson? Or an alternate version of him? Or did he die in that universe too?"

"That's up for you to decide in your own imagination."

"Fuck that," she said, placing her hand on his chest and pushing him into the kitchen. She followed, closing the door behind her before resting her fists on her hips. "I have zero imagination, Jeremy. None." She held up her hand, touching her index finger to her thumb to form a circle. "You can't do this to me."

Chuckling, he reached for her and attempted to pull her close. "Man, you are so hot right now with those flushed cheeks and fire in your eyes. I should've asked you to read *Alternate Destinies* months ago."

"You want sex? Then you're giving me answers, buddy. Come on."

Disengaging, she encircled his wrist and led him to the foot of the stairs.

"Where are you dragging me, woman?"

Turning, she stared into his eyes and lifted her chin. "We're bypassing the couch and heading straight for the bed, which I know will incentivize you. I'm going to seduce you into telling me what happens. Come on." She tugged his wrist.

"Heather, I'm on a deadline. I need two more hours—"

Moving her hand to his crotch, she placed it over his zipper and gently squeezed. "Answers," she said, her voice sultry as lust blazed in his eyes. "Now."

Mirth swam in his green orbs as he silently debated before muttering, "Fuck it," and lowered to lift her in his arms. Heather squealed, already anticipating their sexy times as he carried her up the stairs. When they were beside the bed, he set her on her feet and she gently pushed him to sit on the edge of the bed. Reaching down, she slid off her sandals, tossing them aside.

"Heather, I don't want you to hurt yourself."

"I'm just fine, Mr. Famous Author," she said, grasping the hem of her shirt and dragging it off. He reached for her and she swatted his hands away. "Shannon and Jackson. Parallel universe. Go."

Grinning, he leaned back, resting his palms on the bed. "It's honestly supposed to be up to the reader what happens, but if I had to guess, I'd say Shannon is doing well in the parallel universe."

"That's good," she purred, clutching the button of her jeans. Popping it open, her skin tingled as he gazed at her, desire lacing his handsome features. "And where's Jackson?"

"His future is tougher to foresee. Since he died in the original universe, he may perish in the new universe too."

Frowning, Heather shook her head and stilled her hands. "I don't like that ending."

"Or...he might actually survive in the new timeline."

Rewarding him, she slowly unzipped her jeans. "Yes, that's much better." Careful not to dislodge her ankle bandage, she dragged off her pants and faced him before reaching for her bra hook. "Go on."

"They continue to search for the evil overlord, working together to..."

Heather removed her bra, tossing it to the floor before hooking her fingers over her underwear. "Yes?"

Clearing his throat, he continued. "Working together to save the world."

"That's more like it." Dragging the panties down her legs, she kicked them off and stepped toward him. Grasping his shirt, she pulled it off before tugging his pants. Making quick work of his pants and underwear, she tossed them to the floor.

"Sweetheart," he whispered, placing his hands on her hips. "Let me touch you."

"Not yet." Encircling his wrists, she held them in place as she lowered to her knees. Guiding his hands to rest on either side of the bed, she placed her palms on his thighs and spread his legs before easing in between them.

"Holy shit," he breathed.

Reaching for his semi-hard cock, she took him in her hand, reveling in his desire-laden hiss. Gaze cemented to his, she began to gently jerk him as she lowered her lips to his inner thigh. Running her tongue over his skin, she tasted him, closing her eyes at his scent, musky and heady.

"Do they eventually catch the overlord and bring him to justice?" she murmured against his skin.

"That's hard to know for certain," he growled, threading the fingers of one hand through her hair. "It would require a massive effort and several alliances in the new universe."

She formed a sultry pout. "I want him to pay for his crimes."

Expelling a laugh, Jeremy's hips surged toward her. "I mean, I guess he could eventually be captured and put on trial."

Kissing a trail up his thigh, Heather reached his shaft, nudging it with her nose. Opening her mouth, she huffed out a warm breath. Jeremy's fingers tightened in her hair at the feel of her breath on his cock. "Jesus, Heather."

"Tell me he suffers." Placing her lips on the sensitive head, they brushed against him as she spoke. "Tell me he's brought to justice and Shannon and Jackson live happily ever after."

Jeremy's tongue darted out to bathe his lips before he thrust his other hand in her hair. "I thought you didn't believe in happily ever after."

Grasping his cock, she brought the head to rest between her lips, gently touching as she hovered, ready to suck him deep. "Make me believe."

His resulting smile was so fucking sexy, Heather felt a gush of wetness between her thighs. "The overlord dies a painful death and Shannon and Jackson live their best fucking lives."

Breaking into a huge grin, she whispered against his cock, "Good boy." Then, she widened her lips and slid over him, impaling him in her mouth in one smooth, luscious glide.

Jeremy's hips surged high as he groaned, pushing his shaft into the wet depths of her mouth before drawing back. Heather followed his movements, moving her head in tandem with his gentle thrusts as he breathed her name. Enraptured by the intimate moment, she closed her eyes, delighting in his sexy grunts and breathy moans.

"Yeah, sweetheart," he whispered, causing her to lift her lids and stare into his eyes. "That feels so good."

Heather mewled around his cock as she worked him over her tongue and lips, spurring a deep rumble in his chest. His hands were firm but tender, locked in her hair as he guided her around his glistening shaft. Gazing deep into her eyes, he jutted against the back of her throat.

Trusting him, she relaxed, staring into his green orbs as he slid the tip of his cock past the tight ring of her throat.

"Too much?" he asked, drawing back.

She shook her head, sliding her lips to the tip of his shaft and popping him free. "Go for it. You earned it with that perfect ending." Waggling her brows, she opened wide and glided over his length once more.

"Damn, hon," he said, easing to the back of her throat. "You're the one who's fucking perfect. Look at you." Red splotches seemed to burn his chest and cheeks as he pushed deep, gritting his teeth before pulling back. They fell into a rhythm, Heather alternating her breaths and swipes of her tongue with his measured thrusts. Eventually, he closed his eyes, groaning as his head fell back.

"I'm going to come," he rasped, fingers tightening in her hair. "Fuck, hon."

She purred around him, giving her consent. Lifting his head, he gazed down at her as his hips jutted his cock into her mouth. "*Heather*," he whispered.

Whimpering, she dug her nails into his thigh, acknowledging how ready her body was to be claimed. Slickness coated her core as she waited for him to explode. A muscle tightened in his neck as he clenched his teeth, and then he uttered a ragged cry as the climax took over.

Heather latched onto him, hollowing her cheeks to add to the pleasure. Blissful shouts echoed off the bedroom walls as he emptied jets of release against the back of her throat. Dying to please him, she soaked up every drop, loving the tiny pulses of his sensitive shaft between her lips. Feeling him soften as the tremors eased, she eventually drew back, releasing him.

He panted atop the bed, heaving breaths into his lungs as he released the death grip on her hair. Sliding his hands to cup her jaw, he shook his head. "Good lord, woman, are you trying to kill me?"

Arching a brow, she pondered. "It would serve you right for that cliffhanger. I was really pissed."

"Yeah, it seems like you hate me right now," he teased, running his finger over her lip.

"I'm over it." Grinning, she caressed his thighs, running her palms over the scratchy hairs. "That was fun," she said with a wink.

Craning his neck, he glanced at her ankle. "Are you okay? I know you're still healing."

"I'm fine. Help me get on the bed."

He tugged her up and pulled back the covers before urging her between the sheets. Once there, he drew her into his arms and sighed. "That was much more enjoyable than meeting my deadline."

"I mean, we were supposed to have a low-key date night since the girls are with Jen," she said, gently running her nails over his chest. "I just arrived a little early."

"Did you ever," he murmured, releasing a deep breath. Turning his head on the pillow, he grinned. "I think you liked sucking me," he said, gliding his hand to the back of her knee and drawing her leg over his thighs. Sliding his palm over her ass, his fingers slid between the swells, landing on her drenched folds.

"Oh, yeah," he murmured, his deep voice vibrating against her body. "Somebody enjoyed having my cock in their mouth, didn't they, honey?"

"Yes," she whispered, pushing against his fingers.

Palming the cheeks of her ass with both hands, he spread them apart before gliding his index finger to her silken opening. Easing inside, he gazed at her through half-lidded eyes as she began to ride his finger. Jeremy impaled her with each slow slide before adding another finger, enhancing the sensation. Whimpering, she wriggled against him, needing more.

Withdrawing, he gently eased her on her back before looming over her. Resting his chin on his hand, his eyes latched onto hers as he urged her legs apart with his other hand. Delving between her folds, he found her clit and began to stimulate it with firm, concentric pressure.

"I was beginning to think there weren't any men left who knew how to find that spot," she rasped.

"I'm the last one," he growled, working his finger against her tight little bud. "Nobody else is allowed to touch you here."

Tossing her head back, she moaned. "Keep doing that and I'll agree to anything."

His fingers were magic, urging her higher and higher toward the peak as he rested his lips against the shell of her ear. "You're mine, sweetheart. Do you hear me?"

"Jeremy..."

"That's right, honey. Scream my name when you come. Fuck, you're so damn gorgeous."

Heather's hips gyrated to meet his hand and her body heated as she neared the peak. Jeremy spoke words of desire and lust in her ear, furthering her arousal, until she was balancing on the precipice, ready to ignite.

"I want to fuck you raw, Heather," he rumbled in her ear. "Skin to skin so I feel this slick, hot pussy wrapped around me."

"I want that too...*oh, god...Jeremy...*"

"Come," he demanded, his fingers frenzied and firm on her clit. "Come on my fingers, Heather."

Suddenly, her back snapped, arching into the air as she dove headlong into the orgasm. Jeremy's fingers ceased the maddening actions, and he cupped her mound, holding her deepest place as stars burst beneath her eyelids. Joyful laughter bounded from her throat as she quaked and shuddered atop the bed, drowning in the warmth of his body and the pleasure from the orgasm.

Sighing as her muscles melted, she relaxed as contentment washed over her. Lifting her lids, she gazed into Jeremy's sated eyes.

"Good job," she said, biting her lip. "You're definitely forgiven for whatever I was mad about when I got here."

Chuckling, he nudged her nose with his. "You were mad about the cliffhanger."

"Oh, right...that." Sighing, she shook her head. "Dust in the wind."

Grinning, he slid his hand up her body, causing her muscles to quiver beneath his touch. Resting his palm over her pounding heart, he spoke softly. "I meant what I said. I want to be monogamous with you, Heather. I don't want anyone else."

Heather waited for the rush of fear, surprised when it didn't flare. Gnawing her lip, she contemplated why. Was she actually considering taking this thing with Jeremy a step further? Where was her instinct to run?

The curve of his lips was so sexy under his tousled hair. "You're actually considering it."

"Yep," she said softly.

"Are you on the pill? We could get tested and have condom-less sex." He waggled his eyebrows. "And I promise to always find your spot."

A laugh escaped her lips. "I have no doubt. And yes, I'm on the pill."

"So?" Excitement danced in his eyes, making him look so hand-some and so *young* for some reason.

"Do you care that I'm older than you? If we do this, you're settling for an older woman who will never have kids."

"I told you I'm done having kids, hon," he said, brushing a kiss over her lips. "And four years isn't *that* big of a difference."

"You're very sweet but this is as good as it's going to get." She circled her hand over her face. "My looks are only going to go downhill from here."

Sighing, he lowered his head so she could feel his warm breath on her lips. "Heather, I don't want you for your looks. Don't get me wrong, you're gorgeous, but I want you for what's in here." He tapped his fingers over her heart.

"I convinced myself what was in there wasn't all that great."

"Well, you've convinced me of the opposite." Kissing her nose, he drew back and smiled. "Let's do this, hon. I want to make this official. You can meet Jen and Lou, and spend more time here. The girls will be thrilled."

Gliding her fingers over his cheek, she couldn't contain her smile. "Why are you so fucking adorable? I never thought men were adorable before you."

He wrinkled his nose. "I am pretty adorable."

Rolling her eyes, she shook her head. "You're too much. Okay, fine, let's do it."

His eyes widened. "Really?"

"Really. I'm probably going to freak out when I'm alone again, but let's do it."

Smacking his lips to hers, he enveloped her in his arms and hugged her tight. Giving into emotions she didn't quite understand, she squeezed back, wondering when the fear and doubt would return.

Chapter 18

A week later, Heather sat in the passenger seat while Jeremy drove to Jennifer's house in Battle Falls. Checking in with herself, she realized she was equal parts nervous, anxious and excited to meet the mother of the two girls she was coming to care for very much.

Since Lou was still recovering from his surgery and Jen was still in a cast, they decided it would be easier to have dinner at home. Jen loved to cook, according to Jeremy, and was making a big Italian meal so the girls could have leftovers throughout the week.

Jeremy's phone dinged and he glanced at it while they were at a red light.

"That's Kara. She says the girls are settled in and ready to binge their favorite series. She's going to order from Nick's Diner with the money I left her."

"Sweet," Heather said, smiling at him as her head tilted on the seat. "I guess it's good for the adults to have dinner first so we can ease any awkwardness without children present."

"Is there going to be awkwardness?" he asked with a goofy grin.

"Let's see…" She began tapping things off on her fingers. "You're introducing your new flame to your ex-wife, who's basically your best friend and the mother of your children. She's cooking dinner for us and her fiancé will be there, so it will be one big happy family. Nope, not weird at all."

"I think it's cool that Jen and I get along so well," he said, his lips forming a slight pout. "It's so good for the girls and I have no desire to hate my ex-wife."

"Well, we're not having dinner with Butch anytime soon. Like ever. Unless he offers me a billion dollars and the map to the fountain of youth."

Breathing a laugh, he winked. "Not to sound like a possessive jerk, but I'm kind of glad you want nothing to do with him. I don't like the idea of anyone else being married to you."

"Said by the man who's forcing me to meet his ex-wife," she droned, scrunching her features.

"Am I forcing you?" he rubbed his chin.

"Yes. And I hate it. Thank god we have wine."

He glanced over and assessed her. "Are you really dreading it? Because I can call it off."

Expelling a breath, she shook her head. "I'm actually excited to meet her. I think it will be cool to see what traits of hers the girls have, and she sounds hella awesome."

He grabbed her hand, squeezing so she would look at him. "You've really taken to the girls. It's awesome, Heather. You'll never know how much it means to me."

"I have pamphlets at home that showcase some lovely boarding schools in Europe," she teased. "We can pick the nicest one and spend a few days with them at Christmas. Sounds perfect."

"Or, you could be the evil stepmother." Amusement sparkled in his eyes as he kissed the back of her hand.

"You think that's an insult but it's actually the perfect role for me." She dramatically flipped her hair. "I'd probably win an Oscar."

They continued the gentle ribbing until Jeremy pulled into Jen's driveway. When he jogged around to open her door, Heather took his offered hand and rose to place a sweet peck on his lips. "Thank you for driving and for being so chivalrous. If I give you a signal, that means I've had enough of domesticated life for one evening and you need to take me home immediately."

Closing the car door, he took her hand and led her to the front door. "What signal should I look for?"

Heather arched a brow and he snickered.

"Middle finger?"

"Absolutely. It's the gold standard."

Jeremy knocked on the door before depressing the handle and entering. The house was a pretty three-bedroom in a quiet res-idential neighborhood, and Heather noticed the same array of dollhouses and toys in the living room. Jen hustled down the hallway, one leg resting on a scooter as she pushed with the other.

"I don't use the crutches in the house because they kill my underarms, so I've become a speed demon on this scooter," she announced, extending her hand when she came to a stop in front of them. "Jen Kramer, soon to be Campanella. Nice to meet you."

"A pleasure," Heather said, shaking her hand. "Wow, you really look like Angeline."

"Yep. We always say that the universe gave us each a kid that looks like us to confirm they're ours. Otherwise, I would've ended up marrying the guy I dated before Jeremy and be Mrs. Rooster Jenkins now. Yikes." White teeth flashed as she smiled.

"You dated a guy named Rooster? Sounds like your love life is worse than mine."

"Long story. Suffice it to say, there are only two men I've ever tolerated. This one," she patted Jeremy's arm, "and this one..." Glancing over her shoulder she called, "Lou? Jeremy and Heather are here!"

A man with slicked black hair appeared from the kitchen, his arm in a sling. "Hey, Jeremy," he said, fist-bumping him before turning to Heather. "And you must be the hot broad Jeremy can't stop talking about. I'm Lou, nice to meet you."

Heather laughed and bumped his uninjured elbow with hers. "Nice to meet you. Please tell me more about how obsessed Jeremy is with me. My middle-aged ego needs it." She plumped her hair.

"Okay, okay," Jeremy said, tugging her into the living room. "We brought wine. Want me to open it so we can have a drink in here before we eat?"

"Dinner's pretty much done so I'll open it," Jen said, taking the wine. "This looks like a nice cabernet. Thanks. Be right back."

She tucked the bottle in the crook of her arm before wheeling away while Heather, Jeremy and Lou sat in the living room. Once the four of them were stocked with full glasses, they toasted to getting to know each other better.

"Well, I'm sure this doesn't need to be stated out loud, but our girls love you, Heather," Jen said, peering over the rim of her wineglass from her perch on the couch. "They talk about you all the time and I think they see you as this cool adult who is far superior to their dorky parents."

"I swore I wanted nothing to do with them in the beginning," she shot a droll look at Jeremy as he sat beside her on the loveseat, "but they grow on you, the little buggers. I've come to like them very much."

Jeremy squeezed her thigh, affection in his eyes as he sipped the wine. "Heather has also set up a day for one of our friends to move the playsets from her back yard to ours. It's so thoughtful and the girls are excited."

"It's no big deal," she said, shrugging. "Kids have never been my jam but your girls are special. We have a nice crew of friends with kids in Ardor Creek and they all have some pretty awesome spawns."

"Well, Jeremy and I are grateful for how well you took care of Angeline when you fell down the ravine," Jen said. "I think of how scared she must've been but she said you two bonded. Of course, she won't tell me what you talked about because you're her cool adult friend and I'm her geeky mom."

"Just girl stuff," Heather said with a sympathetic smile. "She's at a tough age with no end in sight. Hell, I'm still figuring out my place in the world. I can't imagine how hard it is for kids in this age of social media and constant bullying. It must be brutal."

"It is but we try our best to maintain open communication with them," Jeremy said. "I think it works half the time."

"I can't believe I'm volunteering for this, but if you ever want me to talk to them about something they don't want to discuss with you, I will. I have no idea if it will help since I'm a disaster with kids, but if I can get through to them, I'd be happy to try."

"That's lovely, Heather," Jen said, her gaze darting to Jeremy as her expression shone with unabashed approval. "Okay, I take it back. She's not nearly as bitchy as you portrayed her."

Heather's mouth dropped open and she swatted Jeremy's arm. "Jerk!"

"Hey," he said, showing her his palm. "That was months ago. You're only slightly bitchy now."

"I'd shoot you the bird but I'm not ready to leave yet because I'm having fun talking to Jen." Facing her, she said, "That's our secret symbol, in case I wanted to bolt if this got too weird."

Tossing back her head, Jen laughed as Lou chuckled beside her. "Fucking perfect. I have a feeling this is going to work out *really* well, guys."

They fell into conversation before moving to the kitchen table to enjoy the feast Jen prepared. Several glasses of wine later, Heather felt full and sated as she struggled to eat the slice of pie Jen served for dessert. Realizing she was full, she set down her fork and emitted a tipsy hiccup.

"Oh, man," Jeremy said, sliding his arm around her shoulders. "That means she's toasted. She had the hiccups the first night she tried to seduce me."

"He turned me down, the bastard," Heather said, swatting him with her napkin, "so we could *date*. My god. I want to barf just thinking about it."

"Sounds like Jeremy," Jen said, relaxing in her chair and rubbing her stomach. "We became roommates in our late twenties when his former roommate moved out unexpectedly. My roommate got engaged and I couldn't afford a place on my own yet. We had mutual friends who introduced us and we got along really well. We were in a jam, so we moved in together. Never thought we'd end up drunkenly hooking up, but I guess that's what's happens sometimes when two single adults cohabitate."

"Plus, she was impressed with my knowledge of Middle Earth," he said, holding up a finger.

"Like, the hot magma center under the layers of crust?" Heather asked, confused.

"It's a Lord of the Rings reference," Lou said, shaking his head. "I need you to make this thing official with Jeremy, Heather, so I'm not the only one who isn't lost in dork-land when these two talk." He pointed back and forth between Jen and Jeremy.

"Hey!" Jen exclaimed. "You love it when I talk about Lord of the Rings. Remember when I put on the pointy ears and spoke Elvish to you on your birthday last year?" She waggled her eyebrows.

"TMI," Jeremy said, plugging his ears. After the resounding chuckles eased, he glanced at Heather and whispered, "But you can wear pointy ears and whisper Elvish in my ear anytime. Like, tonight if you want to."

"I'm pretty sure that would turn my lady parts dry as the Sahara, but you can continue to dream." She batted her eyelashes.

"Anyway," Jen continued, "Jeremy was so sweet, especially when I informed him that I was pregnant."

"She didn't tell me twins ran in her family until we were at the ultrasound appointment though," he said, shooting her a look.

Chuckling, she nodded. "We were both shocked. Jeremy was already in full dad mode and he was so attentive throughout my pregnancy. The girls became our priority once they were born and..." Sighing, she placed her elbow on the table and rested her chin in her hand. "We just never really got around to the romantic stuff. Jeremy was a great husband but we just didn't have a spark. One day, I got the courage to tell him we both deserved to find someone who made us feel the spark." She placed her hand over Lou's and smiled into his eyes.

"I'm glad Jen found her person. I haven't been so lucky," Jeremy teased, scrunching his features at Heather.

Heather responded with a deadpan scowl. "Well, I hope you find her one day. We're only in this for sex," she announced, gesturing between them as he gave her a broad smile.

"I guess there's always hope once we end our sordid affair." Sliding his hand over the back of her neck he squeezed before winking.

Eventually, the conversation wound down. Jeremy and Lou headed into the living room to catch the end of some sports game Heather couldn't care less about so she helped Jen clean the kitchen. When they were done, Jen poured them each a half glass of wine and they spoke as they sat at the kitchen island.

"This has been so fun, Heather. I hope I'm not overstepping here, but I hope things work out with you and Jeremy. He's really into you and the girls are too."

"Thank you," Heather said, inwardly thrilled at her words. "I never expected it to be anything but casual, if I'm being honest. I convinced myself that was all I wanted." Tracing her finger over the counter, she sighed. "I'm not really wired for love and commitment and all that crap."

Her dark eyebrow arched. "I think my girls and their father would disagree. Jeremy mentioned a few things about your past to me. I hope that doesn't anger you, but it seems to me, you just got dealt a shitty hand. As a result, you hardened yourself so you could face the pain of a tough world and fight your battles."

"Maybe, but that makes me sound like a victim." Sipping her wine, she contemplated. "I'm not. I doled out a lot of bad juju myself. I've become a better person as the years progressed—I *think*—but that rotten part of me will always be there."

Tilting her head, Jen smiled. "I'm looking right at you and I can't see anything rotten. Maybe it's finally gone."

Breathing a laugh, she nodded. "Maybe it is."

Jen licked her lips, contemplating. "I want to tell you something about Jeremy. You might have noticed, but he has this incessant need to take care of people, to the point where he tries to save them."

"I've noticed," Heather said, her tone sardonic.

"He's such a great guy but he's never found his person. I have a theory on why, by the way." She lifted a finger.

"Do tell. I'm ready to take advice from my lover's ex-wife." Lifting her glass, she clinked it against Jen's as they chuckled.

"I think it's because no one's ever taken care of him. He's so busy taking care of everyone else, he doesn't really allow space for that. He's amazing with our girls and still takes care of me too. Don't get me wrong, I love that we're so close, but he needs to find someone who will carve out space to prioritize him. Is this making any sense?"

Heather's eyebrows drew together. "I'm digesting. Go on."

"You're pretty direct, Heather, which I absolutely adore. And I'd even call you...*brash*...is that a good word?"

"I've been called worse," Heather droned. "Brash is a picnic."

Laughing, Jen nodded. "I think your brashness is good for him. You're someone who can put your foot down and tell him to stop saving the damn world for a minute. Someone who understands that putting yourself first isn't selfish—it's necessary if you want to take care of others."

Lowering her gaze to the counter, Jen gnawed her lip, searching for the right words. "I never asked him what made him happy when we were married. I just let him make me happy. That was a huge mistake because it led to us becoming passionless." Lifting her gaze, she shrugged. "I don't think he's ever experienced true passion. I want him to find the person who sets his damn soul on fire."

Heather's eyes widened. "And you think that's me?"

"I think it can be," she said with a nod. "Just don't make my mistakes. Ask him what he wants and don't let him tell you *whatever makes you happy*. It's a death sentence for a healthy romantic relationship but so easy to fall into with him."

Inhaling a breath, she pondered. "He does go out of his way for me. I mean, I pretend I hate it—all the *dating and feelings*—" she made quotation marks with her fingers, "but I actually love it. It makes total sense he'd want someone to drill down and go out of their way for him."

"I'm not sure he even realizes he wants it, but trust me, he does." She lifted her glass. "Figure out what makes him tick and he'll probably propose on the spot."

Heather almost choked on her wine. "We're light-years away from a proposal here, Jen. I'm terrified to get married again. I wouldn't be this forthright without all the wine, but there it is."

"Terrified is okay," she said, leaning her head on her fist as her elbow rested on the counter. "That means you care."

Sighing, she ran a hand through her hair. "I care. Too much, if you ask me."

"Sounds exciting." Her lips curved into a tender smile. "I hope we can become friends, Heather. This has been fun."

"Me too." Rising, Heather placed the empty glass on the counter. "Thank you for dinner and the lovely conversation. I will now inform you that I've reached my emotional capacity and must return home. There's a limit to how many *feelings* I can have in one night."

Jen's warm chuckle surrounded her as she stood and maneuvered her leg atop the scooter. "You're freaking hilarious, Heather. Jeremy snagged a good one. Come on, let me wheel you out."

"By the way," Jen said, as she began wheeling down the hallway. "I'm totally fine if you stay over at Jeremy's. He said you felt more comfortable if we discussed it because of the girls. Lou began staying over pretty soon after we started dating, and I have no reservations about you doing the same."

"Thanks. We'll see if I can get to that level of intimacy before I freak out. Stay tuned."

After saying their goodbyes, Jeremy drove them home, where they were met with hugs and limitless energy from Gabby and

Angeline. Jeremy paid Kara and thanked her before she waved and headed home.

Heather sat in the recliner, observing Jeremy as he sat on the couch between the girls, chatting on about their evening with Kara and the show they'd watched. Eventually, they began to yawn, signaling their energy had finally run out.

"Are you sleeping over, Heather?" Angeline asked.

"Not tonight," she said, shaking her head. "I do have my own house, you know?"

The girls shot playful grins at her before looking at Jeremy.

"We're pretty sure Dad wants you to stay over," Gabby said. "Mom let Lou stay over after we had a family meeting about it."

"I'm not sure Heather is ready for that yet," Jeremy said, questions swirling alongside the emotion in his eyes. "That's a big step and we'll make sure we talk about it when the time is right."

"I'm not ready yet but maybe I will be one day soon," Heather said. "When I am, you two will be the first to know." She winked at the girls.

"Okay, ladies. Teeth brushing time and then we can cuddle in my bed and watch one more episode of Stranger Things."

The girls cheered before trailing over to hug Heather. Gabby grabbed Angeline's arm and slung it around her shoulders before helping her sister hobble upstairs. Smiling at the sweet gesture, Heather rose and sauntered over to sit beside Jeremy.

"Tonight was fun," she said, resting her head on his shoulder. "Jen is awesome."

"Told you." He kissed her forehead. "Thank you for enduring the torture."

"I guess having gone through the 'new partner' thing with Lou gives us a good roadmap...I mean, if we're going to make it to 'partner' status someday."

Gently caressing her cheek with the backs of his fingers, he smiled. "I'm already there, hon. Just waiting for you to catch up."

A soft breath escaped her lips. "You do know that monogamy is already a big step for me, right?"

"I know," he said, nodding. "There's no rush, Heather. One day at a time."

Her eyes darted between his. "Can I ask you a weird question?"

"Sure."

"If you had a perfect day, what would you do?"

Narrowing his eyes, he glanced at the floor, contemplating. "Hang out with you and the girls, I guess."

"Boring," she droned, rolling her eyes. "I'm talking a day only for you, where you get to fulfill your deepest desires."

"Where are you going with this?" he asked, perplexed.

"Obviously, no one has ever asked you this question if it's so hard to answer." Straightening, she poked his chest. "Come on, give it to me. The doctor tells you there's one day left to live. What would you do?"

"Honestly?" She nodded. "I'd wake up and jog, which I never do anymore because, you know, work, kids and all that jazz."

"Yep. Keep going."

"Then, I'd get a long massage...and if we're talking deepest fantasy, it would be by a naked Margot Robbie..." He trailed off, eyes widening as he gauged her reaction.

"Sounds about right. She's stunning. Hell, I'd like a naked massage from her. Go on."

"Whew," he said, mimicking wiping sweat from his brow. "I thought that might piss you off. It's *way* hotter that you think she's hot, but whatever."

Heather grinned, overcome with how adorable he was as he ticked off the items.

"Then, I'd make a huge bonfire in the back yard. I'd eat corn dogs and drink a six-pack without beating myself up. Usually, when I have beer, I make myself do an extra thirty minutes on the elliptical in the basement the next day."

"That's your perfect day? That's not too unreasonable."

Leaning forward, he pressed his forehead to hers. "And then, I'd fall asleep with you and you wouldn't freak out that you're sleeping over in my bed. The end."

She cupped his jaw. "Sounds nice."

"Yeah?" Excitement entered his green orbs.

"Yeah."

"Why do you ask anyway?"

"Jeremy, you do so much for everyone else. People should ask what *you* like to do sometimes."

"I guess," he said, shrugging. "I like taking care of people."

"I've noticed."

"Do you hate it?" His lips curved into a cute pout.

"You know I don't," she whispered. "I like it. Too much." Pressing a soft kiss to his lips, she rose and smoothed her hands over her thighs. "I'm going to head home."

Standing, he gripped her hand and yelled, "Girls! I'm walking Heather home. Be right back."

"Okay, Dad!"

Once they were at her back door, he kissed her good night before leaning in and whispering, "You're my Margot Robbie, Heather. She's got nothing on you. Night."

Taken by his romantic words, she fell into bed and began to plan something for the man she was pretty sure owned her heart.

Chapter 19

Two weeks later, Heather's plan was set. She'd spent hours tracking down everything on Jeremy's list and was determined to give him a well-deserved perfect day. Locking the door behind her, she headed to his house.

"Hey, Heather," Gabby said, the words an excited whisper as she opened the door. "Oh my gosh, this is so cool! Dad has no idea!"

"I'm proud of you two for keeping the secret," she said, tugging one of her braided pigtails. "Nice job."

"Heather?" Jeremy asked, trailing into the room and carrying Angeline in a piggyback. "You're about eight hours early for dinner."

Angeline snickered. "We're surprising you, Dad."

Setting her down gently since her leg was in a massive cast, he glanced between them. "What are you guys up to?"

"I'm taking the girls to breakfast so you can go on a jog," Heather said. "Then, I'm dropping them off at Justine's, who will keep them until I pick them up tomorrow."

"Uhhhh, okay..."

"It's your perfect day, Dad," Angeline said, patting his arm. "We all think you deserve it...and we want to play in the new treehouse Scott built for Avery in their back yard."

He glanced at Heather, who promptly decided his excited grin was worth every ounce of effort she'd expended to create the day.

"Come on, girls. Off to the pancake house." Approaching him, she lifted to her toes and pecked his lips. "Have fun on the jog. I'll be back in an hour or two."

Sliding his arm around her waist, he drew her into a deep kiss. The girls giggled as he drew back and shot them playful glances. "Thank you, Heather."

"No big deal." She shot him a salute and ushered the girls out the back door.

Once they were at the pancake house, Heather had a rather enjoyable time catching up on all things nine-year-olds considered important. Then, she headed to Justine's and dropped them off, amused at the mischievous glint in Justine's eyes as she waved from the front door.

"Have fuuuuuun!" she called before ushering the girls inside.

Heather just breathed a laugh, rolling her eyes at her friend's palpable excitement.

When she arrived home, Heather strolled to the living room and called Jeremy.

"Hey, hon. Saw you in the driveway. The girls are at Justine's?"

"Yep. They're just fine. How was your run?"

"Amazing. I haven't had a Saturday morning to myself in ages. It's either the girls or the writing cave. I feel great right now."

Trailing her hand over the massage table that now sat in the middle of her living room, she grinned. "I'm so glad. Take a shower and head over here."

She could almost hear the wheels turning in his brain. "What are you planning, you little tease?"

"Come over and see, lover. The back door is open. Lock it behind you when you arrive." Clicking off the phone, she watched the screen go dark, already feeling her body heat in anticipation.

Padding upstairs, she removed her clothes and slipped on her silkiest robe. After freshening her makeup, she curled her hair, making sure it was extra full and thick. Wanting to be downstairs when he arrived, she headed down to make sure everything was ready.

The curtains were drawn in the living room, giving it a dim glow, and she heard the latch of the back door. His footsteps sounded on the kitchen floor before shuffling over the carpeted hallway. When he crested the living room door, his eyes grew wide.

"Uh, hi," he said, rubbing the back of his neck. "What's all this?"

"This," she said, gesturing to the table, "is your massage area, Mr. Kramer. I believe you requested a naked massage?"

His eyes darted over her in the skimpy robe, glowing with desire.

"Unfortunately, our regular masseuse, Margot, is out sick today. I hope I'm an acceptable replacement?" She pursed her lips and batted her eyelashes.

He reached down, adjusting himself in his casual athletic shorts. "I think you'll do just fine," he said, arching a brow.

"Good. Please remove your clothes and place them on the couch."

Heather almost laughed at the speed with which he tore away his clothes. Once naked, he approached her, sliding his palms over the silk that covered her hips. "You're so sexy, Heather," he whispered, leaning down to brush a kiss on her lips. "I'm so into you."

She made a *tsk, tsk, tsk* sound. "That's not very professional for a new client, Mr. Kramer, but I'll let it slide. Can you help me untie my robe? The knot is just so tight."

He grasped the sash in his fingers, drawing it away from her body and opening the robe. "Doesn't seem that tight to me," he murmured, tracing a finger over the smooth skin of her stomach now exposed by the open robe.

"I guess you don't know your own strength. Your muscles must be very tired. I'm going to give you a full body massage. As long as I have your consent."

"I consent," he growled, stepping closer and aligning their bodies. "I very much consent."

Laughing, she nodded. "Okay. You'll lie on your stomach first." Drawing back, she gripped the robe and slowly shimmied it down her body until it pooled on the floor. Heavy breaths escaped his lips as he stared at her breasts and rapidly pebbling nipples. Lifting the blanket atop the table, she gestured for him to lie down.

He complied, positioning himself on the table. Heather began to cover him with the blanket before catching sight of his luscious ass. Deciding it would be a crime to cover something so glorious, she tossed the blanket to the floor.

Striding to the side table, she lifted the lotion she'd placed there and dispersed a large dollop in her palm. Rubbing her hands together, she approached the table. Standing at his side, she touched her palms to his back and began to massage him.

Deep grumbles exited his lungs with each stroke of her hands. For several minutes, she worked his muscles, releasing the tension as he relaxed under her firm strokes. Eventually, she trailed to the head of the table, massaging his shoulders from above. Jeremy lifted his head and brought his arms around to grip her hips. Pulling her toward him, he rested his forehead on her abdomen.

"Damn, Heather," he murmured against her, "that feels so good."

"Face on the table, sir," she said, tapping his head. "We'll get to the front soon enough."

He blew her a kiss before placing his cheek on the table. Heather moved to the foot of the table, massaging his legs and sexy-as-hell ass before palming one of the globes and squeezing. "It's time to turn over now, Mr. Kramer."

"I don't think you're supposed to squeeze your client's ass," he chided, rolling over and placing his hands behind his head.

"I have my own technique," was her sultry reply. Dispensing more lotion, she began to massage his shins, then his thighs, skipping over his obvious erection to massage his pecs. His breathing was now slightly erratic as he gazed at her through half-lidded eyes. Reaching for her, he ran his fingers over her hip.

"Please, sweetheart. I need you."

The words ripped open something inside her as she stared into his gorgeous eyes. Balancing her palm on his chest, she lifted her leg, sliding it over his waist to straddle him atop the table. Leaning down, she pressed her lips to his before surging her tongue inside his mouth. His arms surrounded her, drawing her close as he pushed his shaft into her abdomen.

Rising, she gazed into his eyes, taking his cock in her hand and beginning to stroke. The remaining lotion on her hand created an extra layer of lubrication, and slickness was rapidly increasing between her thighs. Balancing on her knees, she hovered over him, aligning her center with his cock. Unable to look away, her eyes bore into his as she took him inside her trembling body.

"*Fuck...*" he cried, hips lifting off the table as he arched to push himself fully inside her. Heather took him deep before drawing back and sliding down once more.

His firm hands gripped her ass, the pressure sparking bursts of pleasure as he guided her in a smooth motion that set them both on fire. Undulating her hips, she rode him, vowing to show him with her body that she was *his*.

"Do you know how good it feels to be buried in your tight, wet pussy?" he gritted, the pace of his hips increasing with every thrust. "You're drenching me, honey...*oh, god*...nothing has ever felt this good..."

Reveling in his sexy words and possessive embrace, she leaned forward, resting her palms beside his head. Cementing her lips to his, she drew him into a torrid kiss as their bodies moved in tandem.

"Move me over you," she whispered, willing to give him all control. It was a big step for her, but in that moment, she realized she trusted him completely. With her body...and perhaps her soul too.

"I'm so turned on," he murmured against her lips. "I don't want to hurt you."

"Fuck me as hard as you want in any way you want," she demanded. "This is about you. I won't break."

"Heather—"

"Jeremy," she said, determination in her gaze. "Fuck me."

Suddenly, he shifted, lifting her in one sure stroke as his cock still rested inside her. Carrying her to the foot of the table, he rested her on her back before looming over her. Unsated lust burned in his eyes as he stood, gripping her ankles and holding them high. Aligning the head of his shaft with her opening, he surged inside.

Thick muscles corded in his neck as his hips hammered at a furious pace. Echoes of his flesh slapping against hers vibrated off the walls as Heather gripped the sides of the table for support. Tossing her head back, she opened herself, letting him take everything.

Uttering a ragged groan, he withdrew from her and tugged her to her feet before whirling her around and pressing her chest to the table. Palming her hips, he nudged her feet wider and she felt his dick probing at her center. Clutching the table, she held on for dear life as he began to fuck her from behind, whispering filthy words as he claimed her pulsing body.

Reaching around, his fingers found her clit, sensitive and swollen. Rubbing it in frenzied circles, he brought her closer to the peak as he aligned his chest with her back.

"Look at you taking my cock, you little tease," he breathed into her ear, the deep rumble of his voice sending shivers up her spine. "Do you like being filled up with my cock?"

"Yes," she whimpered, pushing against him with each thrust. "I love it."

"Look at me," he demanded.

Resting her cheek on the table, she gazed into his eyes as he fucked her hard.

"Tell me whose pussy this is." The pressure of his fingers intensified even more on her clit.

"Yours..."

"Mine," he growled, his frenzied thrusts pushing him so deep, Heather's eyes rolled back in her head.

"I'm going to come..." she cried, closing her eyes as she gave into the pleasure. "*Oh, god*...help...I can't..."

"No one can help us now, honey," he grunted. "We're in too deep."

"*Jeremy...*"

"Come on my cock, Heather. I need you to come first, honey. Please..."

Shouting a curse, her neck snapped as her body jolted head-first into a blinding orgasm. Shudder upon shudder coursed through her body as pleasure-filled sparks exploded in every cell. Jeremy bared his teeth before burying his face in her neck and latching onto the sweaty skin.

Overcome with laughter, she squealed as he bit her. Jesus Christ, he was fucking *biting* her. Score another one for sex god next door who paraded around as calm, mild-mannered dad. Who freaking knew?

His body quaked as he emptied himself deep in her body. Losing control of her muscles, Heather hoped like hell he'd support her. Otherwise, she'd certainly melt to the ground in a puddle of sated lust.

Eventually, his spasms abated and he released her neck, gently licking the spot where he'd bitten her. There was something so sweet...so primal...about the gesture, causing her to emit a sated chuckle.

"Why are you laughing, woman?" he murmured against her neck.

"Because you're licking me."

"I like licking you," he said, swiping his tongue over her skin. "You taste good."

"Mmm-hmm..."

They lay entwined for what seemed like hours before he lifted his head and searched the room. Locating a box of tissues, he emitted a sated groan, withdrawing before grabbing a few and wiping himself. Placing them on the table, he plucked a few more and strode to her, kneeling between her legs and cleaning away the evidence of their lovemaking as she still lay half atop the table.

"Can't move," she muttered, the words garbled by her cheek pressed to the cushioned table.

His strong arms surrounded her, lifting her and carrying her to the couch. Lowering, he reached for the blanket on the back of the couch and covered their cooling bodies. Heather snuggled into him, realizing she was two seconds away from falling asleep.

"I don't know why I'm so tired," she said, yawning. "Perhaps it was my very extensive massage."

Chuckling, he stroked her hair. "I could use a nap too. We're adding that to the perfect day list. Holding you after making love is definitely on the list."

"Aw. I don't even have the energy to pretend I hate that you're making me feel things."

He kissed her hair. "One day, you won't hate it at all. Trust me."

"I do," she whispered, nuzzling into his chest.

Closing her eyes, she admitted she trusted Jeremy more than any man she'd known in her long, solitary life.

After their nap, they showered together at Heather's house, which promptly led to another round of mind-blowing sex. Eventually, the sun began to set and they dressed before heading to Jeremy's house. Heather led him to the back yard, which now housed a huge stack of logs ready to be set ablaze. Turning to her, his excitement was palpable.

"Damn, Heather, you set up a bonfire?"

"Technically, the Ridenhour boys set it up. Best eighty bucks I've ever spent. They were given strict instructions to set it up while you were at my house today." Tugging him over, she observed the stacked wood. "Do you know how to light these things?"

"Sure do. I love bonfires but they're not really conducive with kids around."

"Chad has already set up an appointment with Waste Management to come and clean it up on Monday," she said, giving him a cheeky smile. "He has contacts from his years as mayor and jumped at the opportunity to help. I think he secretly wants Abby to put one in their back yard too, so this is a good trial run."

"Smart man. I'll make sure to report back to Abby that it was a success." Facing her, his features were laced with the excitement of a kid about to ride his first roller coaster. "Thank you, sweetheart. This is so thoughtful."

Palming his cheek, she smiled, admiring the radiant flecks in his eyes from the setting sun. "I'm glad you like it. You deserve for people to make you happy too, Jeremy."

"This is a *very* serious gesture, Ms. Combs," he said, lifting her hand and kissing her knuckles. "I think we're venturing into partner territory."

"Don't ruin it," she said, placing two gentle smacks on his cheek. "Come on, the beer's in the cooler. I had the boys set everything up."

They popped open some beer from the nearby blue cooler before Jeremy got down to business and began lighting the bonfire. Heather watched him, his features etched with glee, and she realized how truly selfless he was. If living his dream day inspired this much joy, how many days did he brush aside his own desires to put everyone else first? Awed by his generous spirit, she couldn't contain her laughter as he eagerly lit the wood.

Eventually, the rusty orange sun dropped below the horizon and they pulled up two chairs beside the fire. The flames crackled as they held hands and lazily sipped. A car engine sounded in the driveway and Heather stood, setting her beer in the grass.

"Be right back."

Jeremy shot her a curious look as she sprinted to the driveway to meet Ashlyn.

"Okay," Ashlyn said, tapping the top of the disposable metal tray in her hands. "We've got corn dogs, baked beans, coleslaw and a homemade apple pie. Yum!"

"Thanks so much, Ashlyn," Heather said, taking the tray. "Condiments?"

Ashlyn placed a plastic bag on top. "And disposable silverware too. You're all set."

"Sweet. You got the Venmo I sent to the Grandma Jean's Gourmet account, right?"

"Got it," she said with a nod. "Enjoy!" With a wave, she hopped back in her car and puttered away.

Heather carried the tray to the small table she'd set up beside their lounging chairs and set it on top. "Dinner's ready."

Jeremy rose, looking over the meal Ashlyn had prepared once Heather removed the covering. Sliding his arm around her waist, he kissed her temple. "Corn dogs," he sighed, nuzzling her hair. "At this point, I'm ready to propose."

"Stop it," she said, swatting him as the words jolted her heartbeat. "Come on, let's eat."

They spent hours by the fire, eating the delicious food and getting slightly tipsy from the beer. Conversation flowed—alternating between serious and silly—and Heather had the insane thought she never wanted the night to end. As the flames began to lose their glow, Jeremy doused the fire and led her inside.

At the bottom of the stairs, he held her hand, a question in his eyes as he waited. She nodded and he led her upstairs to his room.

Slowly, they undressed each other, silent as the latent contentment from the day surrounded them. Once they were naked, Jeremy urged her into bed, sliding over her as he gazed into her eyes. Threading his fingers in her hair as it splayed atop the pillow, he wedged her thighs apart.

Finding her wet and ready, he nudged the head of his shaft inside, those green orbs locked with hers.

"Heather..." he whispered, sliding inside her inch by inch. "Thank you."

"Thank me by fucking me," she murmured, digging her nails into his back.

Emotion flared in his eyes as he dragged the smooth steel of his cock through her soft, wet core. "This is so much more than fucking, Heather—"

Unable to comprehend the deep sentiment in his eyes, she tugged him into a kiss, inhaling words she wasn't ready to hear. Jeremy made love to her, slow and tender, until they both collapsed in an exhausted heap on his bed.

Reaching over, he plucked some tissues, cleaning them both before settling on the mattress. Drawing her close, he pressed his front to her back, spooning her as they shared a pillow.

"This okay?" he murmured against the back of her neck.

Heather nodded, although inside the old terror flared. Once she'd spent the night in his bed, there would be no excuse not to. No more pretending their connection was casual. Heather's heart pounded as she pondered the implications.

Sleeping overnight in a lover's bed might not be daunting for some, but for someone like her, who'd never understood true intimacy, it was petrifying. It signified a meaningful and important step to her. Thankfully, Jeremy seemed to comprehend her struggle.

"It's okay, sweetheart," he whispered, his lips brushing the shell of her ear. "You're safe with me. I promise."

Squeezing her eyes shut, she railed at the tears that formed behind her eyelids. God, she hated tears.

"You deserve to be loved, just like I deserve to have someone take care of me." Covering her heart, he gently ran his thumb over the skin above her breast. "Maybe fate brought us together to teach each other those lessons. But I know one thing for sure..."

"What?" she whispered.

"If your heart doesn't stop pounding like this, you're never going to sleep." His thumb moved in slow, measured strokes upon her skin. "Relax, Heather. I've got you, hon."

Inhaling a deep breath, she slowly released it, willing her muscles to relax.

"That's good. Again."

She continued the careful breaths, feeling her muscles loosen with each exhale. Finally, her heartbeat ceased its ragged pace and she nuzzled into his body.

"Good night, sweetheart," he murmured.

"Night," she mumbled.

Lulled by his smooth strokes, she melted against him in the dark.

Heather awoke with a jolt, her eyes darting to every corner of the unfamiliar room. Sucking in a breath, she sat up and swiped the mussed hair from her face. Exhaling, she realized she was in Jeremy's bed...and she'd stayed the night...and the world hadn't collapsed.

Go figure.

Crawling from the bed, she tugged on her clothes and headed downstairs, surprised to hear two chipper voices chatting as the smell of pancakes filled her nostrils. Entering the kitchen, she observed Gabby and Angeline chatting away as Jeremy stood at the griddle, making pancakes.

"Hey, Heather," Gabby said excitedly. "Dad said you guys had a fun sleepover."

Heather glanced at Jeremy who shot a mischievous grin over his shoulder. "Avery woke up sick and Justine said it's a barf fest so Gary brought the girls home early." Gesturing to the table with the spatula, he said, "Sit down. The girls are prepared to grill you about last night's bonfire experience."

"I..." She ran her hand through her hair. "I should probably head home and let you all eat together—"

"Please, Heather?" Angeline asked. "Dad said he had so much fun and we want to hear about it. Was the bonfire awesome? We want to keep it."

"The bonfire was a one-time thing. Maybe we'll have one again when you two are older," he said, his tone firm. "For now, who's hungry?"

The girls raised their hands, giggling as Jeremy strode over with a plate full of steaming pancakes. Leaning down, he kissed Heather on the cheek. "I made this one for you." He pointed to the largest pancake atop the pile and winked. "Come on. We don't bite."

Heather cocked a brow, returning his heated gaze as they both remembered the previous day where he most certainly *did* bite her atop the massage table. Capitulating, she sat, observing the plate and fork atop the placemat.

"Okay, ladies," Jeremy said, scooping pancakes onto everyone's plate, including his in front of the vacant seat. "Eat while it's warm. I'm going throw some stuff in the sink to soak and I'll be over."

Heather observed the girls douse their pancakes with syrup before Gabby passed her the bottle. Pouring on a less generous portion, she settled in and began to eat.

"Petunia is getting so big," Angeline said between bites. "We had so much fun at Avery's. We took her on a walk in the woods and found this creepy old bridge by the creek…"

Heather nodded and murmured the occasional "Mmm-hmm," as the girls chatted about their night with Avery. Jeremy eventually joined them, munching the pancakes as they carried on. He told them about his day with Heather—leaving out the sexy times, obviously—and excitement glowed in his eyes as he seemed to relish her presence at the breakfast table.

When the meal was finished, Jeremy sat back and patted his stomach. "Okay, girls, time to clean up. You know the rules."

"Dad cooks and we clean," they droned in unison.

"Exactly. Gabby, can you help your sister pull a chair over so she can sit while she dries the dishes?" he asked.

"I don't understand why we have to wash and dry dishes since we have a dishwasher," Angeline said, rolling her eyes.

"*We* don't have a dishwasher," Jeremy said, "I have a dishwasher. When you make enough money to pay the mortgage, you can buy a dishwasher."

"I'm nine!" she exclaimed.

"And that's a perfectly fine age to learn responsibility," he said with a nod. "Go on. Get the dishes washed and we'll go see the new Marvel movie."

The girls stood and cleared the plates before heading toward the sink. Once Angeline was situated, they began to wash and dry as Jeremy smiled at Heather.

"I'm determined to teach them manners and work ethic. They think I'm a tyrant."

"You're not so bad."

He extended his hand, palm up, and she covered it with her own before squeezing. "Thanks for breakfast. I think I should head home. I've got an appointment at three and I need to get some form of exercise in today."

"You don't want to come to the movie with us?" he asked, arching a brow.

"Um, no. I've met my fun-family-time quota for the week."

Chuckling, he laced their fingers as his gaze simmered. "Thank you for yesterday. It was awesome. And thanks for staying for breakfast. I was worried you were going to bolt there for a sec."

Sighing, she shook her head. "This is all so weird for me," she said softly, not wanting the girls to hear. "I'm not sure I fit...and I'm not sure I want to. I need to be honest about that, Jeremy. I don't want to enter into something I'm not equipped for or that I don't really want."

His expression slowly morphed into something equal parts sad, wistful, and hopeful as his thumb caressed her hand. "I think you're already in it, sweetheart. The question is: do you want to stay or do you want to run?"

Swallowing thickly, she dropped her gaze, overcome with how well he knew her. Heather had realized ages ago her basic instinct was to run. She'd run from her parents...run from her marriage...and run from anything remotely involving emotion because it always led to pain.

Only recently, after lots of reflection, had she gained the ability to chart a different path. Returning to Ardor Creek had been the first step in that journey. Was she ready to take another huge step so soon?

Raising her eyes to his, she shrugged. "I don't know," she whispered.

His lips curved, causing her heart to pound since it transformed his features into something so freaking sexy. Somewhere along the way, he'd gone from the geeky-sexy author next door to the hottest man she'd ever been with. Perhaps it was the mind-blowing sex. Yep, that was definitely it.

"'*I don't know*' is better than a lot of other options, so I'll take it." Squeezing her hand, he cocked his head as affection swam in his eyes. "I'll let you off the hook. I think you've more than earned a day to regroup and have some alone time. You rarely get that as a parent or when you have a family. I can see how daunting it could be."

"It is daunting, especially when you have zero foundation to build upon."

"It's never too late to build a new foundation, Heather. One where you still maintain your values and what you want, but also allow yourself to consider something new."

She nodded, digesting his words.

"I love that you stood firm in your choice to not have kids. I think it's a good example for the girls to prove a person can build the life they want. A life they *choose*. But sometimes, we can choose to make adjustments along the way, right?"

Breathing a laugh, she nodded. "Right. I get the sense you're trying to butter me up to the idea of being a...*stepmom*...uggh," She coughed as she choked on the word. "I think I just threw up in my mouth."

Playfully rolling his eyes, he stood, tugging her to her feet. "Come on. I'll walk you home before you get too spooked and call this off for good." Craning his neck, he called, "Be right back, girls. I'm going to walk Heather home."

Their cheerful, "Okay! Bye, Heather!" sounded above the clanking dishes and Jeremy led her out the back door.

Once they reached her back porch, he leaned in and pressed a sweet kiss to her lips. "Have a good day, sweetheart. Don't freak out, okay? We can do this. People enter into serious relationships all the time and it doesn't end in catastrophe."

Wrinkling her nose, she asked, "Do they?"

Laughing, he nodded. "So I've heard. I'm not really the poster child for long-lasting relationships myself. Maybe that will change soon." Giving a salute, he released her hand and trailed away.

Grasping her upper arms, Heather rubbed them as she stared at the clear blue sky. Expelling a deep breath, she muttered, "Damn, Heather, you somehow maneuvered yourself into a serious relationship with a dude with two kids. Holy shit. You definitely win the award for *Worst Casual Dater Ever*."

Smirking, she headed inside, determined to forge ahead in a life that was now filled with complexities and unknowns. Ones that terrified parts of her soul she hadn't realized existed before she began the slow slide into *feelings* for Jeremy Kramer.

Chapter 20

♥

The long summer days began to cool as summer turned to fall. Heather continued her slow descent into *serious relationship* territory, continuing to stay over on weekends Jeremy didn't have the girls. Sometimes, she would also stay when they were there, usually after they all watched a movie together and the girls fell asleep. Jeremy would urge everyone upstairs—Heather included—and since she was already half-asleep, she just went with the flow.

There was something to be said for becoming comfortable around Jeremy and his kids. She often wore sweats and a bare smattering of makeup—much less than she'd ever worn around her other lovers, except Butch. Somewhere along the way, she'd lost the need to cultivate her appearance for Jeremy. It was another big step that meant she was slowly accepting he cared for her regardless of her appearance.

For someone whose early identity had revolved around that carefully manicured outer shell, it should have been disconcerting. Instead, it was just...*normal.* Jeremy seemed to care for the person inside just as much as the outer layer, and it was equal parts baffling and humbling. Perhaps, after all this time, she had morphed into a better person, worthy of love and affection.

One day in mid-September, Heather's phone chimed and she grinned at the caller ID before lifting it to her ear as she locked the front door of the home she'd just shown. The perspective clients, a young couple with a child on the way, had just driven off and she wanted to secure the home before heading to her next appointment.

"Hey, Carrie. You must have gossip for me. Spill."

"Well, I guess I should stop insisting I never gossip," Carrie chimed, amusement in her tone. "Although, I swear, I'm not *that* bad."

"Are you kidding?" Heather asked, trailing to her car and lowering behind the wheel. "I love it. You get the best dirt. Just hold on a sec and let me start the car so Bluetooth picks you up." Once the engine was purring, she called, "Okay, go for it."

"Soooo, I don't know how to tell you this..."

"Is it about me?" she asked, intrigued. "Do tell. Now I'm really excited."

"Um, you could say it's related to you in a weird tangential way."

"Okaaaaaay..."

Carrie cleared her throat. "I just saw Cynthia on Main Street and noticed she had a tiny bump."

Heather's heart slammed in her chest. "Like, a baby bump?"

"Yeah. Of course, I had to approach her and ask, and it turns out she's pregnant. Almost six months along."

Heather's breath caught in her throat as she processed the words.

"She was pretty open and told me about her and Butch's journey. Since she's our age, they had to do IFV. Apparently, they've been trying for a while and it finally took. So, there it is."

"Wow," Heather said, gently rubbing her forehead. "Butch is finally going to be a dad. He always wanted kids and I didn't realize I didn't until after we were married. It was a huge oversight we never discussed because we were young and stupid."

"Hey, it's tough to realize you need to have those discussions when you're eighteen, Heather," Carrie said, sympathy in her voice. "Don't beat yourself up."

"Yeah." Picking a wayward string on her cardigan, she tried to digest the information. It was shocking but she also felt...happy. Yes, strangely enough, she was happy for her ex-husband. Man, aliens really had invaded her body over the past few months. Never in her wildest dreams would she *ever* imagine feeling happy for Butch. Feeling her lips curve, she took a moment to acknowledge how instrumental Jeremy had been in that transformation. His selfless and caring nature had most likely rubbed off on her, and she was grateful.

"Heather? You there?"

"I'm here," she said, glancing at the clock on her dashboard and calculating how much time she had before her next appointment. "Thanks so much for telling me, Carrie. I genuinely wish them well."

"I can tell you mean it," Carrie said, sounding impressed. "That's awesome. Maybe you're fine with it because you're in love yourself, *hmmm?*"

"Okay, let's not toss the L-word around," she teased, secretly wondering if she was in love with Jeremy. How did someone who didn't understand the concept of love know if they were actually in love? A pretty perplexing idea, for sure. "Jeremy is scratching all my itches. Let's leave it at that."

"Oh, I bet he is, honey. Can't wait to see you at Justine and Gary's wedding in a few weeks. We're going to have so much fun. If anyone asks you where you heard the news, just say the mailman, okay? I've got to work on my reputation over here."

Chuckling, Heather nodded. "Understood. See you soon, Carrie. Thanks for calling."

After the screen went dark, Heather put the car in gear and began to drive as the knowledge of where she was headed settled into her bones. Steeling herself for the conversation ahead, she lifted her chin and meandered through Ardor Creek toward Connors Auto Repair Shop.

Ten minutes later, Heather carefully walked through the open garage door, navigating around the various metal pieces that lay on the dirty cement floor. Approaching the car with the open hood, she knocked on the metal side, observing the long legs that stretched from the person hidden underneath the car. The clanking of metal underneath ceased and the person attached to said legs rolled out, glancing at her with wary eyes.

"You used to rap on the car like that when you came here to see me," Butch said, sitting up and wiping his hands on a grease-soaked cloth. "Somehow, I knew it was you."

"Yep. Your bitch ex-wife in the flesh," she said, cocking a sardonic eyebrow. "I'm still convinced you never wash those cloths, by the way."

"Eh, they'll just get dirty again anyway." Tossing the cloth to the ground, he rose and leaned against the car. "So, to what do I owe the pleasure?"

Tilting her head, she studied him. "I'm pretty sure you can guess one of the reasons I'm here."

"Cynthia's showing," he said with a nod. "I knew once she saw Carrie, it would be all over Ardor Creek. I'm fine with that since I'm thrilled. We're having a little girl."

Heather pursed her lips, cognizant of the tears that just barely stung her eyes. After a moment, she broke into a huge grin. "I'm really happy for you, Butch."

His eyes narrowed before his lips curved. "Damn, I think you are. Well, thanks. That means a lot, Heather."

"It does?"

With a slight shrug, he nodded. "Yes. I never set out to have a shitty marriage with you, Heather. It just kind of happened."

"We were so young," she said, her voice gravelly from the sudden rush of emotion. "We never stood a chance."

"Nope." Crossing his arms, he kicked the ground with the toe of his shoe. "And we never discussed what we really wanted. Obviously, we realized we wanted different things when it was too late."

"Yeah." Glancing down, she inhaled a deep breath before reclaiming his gaze. "And then you cheated on me, which was probably a blessing in disguise since it prompted me to file for divorce and hightail it out of Ardor Creek." Her eyes narrowed. "Telling everyone I cheated on you was a low blow. I think you knew that people didn't care much for me and that would affirm their assumptions about my character."

A muscle ticked in his jaw. "That's a fair assessment. They didn't care much for me either and I figured if everyone was focused on you, they wouldn't notice what a shithead I was."

A laugh escaped her throat. "You are a shithead, Butch. That false rumor is one of the things that prompted me to come back and set things straight."

"And look at you now," he said, arching an eyebrow. "Everybody *loves* Heather Combs. You finally won everyone over. I'd ask you how but I don't really give a shit. I always thought the crew you seem to adore so much was pretty stuck up in high school. I've got Cynthia and we're happy with our own little crew."

"Well, I'm glad. You two can make each other miserable until you croak. It's the stuff of dreams," she said, a teasing lilt in her tone.

Butch assessed her before his lips twitched ever so slightly. "I guess so. Anyway, for what it's worth, I'm sorry for the lies. And I'm sorry I cheated on you. You wouldn't have sex with me anymore, so I went looking elsewhere."

"It's hard to have sex with someone who makes you feel like crap, Butch," she murmured.

"I know." Blowing out a breath, his lips fanned together. "You were no picnic either."

"That's true. I had absolutely no foundation to even try to love someone or build a sustainable, healthy relationship. It was shortsighted, so I'll apologize for that."

His blue eyes darted between hers, causing her to feel uncomfortable.

"Just spit it out, Butch. Say what you want to say."

"I'm just wondering..." He lifted a shoulder. "You seem pretty happy with the author guy. It's all over town how serious you two are. Maybe you've finally figured it out."

"*The author guy* is named Jeremy, and yes, I really like him."

Butch smiled. "A dude with two kids. That's a leap for you, Heather. He doesn't want anymore?"

"He says he doesn't so I take him at his word." Gnawing her lip, she pondered. "But the two he has are pretty great. They're going to be ten soon so I might not be able to completely fuck them up if he does something crazy like convince me to marry him."

Butch's eyes widened. "Would you get married again? I thought you were determined to only marry an old rich guy who wouldn't require any emotion in return."

Exhaling, she shook her head. "I don't know. I was so sure I knew what I wanted...and then Jeremy happened." Lifting her hands, she shrugged. "Now, I have no idea. A part of me is terrified. But, yeah, I think I might consider marrying him...down the road...like, when I'm eighty."

Butch chuckled. "Or maybe sooner. I hope you consider it. Regardless of all the shitty things we said to each other in the past, I want you to be happy too, Heather."

Running her damp palms over the soft fabric of the cardigan, she grinned. "It took us two decades to get to the point where we want each other to be happy. Too bad we couldn't have gotten there when we were together, but it's nice to get there now."

Placing a hand on his hip, he nodded. "It is. Is that why you stopped by?"

Heather's brow furrowed as she contemplated. "Yes. I felt this need to see you—once I found out about Cynthia—and to wish you both well. I still hate her guts, mind you," she lifted a finger, indicating her teasing, "but I wish you both well. Ardor Creek is a small town and I plan to stay here. I don't want to waste any more time detesting you. It requires too much energy."

"Well, then I won't detest you either." Glancing at his hand, he said, "I'd offer to shake on it but you always hated my greasy hands."

She showed him her palms. "Still do, buddy. I think verbal confirmation is fine." Lowering her hands, she gave him one last genuine smile. "Congrats on the baby, Butch. See you around town."

His expression was soft...clear...open...as he gazed at her before grinning back. "See you around town, Heather. Thanks for stopping by."

Waving, she turned and navigated out of the garage before settling into her car. Once the door was shut, she backed out and drove two blocks before pulling to the side of the road and putting the car in park. Closing her eyes, she took a moment to acknowledge how magnificent it felt to let go of the remaining toxicity for her ex-husband that had simmered like acid in her gut for so many years.

Lifting her lids, she inhaled a deep breath, noting how much lighter she felt. Ready to embrace a future that wasn't bogged down with past anger and regret, she resumed the drive, excited to finish her next appointment and head home to see Jeremy and the girls. They always arrived home from school around four, although she usually didn't stop over on weeknights.

Deciding to make an exception tonight, she texted Jeremy when she arrived at the showing.

Heather: I know it's a school night but I want to have dinner with you guys. If you'll have me.

A small flare of anxiety welled as she awaited his response.

Jeremy: For real? Since it's a school night, it's just dinner, homework and bedtime. Not super exciting.

Heather: Who needs exciting? I'll pick up dinner. Tacos?

Jeremy: Tacos are awesome. The girls love guacamole and queso too. I can pay you back when you get here.

Heather: I'm not a bestselling author but I think I can afford tacos. See you at five?

Jeremy: Perfect. I wasn't expecting school nights. That's pretty rad. You can sleep over if you promise to go to bed on time, young lady.

Heather breathed a laugh.

Heather: I promise to go to bed but I definitely won't be sleeping, if you catch my drift.

He sent a heart-eyes emoji.

Jeremy: Drift caught. Also, thank you, because now I'm definitely finishing the two chapters I plotted. I wasn't rushing because I told myself I could write after the girls were in bed.

Heather: Get to work. I will require your full attention after tacos and bedtime. Family time on a weekday is a lot to handle but I think I can take it.

Jeremy: You'll take it. After family time is over and we're alone. Trust me on that.

Scoffing, she shook her head.

Heather: Too cheesy! How are you considered one of the greatest authors of our time? Go write. See ya later.

Jeremy: Bye, sweetheart.

Grinning, Heather exited the car to prep the house for her last appointment of the day.

Chapter 21

September rolled into October, the full leaves turning to bright yellow and orange before they began to fall to the ground. Heather continued to spend more time with Jeremy, Gabby and Angeline, slowly allowing them to penetrate the wall she'd built around her heart so many years ago.

Justine and Gary's wedding took place on a warm, sunny October Saturday by the lake that sat on the north end of Ardor Creek. They married under the same altar Scott had built for Carrie and Peter years before, while the attendees sat in white folding chairs on the grassy field that surrounded the lake.

Since Justine and Gary were Ardor Creek locals, Heather guessed there were at least two hundred people present. Everyone in town wanted to celebrate the beloved cop and the fun-loving artist who'd escaped her unhappy marriage to find true love.

Abby officiated the wedding, beaming the entire time as she stood behind the altar. When she announced Justine and Gary as husband and wife, they leaned in for a sweet, soulful kiss as Avery jumped with excitement beside them. Drawing back, Gary lifted her and situated her on his hip before clutching Justine's hand and holding it high. The onlookers cheered as they strode between the chairs to the clubhouse where the reception would be held.

Justine hired a local band to perform and the reception was filled with lots of laughter and dancing. While Heather appreciated the sentiment of it all, she'd never been a huge fan of weddings, and several hours in, she stepped outside under the rapidly setting sun to get some fresh air.

Approaching the stone balcony that overlooked the lake, she rested her forearms on the cool surface and closed her eyes, thankful for a moment of peace.

"Had enough of the wedding festivities?" Jeremy's deep voice called beside her, causing her to shiver.

Lifting her lids, she nodded as he joined her, resting his elbows on the balcony.

"It's loud in there," she said, craning her neck toward the clubhouse where the band was still playing. "I love that Jus and Gary kept this informal. The barbeque buffet and band are nice, and the kids seem to be having a great time, but it's a lot for this ol' single lady."

His eyes darted over her face as he grinned. "Are you old? You don't look a day over twenty-five to me."

Rolling her eyes, she scoffed. "Um, you're already getting laid tonight. You don't have to pour it on."

"I mean it," he said, gently ribbing her with his shoulder. "And are you single? I was sure we'd entered semi-serious relationship territory, at least."

Shooting him a look, she sighed. "Maybe we have. I don't know anymore. Somehow, I've gone from craving solace to wanting to be with you and your spawns all the damn time. It's annoying."

His breathy chuckle surrounded her. "Is it?"

"Yes," she muttered, scowling.

Grazing his fingers over her arm, he clutched her hand and tugged. "Dance with me."

"Out here?"

"Mmm-hmm," he said, pulling her to the open stone floor of the patio. "The sun is setting and we have this romantic little patio all to ourselves. The girls are inside dancing with all the other kids. Let's enjoy the moment."

Stepping into his embrace, she slid her arms around his neck as his hands rested on her lower back. Swaying to the music that wafted from inside, she stared into his eyes.

"You look beautiful today," he said, placing a kiss on her forehead. "You're definitely the hottest wedding date I've ever had."

Tossing back her head, she laughed. "Man, you are buttering me up. What gives? I already agreed to stay over the entire weekend."

"I'm glad," he said, gently caressing her back as his fingers roved over the fabric of her dress. "We like having you in our home, Heather."

"I like it too," she whispered, swallowing thickly as her throat tightened.

His light-green orbs studied her as they swayed. "We're not kids anymore, sweetheart, and I'm not a fan of wasting time. Things are starting to move in my life and I don't want to question whether or not you'll be there."

"You know I'm there for you," she said, eyes narrowing as she stroked the back of his neck. "I already agreed to take Angeline to physical therapy every Tuesday and Thursday now that her cast is off. It makes sense because I make my own schedule and you're going to be swamped now that Netflix is in full production of *Alternate Destinies*."

"And I'm so thankful you agreed to do that," he said, placing a peck on her lips. "Jen is too since it's hard for her to get away from work to make those three o'clock appointments."

"I'm happy to do it."

His lips curved into the goofy smile that melted her insides for some insane reason, causing her to laugh. "What?"

"I think it's time we start discussing you moving in with us, Heather," he said, his fingers constricting on her back as he drew her closer.

"I live next door," she said above the intense pounding of her heart. "I'm practically already there."

Lowering his head, he rested his forehead against hers. "It's silly for you to keep paying rent when I have a perfectly good house you can move into. I know this is scaring the crap out of you, but how long are we going to stretch this out, hon? We've both been around the block and know what we want. Well, I do, at least."

Expelling a breath, she shook her head against his. "You son of a bitch. You ask me to dance and rub my back while you suggest things. You're not playing fair."

Laughing, his arms tightened, pulling her flush against his body. "Stop laughing at me."

"You're just so cute right now," he said, nuzzling her nose with his. "Your eyes get all fiery when you freak out. It's hot."

Sighing, she slid her fingers into the thick hair at the base of his neck. "I take it back. You're never getting laid again."

His warm chuckle surrounded her. "I can't wait to prove you wrong when we get home. I'm going to make you scream tonight, sweetheart."

"Don't threaten me with a good time," she murmured, her tone sultry.

Jeremy just gazed at her, raw emotion swirling in the honey flecks that dotted his green orbs.

Her fingers toyed with his hair as she struggled to calm her heartbeat under the dimming sky.

"You seem determined to make me a stepmother," she finally said, her tone teasing but acerbic. "If that happens, I'm never going to forgive you."

Tossing back his head, he gave a joyful laugh. "Yeah, I think I am. I want it all with you, Heather. I'm man enough to say it and to get it out in the open." Tucking a curl behind her ear, he smiled as affection laced his features. "I'm in this, hon. I'll need to travel to New York on occasion now that we're in production and I want you with me. When we have the premiere, I want you by my side."

Her eyes roved between his as she contemplated. "I've never been very good at being someone's partner," she said, her voice raspy as she shook her head. "I can't promise it will work. It's a lot to take on, especially since you have the girls. The stakes are high and it's very possible I'll let you all down."

"Nothing is ever guaranteed, sweetheart," he said, cupping her jaw and running his thumb over her cheek. "But somehow, we seem to fit. I never expected it when we first met but it happened and now, I can't imagine my life without you in it."

Emotion flooded her as genuineness swam in his gaze.

"Jeremy—"

"Just think about it, okay?" he asked, tilting his head. "We don't have to make any decisions now. I just figured it was time I said it so you could start digesting it. Maybe by Christmas, you'll be ready to admit you're crazy about me." He waggled his eyebrows.

Her eyes narrowed. "You're passable."

Laughing, he drew her close, wrapping his body around hers as she pressed her cheek to his chest. Resting her forehead against the warm skin of his neck above his dress shirt, she swayed along to his easy rhythm.

"Mine's pounding too," he said, grasping her hand and flattening her palm over his heart. Firm beats pulsed beneath her hand, although not as ragged and erratic as her own. "I don't want to let you down either, Heather. We've been unlucky in love before but maybe this is our time."

"Maybe it is," she murmured, nuzzling into him.

Closing her eyes, she trusted him to hold her as the song played in the distance. When it was finished, she followed him inside, the swirling emotions lingering long after the band played their last song.

Chapter 22

In early November, the owner of Heather's real estate firm, Chandler Grossman, asked her for a meeting. As she prepared at home on a cool, crisp Tuesday, she took time to ensure she appeared coiffed and professional. Chandler was approaching eighty and she felt he was finally going to offer her a deal to buy out the firm. Running her palms over her black pencil skirt that hugged her legs beneath a black blazer, she rotated in front of the long mirror, affirming she looked fantastic. With a confident nod at her reflection, she grabbed her bag and headed to Main Street.

Arriving at the office, she strode inside, her heels muted on the functional carpet. Chandler's assistant, Hope, smiled as she approached.

"Hi, Heather, he's expecting you. You can go on in."

"Thanks, Hope." Straightening her shoulders, she trailed down the hallway and knocked on his open door.

"Hi, Heather," Chandler said, standing behind the mahogany desk. "Right on time. Come on in."

"Hi, Chandler," she said, shaking his hand before sitting in one of the leather chairs that flanked his desk.

Sitting back in his chair, he smiled, his posture relaxed under his white hair and bushy eyebrows. "So, how's my top agent doing these days? You've already received two offers for the month and we're barely into November. Well done."

"Thank you," she said with a nod. "I was thrilled to get an offer for list price on the home on Meadowbrook Drive. But to be clear, I aim to bring you several more offers this month." She lifted a finger.

"I don't doubt it," he said, twirling his thumbs atop his thighs. "You're by far my best agent, Heather. Who knew when you were head cheerleader at Ardor Creek High all those years ago, you'd end up being so great at closing real estate?"

Chuckling, she rested her chin on her hand as her elbow pressed into the arm of the chair. "I should've gotten my real estate license years ago. It compliments my personality. There's something refreshing about closing deals. The negotiations are perfect for my unemotional, brassy nature. Sales certainly isn't for the meek, that's for sure."

"So true." Brown eyes studied her as he contemplated. "As you know, we're a small firm with only four agents but I've built this business into something I'm very proud of."

"You should be," she said, straightening.

"It's important to me that whomever I sell the firm to maintains its reputation and integrity."

"Agreed."

"Anderson, Craig and Louisa are part-time agents who have no desire to run the firm. Therefore, I'm down to you—my best agent and my only full-time agent. You've been clear you'd like to purchase the firm when I retire, and I'm finally ready."

Elation surged through Heather's frame. "I'm glad you noticed my not-so-subtle hints. I've made enough sales to upgrade to a broker's license instead of just being an agent. I'm ready to take on a new challenge, Chandler."

His lips curved. "You're tough as nails, Heather. I admire your work ethic immensely."

"Thank you."

"Okay, then," he said, rubbing his chin. "I'm prepared to begin the process of selling the firm to you. You've proven yourself for the short time you've been here and you deserve it."

Heather beamed. "I'm thrilled you think so. I work very hard and it's nice to see it pay off."

"My goal is to have the business sold by the end of the year. I'll sell it to you for the fair market rate our attorneys deem reasonable. I have no desire to profit off you—hell, I've made enough money over the years—but I do want my fair share of what I've built. Mary and I have plenty saved and we want to enjoy our remaining years at our home in Florida. I'll also need your help selling my house in Ardor Creek."

"Done," she said, enjoying the feeling of pure elation that pulsed in her veins.

"My lawyer has suggested I price the business at $400,000. Keep that in mind as we begin to negotiate."

Heather swallowed thickly, trying not to choke on the number. No way in hell could she afford that with what she currently had saved. But she was resilient, and if there was a way to purchase the business, she'd find it.

"I will, although you can expect I'll try to negotiate a lower price."

"I'd be disappointed if you didn't," he said, standing and extending his hand. "Let's start the process, Heather. You have a lawyer you can consult?"

"I'll speak to Mark Lancaster and have him refer someone." She rose and shook his hand.

"Perfect. Oh, and on a random note, my grandson just found out he's having his second kid. I'm over the moon to be a great-grandparent again."

"Congratulations," she said, wondering how that related to selling the business.

"He loves the cul-de-sac where your house is located and asked me if anything there was for sale. I figured I'd mention it in case you want to consider selling him your home. I know you worked out a rent-to-buy deal with Justine Lancaster, but it might be prudent to sell it, take the commission, and rent another home."

Heather's brows drew together. Something about that didn't sit well with her since it meant she'd have to move out of the neighborhood...away from Jeremy and the girls. Mulling it over, she tilted her head and lifted a shoulder. "He's welcome to see the house. Give him my cell so I can set up a time."

Figuring showing the home wouldn't kill her, she finished her meeting with Chandler, thrilled at the outcome...except for the nagging knowledge his grandson might want to buy her home. It would be a good deal for Justine, and she wanted to do right by her—as a friend and as a client—but it would leave Heather unsettled once again.

You could move in with Jeremy...

The words wafted through her mind before she could squelch them. Yes, she could move in with her lover...boyfriend...man she was pretty sure she was in love with...but that would mean she wouldn't have an out. Once she took the plunge of cohabitation, she would be entrenched in their lives forever.

And if she fucked up along the way because she sucked at things remotely involving family, emotion or love? Well, she'd be screwed. Tossed out into the big bad world yet again, alone and back at square one.

Sighing, Heather stepped onto Main Street, shrugging on her coat and drawing the flaps together as the chilly wind stung her cheeks. Could she survive failing yet again if things didn't work out with Jeremy? Hell, she had no freaking idea.

Unable to deal with the complex feelings swirling inside, she hopped in her car and headed to her next appointment, resolved to bury herself in work so she wouldn't drown in the multitude of unknowns.

T wo weeks later, Heather showed her house—or *Justine's* house, depending on the perspective—to Chandler's grandson, Andrew, and his pregnant wife as their four-year-old son followed along. As she walked them around the home and expansive back yard, she admitted it was perfect for their growing family.

When the showing was finished, they stood in the foyer as Heather discussed numbers.

"The asking price is fair and we adore this neighborhood," Andrew said, smiling at his wife as she grinned up at him. "We don't want to play games here, Heather. I think we're going to offer twenty thousand under list price to get the ball rolling. Do you think Justine will accept that?"

"As I've stated, I'm her agent and your agent, so I have to ensure I represent you both fairly," Heather said. "But I think it's a great starting offer. Let me present it and we'll go from there."

"Thank you," Andrew's wife Joanna said, shaking her hand. "We absolutely love it."

"You're not supposed to say that to our agent, dear," he teased, kissing her brown hair.

"I'm pretty good at reading people, so I kind of figured it out," Heather said with a cheeky grin. Opening the front door, she held it as they exited. "I'll be in touch next week."

They waved, the little boy at their side as they trailed to the car and loaded inside before driving off. Closing the door, Heather stood in the foyer, a bit stunned as the realization settled in that she was going to lose the home she'd become quite comfortable in.

Her phone chimed, jarring her from the musings, and she grinned at the caller ID.

"Hey, Ashlyn."

"Hey, Heather. How's it hanging?"

"A bit to the left but who wants to be normal?"

Ashlyn's warm laugh echoed through the phone. "Truth. Do you have a sec?"

"Sure do," Heather said, trailing to the kitchen and lowering onto one of the island stools.

"Scott and I host Thanksgiving for the crew every year and we want to invite you, along with Jeremy and the girls. I figured I'd call you first to feel you out since I know you're not a huge fan of family get-togethers. But I figure you've settled in with our resident sexy author enough to want to spend the holidays with him and the girls."

Exhaling a breath, Heather traced her finger over the smooth counter. "They've grown on me like a weed I can't whack away. It's annoying. Help."

Ashlyn chuckled. "I'll take that as a 'yes' that you're down for holiday festivities."

"Fine. Yes. I'm in. Gross, but I'm in."

"I promise, we're harmless. The kids usually play soccer in the back yard with the guys while we ladies consume every bottle of wine in Ardor Creek. I think you're going to enjoy it."

"You had me at wine," Heather said, smirking. "Do you want me to invite Jeremy? He has the girls this Thanksgiving and Jen has them for Christmas, although they usually end up spending holidays together regardless of where the custody falls. But this year, Jen is flying to Colorado with her mom over Thanksgiving to see her sister and her family."

"Scott's going to call him to invite him but you can certainly mention it. You all can arrive around two and stay until the wine is gone."

Heather grinned. "Jeremy will be thrilled to get an invite directly from Scott. He digs the crew."

"Um, Jeremy is kind of a big deal and Scott is fangirling over his movie deal with Netflix. I think it's the other way around."

"That will make my man's day, for sure."

"Your man, *hmmm?*" Ashlyn asked, excited.

"Yeah," she murmured, tapping her fingernails on the counter. "I'm really wrapped up in him...and the girls. I'd usually make some pithy quip at this point, but I'm honestly terrified. What the hell do I know about building something stable with a good guy like Jeremy and two little girls?"

"Oh, sweetie, you don't have to have all the answers. I failed miserably at love before I met Scott. I think you just have to do your best to care for them as genuinely as possible. If you lead with your heart, you can't fuck it up."

"If there's a way to fuck it up, I will," Heather muttered.

"You of all people know that internal dialogue isn't healthy, Heather," she scolded, causing Heather to smile. Ashlyn was a force of nature and Heather appreciated her tough love. It was the sign of true friendship, and she was honored to finally have genuine friends after so many years of failing.

"You're right." Straightening on the stool, squared her shoulders. "I've got to forge ahead in this relationship like I do everything else in my damn life. One step at a time, trusting I've got the will and ability to make it happen."

"Amen, sister!"

Heather breathed a laugh. "I'm excited about Thanksgiving. Thank you so much for the invite."

"Of course. I'm thrilled you're coming. Bring whatever you want to drink and maybe some prosecco for mimosas. I'll take care of everything else. It will be fun. Bye!"

The screen went dark and Heather rested the phone on the counter. Rubbing her forehead, she contemplated the direction of her thoughts.

"Don't talk yourself out of being happy, Heather," she murmured. "You aren't perfect but you've made some epic changes. Hell, you forgave *Butch.*" She snickered. "I think you might finally deserve to be loved."

The words echoed off the kitchen walls as Heather struggled to accept them. Unable to discern whether they truly settled in, she headed upstairs to change into workout gear, hoping a walk would clear her head.

Chapter 23

That evening, Heather strode to Jeremy's house, using the key he'd given her to unlock the back door. It was Friday evening and they planned to watch the new season of Stranger Things with the girls.

Gabby and Angeline greeted her with the beaming smiles she now craved, and Heather hugged them both, listening to them chatter as she unloaded the bags she'd picked up from the Italian restaurant. Once the food was spread on the counter, Jeremy trailed in and pecked her on the cheek.

"Thanks for dinner, sweetheart," he said, glancing over the food that sat on the counter. "I had to get those revisions finished for my editor. You saved me an hour by picking up the food."

"No prob," Heather said, grabbing plates from the cabinet and handing one to Gabby and Angeline. "Dig in, ladies."

As the girls scooped pasta and salad on their plates, Jeremy rested a hand on Heather's lower back and leaned closer. "How did the showing go with Chandler's grandson?"

"Really well. I'm going to present the offer to Justine tomorrow."

Excitement glowed in his eyes, and Heather's throat closed at the discussion they needed to have after the girls were asleep. Jeremy had offered to lend her the money to buy Chandler's firm as soon as she'd told him the news. Although she knew the offer was genuine, it would create another tether between them she wasn't ready to traverse.

In addition, purchasing the firm was a milestone she wanted to accomplish on her own. She'd worked hard to make her own path and relished the opportunity to prove her worth. Whether she was proving it to herself or the world, she wasn't quite sure, but the desire burned deep within and she needed to sate it in her own way.

"Do you want to talk about the loan?" he asked softly, seeming to understand her hesitancy.

"Once the girls go to bed," she said, nodding.

He squeezed her side before letting it go so they could dig into dinner. They decided to eat in the living room, and Heather settled beside Jeremy on the couch, wondering when her idea of a good time had turned into watching weird television with two kids and her favorite sexy-geeky author.

After dinner, the girls lay on the floor, wrapped up in blankets, as she snuggled with Jeremy on the couch. Eventually, the girls headed to bed and once they were settled, he headed back downstairs to the couch before slinging an arm over her shoulder.

"Well, we made it through several episodes. We should be finished soon and your penance will be done."

"It's a weird show but I'm kind of invested now," she said, stretching her thigh over his as she rested her head on the couch, facing him. "I need to know if they're going to save the world and all that jazz."

"I remember how much you hate a cliffhanger," he teased, arching a brow. "Honestly, I don't think I can ever forget."

Chuckling, she gazed at his chest before lifting her eyes to his. "Do you want to discuss the plan I've concocted to buy Chandler's business?"

"Sure." Curiosity laced his tone.

Inhaling, she began to detail the plan, hoping he wouldn't be upset. "I really appreciate you offering to loan me the money when I told you I was buying the firm."

"I'm happy to do it, Heather."

Lifting a finger, she shot him a scolding glare. "Please let me finish. I was already kind of dreading discussing this with you. Don't make it worse."

Exhaling a hesitant breath, he nodded. "Okay. Sorry."

Continuing, she licked her lips. "I truly appreciate your offer, but I can't ask you to do that."

Anger flared in his eyes.

"Don't get upset," she said, her tone firm. "This isn't about you. I would have to figure out a way to buy the business if we weren't together, and I think I have a good solution."

When he remained silent, she continued.

"I'm not going to take any commission when I sell Chandler's home. My commission from that sale will go toward purchasing the business. I'm also going to contribute my commission from selling Justine's home toward the purchase. I'll get double commission for that sale since I'm the buyer's and seller's agent."

His eyebrows drew together. "Those sales will net you roughly fifty thousand, right?"

"Yes," she said with a nod. "Fifty thousand toward the $350,000 price of the firm that Mark so skillfully negotiated for me. He's a saint to take on this project as my attorney since he's so busy as D.A., but he insisted."

"Because we're in the crew," Jeremy said, waggling his brows.

Laughing, she bit her lip. "We're in the crew. I never thought Mark Lancaster would end up being my pro bono attorney twenty years after we barely spoke to each other in high school. He won't accept payment since he's not in private practice anymore and doesn't want a hint of a conflict of interest."

"But you and Justine are such good friends," Jeremy said, rubbing her thigh. "I think that's how friendships work, hon. You do nice things for people you care about, and Mark knows how important you are to Jus."

"Go figure," she muttered. "Haven't experienced much of that but I'll take it. Anyway, I'll find ways to pay him back. And I'm going to buy a bunch of Justine's weird art over the next twenty years, so it will even out eventually."

"There are a lot of corners and walls around here to place her art." He glanced around the room, a question in his green orbs.

"I'll get to the cohabitation thing," she said, giving him a droll look. "But to finish the discussion on the firm, I've spoken to Chandler and I'm going to set up a loan with him."

"He's willing to do that? I thought he wanted everything taken care of by the end of this year."

"He did, but my negotiation skills are impeccable." She dramatically swiped her hair off her shoulder. "He's agreed to a payback of the remaining $300,000 by taking a seventy-five percent cut of my commissions until he's whole."

Jeremy grimaced. "Heather, that's insane. You'll be putting in tons of work for pennies until the loan is paid off. That doesn't make any sense. Let me loan you the money. We can work it out—"

"No," she said, slicing a hand through the air. "I'm not going to financially depend on you, Jeremy. I did that with Butch and it was a disaster. I won't depend on a man that way ever again."

"Heather..."

Straightening, she drew her leg from his lap and stared deep into his eyes. "I've learned a lot of lessons in my life. When I was financially dependent on Butch in those early years, I felt trapped and extremely unhappy. When I left, I vowed to never put myself in that position again. I won't do it, especially with you."

Frustration lined his features as he shifted on the couch. "What the hell does that mean? I want to help you because I care about you, Heather. You're not the same person you were twenty years ago. This bullshit of being stuck in the past is pretty damn annoying."

Anger shot down her spine, causing her to slide to the far corner of the couch, suddenly craving space. "I'm not stuck in the past."

"You are!" he replied, rising and jabbing a finger in her face. "All I ever hear is how much you hate relationships, how you're incapable of love, and how awful it is to be stuck with us. I'm over it."

Jumping to her feet, she smacked his hand away. "I told you all that *bullshit* because being with you is terrifying for me, Jeremy!" she cried, trying to keep her voice low since the girls were sleeping upstairs. "I've done my best to be honest with you. Sorry if it isn't what you want to hear. I thought you'd prefer that to me blowing sunshine up your ass."

"Well, it's getting old." Placing his hands on his hips, he huffed a breath. "I don't know what else you want me to prove. Loving someone means being able to let them care for you." Stepping closer, he cupped her upper arms. "I want to loan you the money and I want you to move in with us once you sell Justine's house. Not because I don't think you can do it on your own, but because we're partners. Aren't we?"

Heather observed his handsome features, laced with such genuineness and hope. Anxiety swirled in her gut as she realized they would never see the situation the same way. For her, it was an opportunity to prove she'd finally reached the point in her life where she could achieve purchasing the firm on her own. But Jeremy saw the world differently. He was used to familial bonds and partnerships. Heather knew his offer was genuine but he didn't understand her drive to forge ahead and implement the lessons she'd learned after so many years of failing.

"I don't want to fight with you," she said, cupping his cheek. "We're so different, Jeremy. I worried this would happen when you forced me to date you all those months ago."

His lips curved into a tender smile. "*Force* is a *bit* excessive."

Laughing, she nodded. "It is, but I'm putting my foot down this time. I'm entering into the loan agreement with Chandler and I'm going to rent the studio above the firm for a year once Justine's house is sold. We can discuss moving in together when the lease is up for renewal."

Expelling a frustrated breath, he dropped his hands and backed away. "I'm not interested in casually dating you for another year, Heather. I thought I'd been clear on that."

Lifting her hands, she scoffed. "Nothing about this situation is casual, Jeremy. I'm binge-watching TV with your kids and hanging out here every other night. What else do you want?"

"I want you to depend on me," he said, ticking his fingers as he spoke. "I want you to structure a loan with me rather than give away your commission. I want you to make this permanent, Heather."

"Seriously, Jeremy, that's a lot. It hasn't even been a year since we started dating—"

"We're in our forties, Heather," he interjected. "How long do you want to 'date?'" He made quotation marks with his hands. "I have two kids and am not really interested in fucking around at this point."

Groaning, she angrily rubbed her forehead with her fingers. "Okay, this discussion is getting us nowhere. We're not going to see eye to eye on this. It's pointless to continue arguing when we're both dug in."

Crossing his arms, he scowled. "Honestly, I think we need to take some time to figure out what we really want here."

Her features contorted. "Seriously? Because I won't accept a loan from you? That's ridiculous, Jeremy."

"It's more than the loan, Heather," he said, shaking his head. "It's your inability to accept this relationship. It's extremely frustrating and I have no desire to continue running in circles with you."

Heather's mouth dropped open. "Are you serious?"

When he remained silent, she latched onto the fury that swelled deep within. "I have given you more than I've given any man in my entire *life*." Lifting her chin, she struggled to remain calm as her body vibrated with anger. "If you can't see that, then you can go screw yourself for all I care." Pivoting, she stalked toward the back door and yanked it open before he grabbed her arm and whirled her around.

"Don't leave like this," he said, a muscle twitching in his jaw. "Don't run, Heather. We can figure this out."

Drawing her arm from his grasp, she gave a defeated shrug. "Honestly, I'm just not sure we can. Don't follow me. I need time to think. Good night." Closing the door behind her, she trailed home as emotion pervaded every muscle in her frame.

Once she was upstairs, she threw on her sweats and stared in the mirror as she held the toothbrush. Staring deep into her father's eyes, she cursed them for the thousandth time, wishing things had been different. Wishing she had the capacity to so easily consider things that were second nature to Jeremy.

Unfortunately, she never had, and although she'd made some stellar progress, she would probably never evolve into a person who embodied everything Jeremy would want in a partner. Sighing, she leaned forward and whispered to her reflection.

"So, where does that leave us? Can two people so different build something that makes them both happy?"

Silence was her only answer as she finished her nightly ritual and gave into exhaustion.

Chapter 24

T hanksgiving week arrived, along with Jeremy's sour mood. Ever since his argument with Heather, he'd become mired in frustration. Add to that his waning creativity—which meant his writing was shit—and things were pretty much disastrous.

Somewhere along the way, Heather had become his muse. His editor was thrilled with his newest manuscript and snippets of his work in progress, and he wanted to keep the momentum going. Sadly, that was tough to manifest when the woman you loved decided to shut you out. Burying his head in his hands, Jeremy stared at the blank page on his laptop before slamming it closed. Resigned to his writer's block, he stood and called to the girls.

"Gabby? Angeline? We need to head to Mom's soon. Last dinner before she leaves for Thanksgiving."

"Coming!" the girls chimed from upstairs.

They headed down, Angeline limping on one leg which was now firmly wrapped in a bandage rather than a cast. Even though he and Heather were barely speaking, she continued to take Angeline to her bi-weekly physical therapy appointments. It showcased her affection for his daughter, which made him feel terrible since he'd basically accused her of not caring.

After the argument, he'd called her the next day, regretting his sudden burst of anger. Although he'd meant much of what he said, he'd also been hard on her and ended up pushing her away. It was the last thing he wanted since he was irrevocably sure about one thing: he was definitely in love with Heather Combs.

If he were a poet, he could probably write flowery prose about her beauty and wit, remarking on her indomitable attitude and unflappable honesty. Since he was a novelist, he'd stick with the basic plot points: she was a force of nature whom he desperately wanted to build a future with and longed to nurture with his whole heart.

They would never be considered a perfect match, but perfect was rather boring in his opinion. Instead, they were opposites in all the right ways. Two people who would push and challenge each other to become the best versions of themselves. He'd become complacent before he met Heather, stuck in a passionless life, content with the monotony of work, kids, repeat. Although he adored his children, they could never fill the void Heather did.

Jeremy had experienced romantic love in the past, but he'd never experienced the whirling vortex of emotions he felt for Heather. She was frustrating and funny...challenging and puzzling...closed and open, all at the same time. A complex enigma he wanted to solve for the rest of his whole damn life if she'd let him.

Unfortunately, when he'd called to apologize, she'd sent him straight to voicemail on the first ring. Annoyed, he left her a heartfelt message:

"Hey, sweetheart. I don't want to fight with you. I'm sorry I lost it. Please call me back. Let's chat about this, okay? I know we can work it out."

Five minutes later, he'd received a text in return.

Heather: I need some time. I've let the anger go but I need to think about what I really want. I'll continue to take Angeline to her appointments.

Jeremy: You don't have to do that if you want space. I'll make other arrangements.

Heather: I want to do it, Jeremy. You've already arranged pick up for me at her school. I'm not ending this. I just need time. Please respect me enough to give it to me.

Sighing, he'd accepted his fate.

Jeremy: Okay. Thank you. I have constant afternoon video calls now that we're in production and having you take her helps. I owe you.

Heather: You don't owe me anything. People like me show we care in our own ways. It won't always be your way. Remember that, okay? I'll see you at Thanksgiving dinner. Let's chat then (once I've had wine).

Chuckling, Jeremy had ended the text chain, slightly encouraged she didn't want to end things for good.

"Dad?" Gabby called from the doorway, jolting him from his thoughts. "We're ready."

"Sweet. Let's roll."

They climbed in the car and headed to Jen's. Since she was leaving for the holiday, she'd wanted to host a family meal before her trip.

"Hey, guys," she said, greeting them in the foyer as they strolled in. "Thanks for grabbing the dinner rolls. I forgot to get them at the store."

"Sure," Jeremy said, handing her the package as the girls headed into the living room to greet Lou. "Thanks for cooking."

Compassion entered her gaze as her lips curved into a sad smile. "Man, you look like crap."

Rolling his eyes, he huffed a breath. "I've been better."

"Come on," she said, gesturing for him to follow her to the kitchen. "We can chat while I finish cooking. Lou will entertain the girls."

Once she'd poured him a glass of wine and placed the buns in the oven, she resumed stirring sauce in the large pot atop the stove. "Okay, hit me with it. You told me you and Heather were taking a break but you never told me the whole story."

Swirling the wine, he scowled. "I'm not sure I want your advice."

"Too bad, buddy. You forget I know you better than anyone and can identify all your blind spots." Lifting the wooden spoon, she circled it, indicating he should get on with it.

"Fine." After taking a hefty sip, he ran a hand through his hair. "We got in an argument and are pretty much at a stalemate. It all started when Chandler Grossman offered to sell her his firm..."

He continued, elaborating as Jen listened, uttering the occasional, "Mmm-hmm," or, "I see."

Finally, when he was finished, he leaned back and threaded his hands behind his head. "So, that's it. She refuses to accept my help and I'm pissed because it proves she isn't as invested in this relationship as I am. And that hurts, Jen. It just really fucking hurts."

Jen pinched some salt between her fingers, throwing it in the pot as she nodded. "I can see how that would hurt."

Feeling his lips thin, he gazed at her through slitted lids. "And?"

"And what?" she asked, lifting a shoulder

Expelling an exasperated breath, he tilted his head. "She's sacrificing the majority of her commissions when I could just help her instead. It's ridiculous."

"Is it?"

Rolling his eyes, he slammed his palm on the counter. "I'm not going to have this cryptic conversation with you all night, Jen. Just tell me. Am I the one being unreasonable because I can't see it."

Placing the lid over the sauce, she sauntered over, pouring herself a glass of wine before sitting beside him. Lifting it, she saluted before drinking. "My dear ex-husband, you have always been oblivious about your rather large savior complex. It takes over before you even realize it, and usually ends in disaster."

His eyebrows drew together as his gaze dropped to the counter. "I don't want to save her. I just want to help her."

"It's all the same, Jeremy," she said, shrugging. "You've mentioned a hundred times how much you admire Heather's fortitude and strength. And yet, when she devises a plan to secure her future on her terms, you ask her to reject it and let you save the day."

Rubbing his eyes in frustration, he shook his head. "That's not what I'm trying to do."

"I'm sure she doesn't doubt your intentions," Jen said, covering the back of his hand once he rested it on the counter. "You always have awesome intentions. But I think it took her a long time to figure out how to thrive on her own. When she finally did, she met you and that threw her for a loop."

"Because I'm so awful," he muttered.

"You're not," she said, chuckling. "You're pretty amazing, Jeremy, but you're not perfect either. Imagine navigating your whole life and finally recognizing your power, only to fall in love with a guy who wants a true partnership. She finally figured it out on her own and now you're asking her to push that aside."

"She has to trust someone eventually," he said, exasperated.

"The thing is, she doesn't," Jen said, eyeing him as she sipped the wine. "She could live her whole life as a solo woman out there crushing it. And yet, she took a chance on you, all the while being incredibly honest how difficult it was for her."

Jeremy mulled her words, letting them sink in as she continued.

"And when she finally trusts you—and loves you and our girls—you accuse her of not caring because she won't let you save her."

"That's not what I said," he muttered, his lips forming a pout.

"It pretty much is," Jen said, flashing a cheeky grin. "Trust me. I'm intimately familiar with your savior complex."

"Whatever." He rolled his eyes. "I think that's pretty unfair."

"Well, imagine how she feels." Jen circled her hand, annoyance in her tone. "There's another way to handle this, Jeremy. One that will empower her and show her you care."

"I'm listening," he muttered.

"The more accepting reaction would've entailed looking her in the eye and telling her how proud you were that she developed a kick-ass plan to take over Chandler's business. You could've told her you supported her and would be there no matter what. That your house was always open whenever she decided to move in rather than accusing her of being a moron for paying rent."

"I just think it's silly when I have a perfectly good home and she's already there a lot," he said as Jen's advice settled in. "But I see your point. I was pretty dismissive of her plan."

"Yep. And then you accused her of not caring, which is really shitty considering she's taking our daughter to physical therapy and obviously loves you and our girls. Love isn't always expressed the way *you* express it, Jeremy."

His lips quirked. "She said the same thing to me over text. I guess I should've listened."

"Hey," Jen said, scooting closer and cupping his shoulder. "I get it. She's super rad, hella funny and gorgeous. I know you're head over heels for her. But you pushed her into this thing pretty fast, and for someone who swears she's not equipped for relationships, she acclimated pretty quickly."

"I did push her," he said, kicking the leg of the stool with his heel. "I felt she needed it because she was so convinced she wasn't wired for genuine connection and I wanted to show her it didn't have to be a disaster."

"You wanted to save her," Jen said, biting her lip.

"No, I didn't."

"Yes, you did." She patted his cheek. "It's cute. But from now on, how about less 'saving' and more 'accepting?' Support her in her plan to buy the business and take your loan off the table. Leave the offer open for her to move in. I think if you stop pushing and just let things evolve, you might end up getting a better outcome."

His lips fluttered as he blew out a breath. "How did you become so smart about relationships anyway? We sucked at being in love."

Tossing back her head, she gave a joyful laugh. "We did. But we're pretty awesome as co-parents and you're still my best friend, Jeremy. I had to navigate my own journey with Lou. You remember when we first started dating. His mom swore she wouldn't let him marry me because I wasn't Italian. Now, she's obsessed with me." She batted her eyelashes.

"True," he said, encircling her wrist and squeezing. "You won them all over. I'm so happy for you, Jen."

"And I'm happy for you." Standing, she placed her glass on the counter and rubbed his upper arm. "It will work out. Just remember to nix the savior complex. Otherwise, you're going to fuck it up."

She trailed over to the stove to finish dinner and he thanked her for the sage advice. After they'd eaten, the girls hugged Jen and Lou goodbye before Jeremy ushered them into the SUV. Once the house was dark, Jeremy lay in his bed, hands beneath his head as he stared at the ceiling. Jen's suggestions played on a constant loop in his head, and he admitted he'd definitely fucked up.

Determined to take her advice, he decided he'd confront Heather at Ashlyn's Thanksgiving dinner and apologize. Then, he'd do his best to support her in whatever path *she* wanted to take. Excited for the discussion, he closed his eyes and tried not to focus on how much he missed feeling her silken skin wrapped around him in the lonely bed.

Chapter 25

J eremy awoke on Thanksgiving morning ready to spend the day with Heather, his daughters, and his friends. Grateful for the opportunity to spend time with them, he formulated what he would say to Heather when they were alone. He would certainly apologize and encourage her to follow the path that made her comfortable. Hoping it would help set things right, he began to shuffle the girls out the door.

He'd texted Heather earlier that week and offered to drive to Ashlyn's. Although they were on a break, he didn't see the need for them to drive separately. She'd sent him a cheeky reply that she was happy to have a designated driver so she could drink more wine, and the plans had been set.

Glancing at his phone once the girls were in the car, he began to compose a text to Heather, closing out the message when she appeared. Trailing around the fence, she wore knee-high brown felt boots over tight jeans and a light blue sweater that complimented her eyes. Silver earrings sparkled beneath her golden curls and desire curled in his gut.

"Well, if it isn't famous author Jeremy Kramer," she said, slowly approaching to stand before him. "My, you look very handsome today."

Reaching for her, he encircled her wrist and gently tugged. She swayed toward him and he pressed a tender kiss to her lips. "You look so pretty, sweetheart."

Gabby chose that moment to slide down the window, and Jeremy cursed himself that he'd already started the car. "No kissing, Dad," she chided, rolling her eyes. "We're going to be late and we told Avery we'd be there by two o'clock."

Grinning at Heather, he muttered, "Do you still have the boarding school applications?"

Laughter bounded from her throat. "Sorry, but I'm kind of attached to them now. I think you have to keep them."

"Okay," he said, squeezing her arm. "I do kind of love them. Ready to go?"

"Ready." She headed to the passenger side, sliding in and fastening the seatbelt as Jeremy sat behind the wheel. As they puttered across town, he was taken with how easy the conversation was between Heather and the girls. They chatted away, Angeline telling her about a new friend she'd made in school who was *way* better than Debbie. Gabby detailed everyone on her upcoming Christmas dance recital, where she'd scored a solo. Eventually, they arrived at Ashlyn and Scott's, where the kids dispersed to the back yard to play before the sun went down.

Jeremy gave Heather space as he sat in the living room with the guys, watching football for a few minutes before they headed outside to join the kids. The ladies all congregated in the kitchen, wine flowing as Carrie caught them up all the juicy gossip in Ardor Creek.

A few minutes before dinner, Jeremy finally caught Heather as she was exiting the bathroom near the front door. Crooking his finger, he urged her to follow him into the small den and closed the door behind them.

"Are you summoning me, Mr. Kramer?" she asked, in that silken tone that drove him wild.

"Yes," he murmured, sliding his arms around her waist. "I needed to hold you since you won't speak to me." His lips formed a teasing pout and she chuckled.

"I needed some space," she said, gliding her arms around his neck. "But I've really missed you, Jeremy."

"Thank god, because I'm a wreck, Heather. I can't write a fucking word. If you don't take me back, I'm going to go broke."

Her brows lifted. "Is it that bad?"

"Terrible," he said, kissing the tip of her nose. "I really fucked up, sweetheart. I'm so sorry."

"You're lucky Ashlyn plied me with wine because I'm very susceptible to apologies from adorable authors right now." She hiccupped, causing him to snicker.

"Already hiccupping," he said, shaking his head. "You're doomed. Thank goodness I'm driving."

"Seriously."

Her nails traced a pattern over his neck, causing his body to harden as they stared deep into each other's eyes.

"I'm sorry too," she finally whispered. "I suck at this."

"You don't suck, Heather." Drawing her close, he aligned his body with hers, needing to feel her against him. "I completely dismissed your plan and I'm sorry. Jen talked some sense into me and I realized my savior complex was in full swing."

"It's so sweet that you want to help me," she said, bringing her hand around to cup his jaw. "But I need to accomplish this in my own way. I hoped you would understand that."

"I do." Easing his fingers into the hair at the base of her neck, he gently tugged her head back. "I'll support you in any way you need, sweetheart." Brushing his lips against hers, he pleaded, "Please just end this stupid break. I miss you."

Rising to her toes, she tightened her arms around his neck, drawing him into a heated kiss. Thrilled to be in her embrace, he slid his tongue over hers...caressing...tasting...dying to make love to her but knowing they only had moments before dinner. Heather purred against his tongue, the sultry sound sending every drop of blood to his dick, and he pressed against her, wishing the world would melt away.

Drawing back, he nibbled her lips, inhaling another hiccup as he chuckled. "Keep drinking because I want to seduce you tonight."

"I don't think you need to get me drunk for that, but I'll have another one or two just in case."

Elated at her admission, he searched her gaze. "So you'll stay tonight?"

Her tongue darted out to bathe her lips as she contemplated, driving him insane with lust. Clenching his fingers in her hair, he arched a brow. "Heather?"

"Ask me when we get home," she said with a wink. "I think I'm might be amenable."

"Woman, you just made my Thanksgiving."

Giving her one last peck as she giggled, he took her hand, lacing their fingers as he led her from the den. A few minutes later, Ashlyn ushered everyone to the large table Scott had built as they all found their seats. Scott stood, lifting his glass of sparkling cider as he addressed the table.

"Welcome to another Thanksgiving dinner, made by my amazing wife who still puts up with me even when I'm grumpy."

"I love Grumpy Scott," Ashlyn sighed, gazing up at him as everyone chuckled.

"Every year, we take a moment to remember those we've lost. Tina and Ella, whom we talk about every day with our kids and do our best to keep their memories alive."

Ashlyn slipped her hand into his, squeezing as their son Grant beamed beside her in his booster seat.

"Grandma Jean, whose spirit still lives on in our home, and Sally Pickens, who I'm convinced will always have a presence here no matter how many times I renovate."

"He's promised me a she-shed in the back yard, guys," Ashlyn chimed, holding up a finger.

"When the kids are older, Ash," he said, shooting her a look. "I'd like to get through this toast before our kids graduate high school."

"Oh, fine." She snatched her hand from his grasp. "Forgive me for adding context—"

Leaning down, he plopped a kiss on her lips and smoothed a hand over her dark hair. "I'm sorry. Do you want to give the toast?"

"No. You're doing a great job. Keep going."

"Nice apology, dude," Peter said, tapping his temple. "Gotta remember that trick. Saying 'I'm sorry' works. Who knew?"

Carrie swatted him as everyone snickered. "No one asked you, Peter Stratford." Covering his mouth with her hand, she yelped when he playfully bit it.

"Peter!"

"What, honey?" Grabbing her hand, he pressed it to his chest. "You know I can't resist biting you—"

"Oh, brother," she interjected, rolling her eyes. "Sorry I got him started, guys. Scott, please continue."

Scott flashed a grin before forging ahead. "Anyway, we remember everyone we've lost, and are thankful for new friends too.

Jeremy, we're happy to have a famous author in our crew and we appreciate you upping our coolness factor."

"According to Heather, I'm geeky," he said, stretching his arm over Heather's shoulders, "but I'm happy you guys think I'm cool."

"And Heather," Scott said, lifting his glass as he smiled. "No one at Ardor Creek High would've guessed we'd all be here twenty years later. We're all really proud of you for having the courage to come back to Ardor Creek and we're so happy you're here."

Heather's eyes glistened as she lifted her glass. "Thank you, Scott."

"And now, I'll shut up before the daggers in my wife's eyes take me out."

"Who needs to eat food when it's hot?" Ashlyn muttered, glancing at the ceiling as she shrugged. "Not me, the person who spent all day cooking it. No, sir."

Laughing, Scott sat down and reached over to cup her cheek. "Thank you, Ash. I love you and am so thankful for you."

Ashlyn all but melted into the chair, blowing him a kiss before reaching over to grab a dish and commence the dinner. Wine and conversation flowed as they feasted on the amazing meal. After dessert, the night wore down as the kids' bedtime drew near.

Long after the sun set, Jeremy loaded his sleepy daughters in the car, along with a still-tipsy Heather, and they drove home under the star-filled sky. Peering over his shoulder as he drove, he noticed both girls passed out in the backseat.

"They're toast," he said, snickering as Heather gazed over her shoulder.

"I'm with them. I'm ready for a nap."

Reaching over, he slid his palm over hers, clutching. "You can take a nap in my bed."

Chuckling, she lifted his hand and kissed it, causing his heart to dissolve into a pile of mush. "Okay."

Thrilled she was staying over, he held her hand until they were parked. After they'd successfully gotten the girls in bed, he offered to have a nightcap with Heather in the kitchen. She glanced down the stairs, features drawn together as she pondered.

"If it's all the same to you, I think I'm ready for bed." Stepping closer, she placed her hand over his heart. "I missed you, Jeremy. I can't believe I'm saying this, but I missed having you hold me as

I slept. That's never happened before. I used to kick Butch in the shin if he came within a foot of me while I was sleeping."

"Yikes," Jeremy said, tugging her toward his bedroom as she trailed behind. Once inside, he closed the door and led her to the side of the bed. Turning back the covers, he glanced over his shoulder. "You'll warn me if you want to kick me, right? In case you haven't noticed, my family is very accident prone and we can't afford another broken leg around here."

Tossing back her head, she laughed. "You guys are really accident-prone. What gives?"

Straightening, he reached over and flipped on the lamp that sat atop the nightstand. "I have no idea. It's strange, for sure."

Her eyes roved over him before she padded to the lamp and shut it off. Trailing to the window, she spread the curtains wide, allowing the light of the full moon to seep into the room. Sauntering toward him, she rested her palms on his pecs. "Let's do this in the moonlight. Where it's just you and me and we can just *feel.*"

Lifting her hand, he kissed her palm. "I thought you didn't want to feel anything. Only sex, remember?" he teased.

"I never did before you." Grasping the hem of her sweater, she tugged it off and tossed it to the floor. "Now, I can't go back. You changed everything and I'm so damn tired of being scared."

Eyes locked with hers, he slowly unbuttoned his shirt, taken with the dark flecks in her blue orbs that glinted in the moonlight. After tossing his shirt to the floor, he unbuckled his belt, loving the flare of desire in her gaze. Once he was naked, he hooked a finger in the waistband of her jeans and pulled her close.

"I never meant to downplay your fears, hon," he whispered, reaching behind to unclasp her lacy bra. Dropping it on the soft carpet, he cupped her breasts, running his thumbs over her pebbling nipples as he stared into her eyes. "You were nothing but honest with me and I lashed out by accusing you of not caring. You trusted me with your fears and I let you down. I'm sorry."

The cadence of her breaths increased as she pushed her breasts into his palms. "Show me."

Tightening his thumb and forefinger, he pinched her nipples, reveling in her gasp. "You little tease," he murmured, tugging the pebbled buds as her lips fell open. "You want me to show you?"

"Yes," she rasped, eyes closing as he toyed with her nipples. "And then I'll show you how sorry I am for...well, whatever it is, I'll figure it out. Keep going."

His low-toned laugh surrounded them. "You don't have to apologize, hon. I'm ready to put this behind us and support you in every way you need." Gliding his fingers down her abdomen, he noticed the muscles quiver before he reached the hem of her jeans. Unbuttoning them, he slid them down her legs, removing her clothes before lifting her onto the bed. Settling her on the soft sheets, he was overcome with how gorgeous she was as her hair splayed over the pillow in the dim moonlight.

"Jeremy," she whispered, sliding her arms around his neck. "I do care about you. You know I'm in this, right? You were so good at seeing past my walls in the beginning. Don't give up on me."

"Never," he murmured, sliding over her and gently brushing a tuft of hair from her forehead. "You're mine, Heather. Forever. Do you hear me?"

Nodding, she speared her nails into his shoulders, spurring him into action.

Pressing his lips to hers, he sucked her tongue between his lips, jutting his shaft into the soft skin of her thigh as she moaned. Breaking away, he trailed soft kisses over her neck and collarbone before grazing the curve of her breast. Hovering over her nipple, he expelled a warm breath, relishing in her resulting tremble.

"*Please...*" she rasped.

Closing his lips over the tight nub, he sucked, dying to give her pleasure as she writhed against him. Lathering her with his tongue, he stroked her nipple, ensuring it was soaked before he flicked it. The rapid movements caused the tiny bud to harden even more, and she dug her nails into his skin, driving him wild.

Kissing a path to her other breast, he repeated his actions, bringing the sensitive bud to a firm peak before he flicked it in sure, rapid strokes. Heather jutted her hips against him, her body begging for more.

Placing soft kisses on the underside of her breast, he continued down her stomach, grinning when she giggled beneath him.

"Tickles," she murmured.

Splaying his hands over her hips, he held her tight as he dipped his tongue in her navel. "You can take it, hon." His tongue circled the tiny indention. "*Fuck*, you taste so good."

Continuing down her body, his lips found the top of her mound, smooth and silky against his mouth.

"I got waxed earlier this week," she said, waggling her eyebrows as she stared down at him from the pillow.

Settling on his knees, he palmed her inner thighs, gently spreading them apart as he gazed at her glistening core. Sliding a finger through the wetness, his lips formed a mischievous grin.

"So sleek and sexy," he said, gazing at her as his finger found her entrance. Sliding inside, he shuddered at the erotic image of claiming her. Adding another finger, he gently glided back and forth in her tight channel, hooking his fingers each time they reached the hilt.

"*Oh, god...*" she moaned, undulating against him. "So good..."

Lowering his head, he spread her folds with his free hand and placed his lips against her sensitive bud. Still working his fingers deep in her body, he began to suck her clit as he gazed deep into her stunning eyes.

Heat radiated from her lithe frame, her skin reddening in the moonlight as he loved her. Dying to make her come, he worked his tongue and fingers, anticipating the moment when he would bury himself deep in her hot, tight body. Once he'd sucked her clit into a taut bud, he flicked it with his tongue, urging her to come with his eyes as his fingers stroked her.

"*Jeremy—*" she cried, threading her fingers in his hair and squeezing so tight, he thought she might rip it out. Hell, who cared when she was drowning in pleasure as he feasted on her delectable body? He'd happily go bald if it made her squirm beneath him like this all day long.

"Come in my mouth, hon," he murmured against her clit, his fingers hooking deep against her inner walls. "I want you gushing inside me. Your pussy is so fucking hot, Heather." Flattening his tongue against her core, he dragged it over her drenched skin before stimulating her clit again with the tip of his tongue.

"Good *lord*," she moaned, drawing his face into her core as he frantically sucked and fucked her with his fingers. "I wasted so much time thinking you were tame in bed when you could've been doing this to me...I'll never forgive myself...*oh, god...*"

Smiling against her wet warmth, he increased the pace, sending her over the edge. Groaning, she clenched his hair, pushing him deeper into her pussy as she quaked and undulated against him. Jeremy took the hint, sucking her clit between his lips as her body exploded beneath him. Her essence surrounded him, drowning him in her scent and taste. Eventually, her shudders eased into trembles and she relaxed the death grip on his hair.

Placing soft kisses on her mound and inner thigh, he gently caressed her as she fell back to Earth. Feeling his body tremble with need, he slowly rose, looming over her as he settled between her legs.

Sliding his hand under her thigh, he wrapped her leg around his waist as he touched the head of his cock to her slick entrance. Balancing on his forearm, he threaded his fingers through her hair as it splayed across the pillow. Gazing deep into her eyes, he began to push inside.

She opened for him, tugging him close with her leg as he worked his hips. When he was fully seated deep inside her luscious body, he gritted his teeth and drew back before slowly surging deep once more.

"*Heather...*"

"I know," she whispered, nodding as he slowly dragged his steel through her softness.

"I want this forever," he rasped, lowering his forehead to hers. "I love you, sweetheart."

Tears clouded her eyes, causing his heart to splinter as her chin trembled. "Jeremy—"

"You don't have to say anything," he interrupted, pressing his lips to hers as he worked her tight channel. "There's no rush, sweetheart. I just needed you to know."

Swiping the tear that slowly ran down her cheek, he shook his head. "Don't cry, honey. It's a good thing, I promise." Leaning down, he rested his lips on the shell of her ear. "Now open that sweet pussy and let me fuck you. I missed being inside you."

Her breathy laugh rumbled against his chest. "If you'd shut up for two fucking seconds, you could concentrate on fucking me—"

She yelped beneath him as he shifted, rising to his knees and sliding his hands beneath her legs. Lifting them high, he pressed them toward the bed, planting his palms so he could anchor them.

"Careful what you ask for, hon," he grunted, rearing back before thrusting inside her tight warmth.

The little minx lifted her arms high, flattening her palms against the headboard. Grinning at her sultry expression, he began to fuck her in firm rapid strokes, increasing the pace as she mewled beneath him. Grasping her ankles, he brought them to his shoulders, holding them close as he pounded her ravaged body.

The sounds of their lovemaking pierced the quiet room, and Jeremy was overcome with the sight of her sweet honey covering his cock every time he withdrew before plunging back in. Tossing back his head, he closed his eyes, feeling his balls tighten as he prepared to empty everything inside her. Moaning her name, he began to come, choppy laughs escaping his lungs as her pussy milked his cock.

His hips pressed into her with every pulsing jet, wanting to mark her as *his*...the primal need almost overwhelming. Expelling a breath, he lowered her legs, letting them fall to the bed as his muscles lost the ability to support his weight. Lowering over her, he encircled her with his arms, drawing her close as the last pulses of release exited his body.

Heather wrapped a silken leg over the back of his thigh, holding him close as he relaxed against her. Nuzzling her neck with his nose, his thumb caressed her upper back as she ran her nails over his shoulder blade, causing tiny bumps to rise on his skin. Content to lay there forever, he emitted a frustrated groan when he began to slip from her.

"Son of a bitch," he muttered. "Sex with you is messy."

"Only with me?" she teased, pressing a nail into his shoulder.

"Ouch, woman." Rising, he pecked her lips. "No stabbing, okay?"

Reaching for the tissues, he mourned the loss of her tight warmth around him as he cleaned them up. Tossing the tissues aside, he drew the covers over them and settled on his back. Heather slithered over him, gliding her leg over his thighs and resting her cheek on his chest.

"Good night, sweetheart," he said, kissing her forehead as he stroked her hair. "I'm so glad you stayed."

"Me too," she mumbled.

Silence stretched as their breaths grew longer and deeper.

"Just need a little more time to say it back," she murmured, her voice laced with sleep. "Don't get mad. It's a big step for me."

"I'm over being mad, Heather," he said, tenderly stroking her soft tresses. "And I think you love me too. If you're ever ready to tell me, I'll be ready to hear it, but there's no pressure."

"You're awfully sure of yourself," she teased.

Chuckling, he kissed her forehead.

His eyelids drooped as her body melted into his.

"The overblown ego thing is kind of hot for some reason. Keep it up."

Laughing, he tightened his arms around her. "Yes, ma'am, Ms. Combs. I'm at your service."

Jeremy felt her grin against his chest before she nestled deeper into his side. And then, he closed his eyes, cherishing the feel of having her back in his arms.

Chapter 26

Heather barreled into December, prepared to accomplish a multitude of tasks before the Christmas holiday. First, she had to sell Justine's and Chandler's homes. Then, she needed to prepare the lease for the studio above Chandler's business so she could move in. Lastly, she needed to upgrade her real estate license to a broker's license so she could sponsor the other agents' licenses at the firm. That was the owner's job, and since Chandler was retiring, it was now her responsibility.

On top of that, she had to figure out how to deal with her ever-growing feelings for Jeremy and his girls. When he'd gazed at her so reverently while they made love and spoken the three little words she'd rarely heard, her heart had nearly burst. Finally, after so many years of heartache, Heather was *loved.* It was a small miracle that made her giddy every time she remembered the sweet words said in Jeremy's deep, sexy voice.

Heather was pretty sure she loved him too, but change took time and she was determined not to rush into something she wasn't ready for. She wanted to say the words back when she held no reservation; no fear. Until that time came, she would hold them close, trusting Jeremy to be patient with her.

It was a lot to ask, but she finally understood that love was patient. After their steamy Thanksgiving night and soulful apologies, Jeremy had completely let the argument go, allowing her to chart her own path. He didn't mention the loan offer again and he made it clear she could move in whenever she was ready. The subject was officially closed and hadn't been referenced by either of them again.

That was fine with Heather because it gave her space to think...space to breathe...and space to accept that she could enter into something that would last forever with Jeremy. With all her reservations, she needed the extra contemplation and was grateful to have a partner who finally got her.

As the month wore on, Heather closed the sale on Justine's home, and then Chandler's. Sitting in Chandler's office—soon to be *her* office—she typed the finishing touches for the lease on the studio above the business. It was tiny and was currently used as a storage space, but it was a perfectly fine place for Heather to live for a year before considering moving in with Jeremy. She stayed at his house quite often, and having the studio would give her the additional breathing room she craved.

Printing out the lease, she looked it over, satisfied with the changes. She would technically be renting to herself since she would own the real estate LLC on January 1st, but she wanted the documentation for tax purposes. Peter was her accountant and had advised her to keep her personal and business finances separate. Glancing at the lease, she felt an urge to see the studio. Grabbing the papers, she trailed down the office hallway and up the back stairs.

The door was unlocked so she stepped inside, noting the dust that filtered through the sunlight that wafted through the lone window. She would definitely need to clean before moving in. Striding around the small space, she observed the kitchenette and microwave, noting they'd seen better days but were functional.

Stepping into the small bathroom, she observed the tiny shower, wrinkling her nose at the chipped tile. Testing the water pressure, she affirmed it was strong, so at least that was a plus. Padding back toward the living space, she stood on the semi-worn carpet and slowly turned to take in the studio.

After a full rotation, she stood still, closing her eyes as silence filled her ears. Lifting her lids, she glanced at the lease in her hand. Narrowing her eyes, she murmured, "What the hell are you doing, Heather?"

Clenching the papers, she acknowledged her pulse, ragged and strong in her neck. Overcome with realization, she let it wash over her, understanding the gravity of the moment. Inhaling deeply, she straightened her shoulders and surveyed the studio one last time.

And then, she beelined down the steps, through the back door to her car, and straight to Jeremy's house.

Jeremy's fingers roved over the keyboard as he finished a suspenseful chapter. He loved the thrill of writing twisty stories, and thankfully, his creativity had returned tenfold after repairing things with Heather. Pleased with the flow of the story, he was so lost in the words that he barely heard the voice calling his name from the kitchen.

Freezing, he perked his ears and listened, wondering if he was hearing things.

"Jeremy?"

Confusion ran through him as he checked the clock on his laptop. It was two in the afternoon and she wasn't due until five o'clock. Jen had the girls for the weekend so he'd made dinner reservations at the fancy restaurant on Main Street, wanting to treat Heather for her help with Angeline's physical therapy. And also to wine and dine her so he could seduce her later. Yes, seduction was *definitely* in the plan.

Rising, he called, "Heather?"

"I'm in the living room!"

Striding out of his office, he trailed down the hall, cresting the doorway of the living room to find her standing in the middle of the carpet, clutching several papers in her hand.

"Um, hi," he said, rubbing the back of his neck. "You're about three hours early."

She studied him as he tried to discern her strange expression.

"Did I interrupt your writing?"

"Yeah," he said, shrugging, "but you're way better than my serial killer soccer mom." Approaching her, he stopped a foot away and narrowed his eyes. "Are you okay?"

Her cheeks puffed as she expelled a large breath before nodding. "I'm good."

"Okay." He arched a brow. "Because you're kind of pale and look like you're going to pass out."

She ran a hand over her face before cupping her chin. "I might pass out. Let's definitely *not* rule that out."

Closing the distance between them, he cupped her upper arms. "Is it the business? Or did one of your deals fall through? Whatever it is, we'll figure it out."

Blue eyes sparkled as she broke into a gorgeous smile. "Nope, it's neither of those things."

Jeremy's brow furrowed as he waited.

"The thing is, Jeremy," she said, lifting the papers, "I was all set to sign this lease."

He glanced at her hand. "All right."

Huffing, she placed her hand on her hip. "No, it's not all right. Because I don't want to live in a musty studio apartment."

Joy welled in his chest as he struggled to comprehend what she was saying. "You don't?"

"No." Eyes full of fear...and hope...and *love* stared back at him as short breaths exited her lungs. "I want to live with you. And the girls. That's where I want to be."

Jeremy pursed his lips, hope blooming in his chest as his eyes darted between hers.

"Damn it, you're going to make me say it, aren't you?"

Breathing a laugh, he asked, "Say what?"

Lifting her hand, she tenderly placed her palm on his cheek.

"That I love you, you daft man. There. It's done." Closing her eyes, she shook her head. "Yep, I'm two seconds away from passing out."

Overcome with laughter, he slid his arms around her waist and pulled her into his body. Her arm encircled his neck as she clutched the papers in her other hand.

"I've got you, sweetheart. I won't let you fall. Holy shit, you finally said it."

Gazing up at him, she nodded. "I finally said it." Flicking her wrist, she tossed the papers, both of them laughing as they flitted to the floor. "I'm ready. Let's fucking do this. I might suck at everything having to do with love and relationships, but I'm ready to give it a go."

"You're going to be so great, Heather," he said, smoothing her hair. "I think we can accomplish anything as long as we do it together."

"Me too," she whispered, lifting to her toes to brush a kiss on his lips. "And, I might forgive you one day for making me a...uggh...*stepmother*." Staring at the ceiling, she groaned. "Goddammit. I love those little beasts. I can't wait to help you raise them and do the best I can to help them grow into strong, remarkable women."

Jeremy's eyes welled like a damn sap at the reverent way she spoke about his daughters. "Heather," he whispered, resting his forehead against hers. "You can't possibly know how much that means to me. The fact that you love them too is amazing."

"I do," she said, nodding against him. "Damn it, I love all three of you. It's annoying."

Threading his fingers through her hair, he gently tugged her head back before nuzzling her nose with his. "I hope you'll forgive me one day."

"The only thing that's saving you right now is your ability to whisper dirty words in my ear and fuck me like I'm the last woman on Earth. Mind-blowing sex is part of this relationship deal, Jeremy. I mean it—"

Enchanted by her teasing, he pressed his lips to hers, inhaling the words as she moaned under his touch. Finding her tongue with his, he stroked and tasted, drowning in the fact she'd finally accepted everything they could build together.

Life with her wouldn't always be easy, but it would be filled with affection, honesty and her unflappable sense of humor. Thanking the universe for placing her in his path, he couldn't imagine entwining his future with anyone who complimented him more. His heart now belonged to her, and since she'd finally given hers in return, Jeremy vowed to spend the rest of his days safeguarding Heather Combs' tender heart.

Epilogue

Jeremy fiddled with the bow tie that constricted his airway, two seconds away from ripping the damn thing off and stomping on it. Gritting his teeth, he tried again to straighten it but it was still crooked.

"Here," Heather said, inserting herself between him and the mirror. "You look like you're going to punch someone. Let me do it for you." Her fingers worked methodically to arrange and straighten the bow tie. Stepping back, she nodded. "Perfect. You look very handsome, Mr. Kramer."

"Thank you." Brushing a kiss on her lips, he checked his phone before slipping it into the pocket of his tux. "It's 6:50. We need to head downstairs."

"Aye, aye," she said, saluting. Grabbing her clutch from the hotel bed, she held it at her side as she flashed a sultry grin. "How do I look?"

Jeremy's eyes roved over her black sequined dress that hugged every curve, and her full golden hair which was curled into some fancy updo he couldn't wait to thrust his hands into later.

"So damn hot," he murmured, stalking toward her and sliding a hand over her waist. "Man, I wish I had time to fuck you right now."

"Later, lover," she said, easing away from his grasp. "Your fans await."

Gathering their things, they closed the door behind them and Jeremy took her hand as they strode toward the elevator. Once they were inside, he gazed at her and grinned. "Are you ready for this?"

"No one cares about me," she said, shrugging. "You're the famous author."

"Um, I'm not sure if you've *seen* you in that dress, but trust me, no one's going to be looking at me."

Chuckling, she cocked a brow. "I'm no Margot Robbie."

"Sweetheart, you put her to shame." Pressing a kiss to her temple, he squeezed her hand. "Okay, here we go."

The elevator doors slid open and they walked through the lobby to the expansive ballroom that had been decorated for the occasion. Jeremy's agent, Dorothy, waved them over and they walked toward the red carpet.

"Just be yourself," Dorothy said, smoothing her palms over Jeremy's arms to straighten the fabric. "You're going to be fine."

"Thank goodness Heather agreed to walk with me. Geeky authors aren't really into this kind of thing."

"I've got you," Heather said, squeezing his hand. "From one end of this damn carpet to the other. Let's go."

"Mr. Kramer?" a man wearing a headset called. "You're next in the press line. Please step forward."

Expelling a huge breath, he walked past the hanging black felt curtain as noise from the throng of reporters and photographers flooded his ears. Clutching Heather's hand, he stepped onto the red carpet.

"Well, folks, here we have author J.R. Kramer himself," a woman said into a microphone as she stood behind the divider. A man filmed her with a TV camera atop his shoulder etched with the words *Hollywood Minute*. "Are you excited to be attending the premiere of *Alternate Destinies*?"

Overcome with how loud it was, Jeremy nodded, reminding himself that tomorrow he'd be home with Heather and the girls and the stressful night would be over. He was extremely proud of the movie and wanted to promote it, but hanging out with his family was about a hundred times higher on his list than speaking to the twenty reporters lined up for the premiere.

"I'm really excited about it. The cast did a fantastic job and they brought the story to life."

"And who is your gorgeous date? Is this your wife, Mr. Kramer?"

"Heather Kramer," she said with a nod. "Just here to support my husband. I get the feeling he's not really into the whole press junket thing, so go easy on him, okay?"

The reporter grinned. "Well, this is breaking news. Were you recently married? I didn't find any mention of a wife when I did my research."

"Just last weekend by the mayor of our quaint little town in Pennsylvania," Heather said, grinning up at Jeremy as she slid her arm around his waist.

"Congratulations! I'm sure there's a wonderful story behind your courtship. I'd love to interview you about it at a later date. I'll contact your agent, Mr. Kramer."

"Actually," Jeremy said, tugging Heather close, "that's something we'd like to keep between us..."

"Lacey from *Hollywood Minute*," the reporter said.

"Well, Lacey from *Hollywood Minute*, you seem great, but the story of how I fell in love with my wife is one I'm keeping for myself." He tapped his temple. "It's my favorite and sometimes an author wants to keep those private."

"Well, you make a gorgeous couple," Lacey said into the microphone. "I wish you the best of luck with the premiere."

"Thank you," Jeremy said, tightening his hand on Heather's hip. Glancing down, he asked, "Ready to continue, Mrs. Kramer?"

Love glowed in her eyes as she smiled. "Ready, Mr. Kramer."

Holding her close for moral support, Jeremy eased down the red carpet, tackling the reporters' questions one by one...exceptionally thankful his wife was in the bunker with him the entire time.

Series Epilogue

Three years later...

"That's enough with the poppers, young man," Carrie said, scolding Charlie after he threw another one on the patio, resulting in a loud bang that made everyone flinch. "Go play soccer with the rest of the kids."

"I suck at soccer," Charlie said, kicking the ground with the toe of his sneaker. "I wish it was basketball season already."

"Well then, go play basketball out front. Lord knows, your dad insisted we put up the hoop by the garage but you all barely use it."

"Am I in trouble?" Peter asked, appearing behind her and hugging her close. "What gives, kid? I got Mom to approve the poppers and you still got me in trouble? We had a deal."

Charlie's lips twitched. "Sorry, Dad. The poppers are cool. Mom says I have to stop so I'll get Gabby to play basketball with me out front. She's the only one who hates soccer like I do."

"I have a feeling you only hate soccer because your brother loves it so much," Carrie said, reaching over and wiping black popper residue from his cheek. "You should be happy for your brother that he got a soccer scholarship to UPenn."

"I'm happy for him, Mom. He just never wants to play with me because I suck."

"Well, you're better than him at basketball and tennis, although it isn't a contest." She shot him a stern look.

"I know. Sorry about the poppers. I won't use them again until everyone leaves."

"Thank you, sweetie."

Charlie nodded before jogging around the house toward the hoop.

Peter leaned down, nuzzling her ear before whispering, "Holy shit, Care Bear. I'm about two seconds from dragging you inside."

Her features scrunched. "Why?"

"Because you used the stern mommy tone on our kid, woman. Man, it does it for me every time—"

"Oh, stop." She swatted his shoulder, causing him to laugh. "I worry that Charlie compares himself to Sebastian. When Sebastian goes to college next year, maybe Charlie will finally come into his own a bit more."

"Charlie's fifteen going on fifty, honey. He's going to be fine," Peter said. "Kids have to go through their own struggles to learn lessons. Remember how much we learned in high school? I mean, you were crazy about me and I could barely tolerate you—"

"Do you *want* to get laid tonight?" she asked, arching her eyebrows. "Because you're on thin ice, Peter Stratford—"

Yelping, Carrie held on for dear life as her husband dipped her and cemented his lips to hers. "I take it all back," he murmured after breaking the kiss. "I love you, Carrie. Please take pity on your husband and give him sexy times once our kids pass out from all the caffeine they're not supposed to have. Pleeeeeease?"

Laughing, she nodded. "Okay. Let me up, please. I'll take pity on you." He lifted her and she slid her arms around his neck. "I might even bring out the sexy nurse costume..."

"Well, that's my cue to tell everyone to leave—"

"Shhh," she scolded, slapping his chest. "It's the middle of the day, Peter. Good grief."

"Uh, sorry to interrupt this display of happy matrimony, but I need more booze," Heather said, shaking her empty cup. "You guys are standing directly in front of the booze table and it's not cool."

"After you," Peter said, stepping away and gesturing toward the table.

"Are you making mimosas, Heather?" Ashlyn asked from several feet away where she was playing soccer with the kids. "I'll have one too if you don't mind."

"Sure thing," Heather called, mixing the drinks as Jeremy appeared at her side.

"Having a good time?"

"Yep," she said, placing the cap back on the orange juice. "The crew is hella cool. I have no idea why I hated everyone so much in high school." Squinting, she rubbed her chin.

"Probably because I didn't ask you out," Chad said, walking toward the table and rummaging in the cooler for another beer. Rising, he popped open the can and took a sip before patting his stomach. "Everybody wanted to date good ol' Chad but there was only so much of me to go around. It's tragic really—"

A soccer ball flew from the yard, pelting Chad in the chest, causing him to emit an "*oomph*" and drop his beer. Holding his hand to his chest, he gulped in air as he stared wide-eyed at Abby.

"Oh, no," she cried, batting her eyelashes. "Did the soccer ball hit you, dear husband? And while you were telling that tender story about your high school days..."

Chad's mouth fell open. "You little imp. Did you intentionally kick that ball at me?"

Abby's features contorted with mock exasperation. "Me? Your loving wife? Never." She drew an X over her heart.

"Oh, you've done it now, babe," Chad said, slowly stepping toward her. "I'm giving you a three-second head start and then it's on."

Squealing, Abby took off across the yard and Chad sprinted after her, tackling her on the far side of the property as their laughter echoed across the lawn.

"They'll be making out for a while," Ashlyn said, trailing over to grab her mimosa from Heather. "Thank god we all have awesome kids who don't need a lot of supervision since our maturity level is somewhere between infant and toddler."

"Speak for yourself," Teresa said, sauntering over to refill her wine. "As the oldest of the crew, I think I have *some* level of maturity." Replacing the cork, she lifted her glass in a toast. "But I think it's adorable that you're all so affectionate. I use this crew as an example for my clients quite often."

"Amen to that," Ashlyn said. "Look at how cute Scott, Mark and Gary are playing with the kids. It's pretty rad we still think our husbands are hot, right?"

"I think so," Teresa said with a nod. "And Mark is by far the sexiest man I've ever been with, so I'm on that page, sister."

"Do you feel that way about me?" Jeremy asked Heather, his lips forming a cute pout.

"Let me have one more of these and I'll answer," she teased, lifting her cup.

Jeremy just stared at her with an adorable puppy dog expression.

"I have no idea why you're fishing for compliments when you know you're my secret sex god," she said, grinning. "Now, go play with the other husbands and kids so the ladies can stand here and gossip about you all from afar."

"Oh, and your sex god status isn't really secret," Carrie whispered loudly, holding her hand to the side of her mouth as everyone chuckled.

Peter and Jeremy jogged over to join Scott, Mark, Gary and the kids in the yard. A few minutes later, Abby trailed over, plucking strands of grass from her mussed hair.

"Are we having gossip time?" Abby asked excitedly. "I figured we were so I told Chad to stay with the kids."

"We are," Carrie said, lifting her cup. "To our sometimes annoying, always loving, definitely gorgeous husbands. May we never stop gossiping about them."

"Hey!" Justine said, walking down the porch stairs from the kitchen. "A girl goes to pee and you all toast without me? What gives?"

"Sorry, Jus," Heather said, pointing to the table. "Need a mimosa?"

"Damn straight I do."

Heather concocted the drink and handed it to Justine. Regrouping, the six ladies lifted their solo cups high and toasted to their husbands and children, their beloved town of Ardor Creek, and finally, their unbreakable friendship.

After sipping, they fell into the comfortable chairs that formed a semi-circle on the stone patio. As the sun set, they reminisced about how each of them had fallen in love in Ardor Creek.

Ashlyn when she'd moved to town after her grandma passed, unable to squelch her feelings for her grumpy contractor.

Carrie, who had always loved Peter, but the timing had just never been right...until it finally was.

Teresa, who'd accepted contentment over happiness because she thought she'd run out of time...until she met Mark, who loved her exactly as she was.

Abby, who returned to Ardor Creek to finally beat Chad, only to lose her heart to him in the process.

Justine, who overcame an abusive past to create a new life with the soul mate who'd been right in front of her the whole time.

And Heather, who'd always fought her battles alone until she gained the courage to love...and to be loved in return.

Sighing, Ashlyn stared at the rapidly dimming sky, lifting her cup as she murmured, "To our freaking husbands."

Hiccupping, Heather raised her cup. "I think you're drunk, Ashlyn."

"Ummm, news flash," Carrie chimed. "We're all drunk. Our men are getting sooooo lucky tonight!"

Snickering, the six friends fell back into easy conversation before the night eventually wound down and everyone headed home. In the morning, they each awoke to a text on the group chain that was blank.

Perplexed, the ladies texted each other, wondering how someone had managed to send a blank text since they'd all pretty much passed out. It was a mystery that remained unsolved as they each resumed their busy lives with their beloved husbands and kids.

Until one day, several weeks later, when Ashlyn gingerly walked up the stairs to the attic. It was still untouched since she wanted to leave it exactly as Grandma Jean had desired, with Sally Pickens' chair resting in the middle of the dusty wooden floor.

"Sally?" Ashlyn whispered, holding up her phone. "Did you have something to do with the blank text?"

Silence answered as a chill ran down her spine. Rubbing the bumps on her arms, she swallowed thickly as her children called to her from downstairs.

"Coming!" she answered, unable to shake the strange feeling that Sally's presence still lingered in their home. And hey, maybe she wanted to be part of the crew too? After all, the crew *was* pretty damn awesome.

Turning, Ashlyn approached the stairs, noting it was time for lunch. Feeling the hairs stand up on the back of her neck, she glanced over her shoulder one last time. Slow and steady, the old wooden chair began to rock...back and forth over the withered floor.

"Holy shit," Ashlyn whispered, eyes growing wide as she observed the movements. "You did send the text. *Ohmygod*, this is so cool!"

Suddenly, the chair creaked back into place and froze, causing Ashlyn to rapidly shake her head. Had she imagined it or had it been real?

"Mommy? Can I have a peanut butter and jelly?"

Expelling a breath, Ashlyn started down the stairs, closing the attic door behind her. When she reached the kitchen, she pulled the ingredients from the fridge, ready to make sandwiches for her kids. Scott strolled into the kitchen and planted a kiss on her head.

"Hey, hon. Making PB&Js?"

"Yep," she said, heart still pounding from the incident in the attic.

"You're quiet," he said, eyes narrowing as he sipped a can of soda. "You're never quiet. What's up?"

Chuckling, she lifted her gaze to his. "What would you say if I told you I think Sally wants to be in our crew?"

"Sally Pickens?"

"Yes, Scott. What other Sally do you know?"

Laughing, he strode over and slid his arm around her waist. "I'd say she has really good taste. Our crew is awesome. They're our family and we're so lucky to have them."

Smiling into his eyes, she asked, "They are our family, aren't they?"

Nodding, he squeezed her hip. "Every single one of them."

"Ardor Creek is pretty freaking special to have drawn us all together, isn't it? I mean, what an awesome town."

"It's the best," he said, lifting a shoulder. "I challenge anyone to find a more amazing town than Ardor Creek."

Gazing at her husband, Ashlyn's lips curved in agreement, thankful for their tiny town and the lives she and her friends had built in Ardor Creek.

Before You Go

W ell, dear readers, I'm not crying, that's just a speck of dust in my eye...or something. Okay, who am I kidding? I'm bawling over here as I wrap up this amazing series where every character stole my heart. I hope they inhabited a tiny piece of your heart too, and I thank you so much for spending some time in Ardor Creek with me.

Rest assured, there will be more series and more stories from me. Perhaps none quite like Ardor Creek, because it's so special, but each series allows me to create something new, so I'll cherish that excitement as I forge ahead.

Not ready to leave Ardor Creek yet? I wrote a bonus scene featuring Heather and Jeremy's wedding reception exclusively for my newsletter subscribers. Follow the link below to be added to my newsletter and the scene will be emailed to you right away. All the Ardor Creek lifers make an appearance!

Use this link to read Heather and Jeremy's bonus scene:
https://BookHip.com/VBGSZNR
or find it on my website:
www.aylaasher.com

About the Author

Ayla Asher is the pen name for a USA Today bestselling author who writes steamy fantasy romance under a different pseudonym. However, she loves a spicy, fast-paced contemporary romance too! Therefore, she's decided to share some of her contemporary stories, hoping to spread a little joy one HEA at a time. She would love to connect with you on social media, where she enjoys making dorky TikToks, FB/IG posts and fun book trailers!

ALSO BY AYLA ASHER

Manhattan Holiday Loves Trilogy
Book 1: His Holiday Pact
Book 2: Her Valentine Surprise
Book 3: Her Patriotic Prince

Ardor Creek Series
Book 1: Hearts Reclaimed
Book 2: Illusions Unveiled
Book 3: Desires Uncovered
Book 4: Resolutions Embraced
Book 5: Passions Fulfilled
Book 6: Futures Entwined